malicious

USA TODAY BESTSELLING AUTHORS
ALEX GRAYSON
MELISSA TOPPEN

Malicious

Copyright © 2020 by Alex Grayson & Melissa Toppen.

All rights reserved.

Cover Design by Melissa Gill Designs. Interior Formatting by Alex Grayson. Editing by Rose David Editing.

All rights reserved. No part of this publication may be reproduced, distributed, or transmitted in any form or by any means, including photocopying, recording, or other electronic or mechanical methods, without the prior written permission of the publisher, except in the case of brief quotations embodied in critical reviews and certain other noncommercial uses permitted by copyright law.

The scanning, uploading, and/or distribution of this document via the internet or via any other means without the permission of the publisher is illegal and is punishable by law.

Please purchase only authorized editions and do not participate in or encourage electronic piracy of copyrightable materials.

All characters and events appearing in this work are fictitious. Any resemblance to real events or persons, living or dead, is purely coincidental.

one

OLIVER

With a growl of frustration, I drop my phone on the table beside my bed and kick a stack of books across the room. I rake my fingers through my hair and lean my elbows on my knees.

Why the hell isn't she answering my calls? When we last spoke two weeks ago, we made plans for me to come visit her for Thanksgiving. It pisses me off because that was my excuse to avoid going to my father's for the holiday. To say things are tense between him and me is putting it mildly. We've always had a strained relationship, but when shit went down with him and my mother, things got worse. My and my father's relationship went into the bowels of hell the night I overheard them arguing over his affair, the same night he asked for a divorce. And what do you know, the ink wasn't even dry on the divorce papers before he brought his mistress home as his new wife. My resentment toward him has only manifested since then. How the fuck could he go from being married to my mother for twenty years, to demanding a divorce, and then marrying another woman so quickly?

To add the rotten cherry on top of the moldy cake, he not only brought a new wife into the house he shared with my mother, but also a stepdaughter my age. Those first couple of months were bad. Angry at my father, but unable to take it out on him, I directed my wrath at Rylee, my new stepsister. It was her mother who fucked up my parents' marriage. I was miserable, and I made damn sure she was too.

Call me a whiney little bitch and see how many fucks it produces. Yes, I was an asshole for all the shit I did to Rylee, and I now regret taking my anger out on her. She was the one innocent person in all of this, and it was wrong of me to assume she wasn't. Even her mom, Evelyn, isn't who I thought she was. She actually seems like a decent person. No, it's my father who's at fault here. He's the asshole who cheated on my mother. The one who tore our family apart. It's something I'll never forgive him for.

And now, on top of all that shit, my mother hasn't answered any of my phone calls for the last two weeks.

When she and my father divorced, my mother moved in with my aunt in Utah. She's only come back home to visit a few times. I'm supposed to spend Thanksgiving with her and Aunt Rina, but fuck if I know if that's still the plan. I've tried calling my aunt, but she always says my mother's busy and will pass along the message to call me.

Thanksgiving break starts tomorrow, and I'm tempted to just fly there without confirming with my mother, but the last thing I want to do is spend a week alone with my aunt if my mother won't be there. My aunt's a major bitch that I can barely tolerate with my mother present. There's not a chance in hell I'll be able to without her around.

My father's been up my ass about coming home, something I try to avoid when possible. Now that I'm in college and don't have to put up with his shit, the less I see of him, the better. With my mother not answering my calls, I have no good excuse to not show up. And knowing my father, if I don't come home, he'll recruit Zayden, my best friend, to come get my ass.

The only silver lining is Rylee and Zayden will be there. I still feel guilty as shit for what I did to them, and what almost happened to Rylee because of my actions. Our relationship is still on rocky ground. I've got a lot of making up to do. Thankfully, she's coming around better than I would have in her shoes.

My and Zayden's friendship was shaken too, something else I regret.

Yeah, I know. I was a bastard.

Any chance I get to show Rylee and Zayden I'm over my rift with Rylee, I take it. This week will give me another.

There's a loud bang against my door, followed by a shout of laughter. Why I thought moving into a dorm would be a good idea beats me. Oh yeah, it was my dick that convinced me. Co-ed dorms meant plenty of girls at my disposal. And while that's still the case, most of the girls here don't interest me. Or they don't anymore. When I moved in at the beginning of the term, I had a new girl in my bed every night. It was fun at first, but it soon turned lackluster.

The image of stunning green eyes and soft blonde hair comes to mind. Shaking my head, I force away the thought before the rest of her can fully form in my mind. I've got no business thinking about Savannah. She's a bitch who thinks I'm the scum of the earth and would love nothing more than to squash me beneath her fancy heels. Rylee's best friend and protector. Because of my prior treatment of Rylee, who has *mostly* forgiven me, Savannah's hated me from the start. I've tried talking to her, being nice and all that shit, but she won't have any of it.

Evidently, my body doesn't care if she'd rather eat slugs than put her gorgeous eyes on me, because if she's near, or I get even a hint of her unique scent, I grow hard.

Stupid fucking dick.

Whatever.

I stalk to my door after there's another thump and yank it open. Belamy catches himself on the door frame before he ass plants on the floor.

"Do you fucking mind?" I growl.

He steps away, holding his hands up in the air defensively. "Shit, Oliver. Is that your door? I wasn't paying attention."

"It's the same door I've had since I moved in, you idiot."

"Sorry, man. It won't happen again."

Shooting a glare from him to Brett, who's holding a football, I slam the door. Heading toward my closet, I pull out a duffle bag to pack my shit for the next week.

As a freshman, I shouldn't have as much pull as I do here, but having the last name Conley has afforded me many things. Ruling the roost at Seattle University is one of them. Having a dorm room to myself is another.

Dropping the duffle on my bed, I start pulling clothes from my closet and stuffing them inside. As I'm zipping it closed, my phone rings. I grit my teeth when I see Zayden's name instead of my mother's.

"Sup, Z?"

"Rylee and I are hitting the road in the morning. You wanna hitch or are you still going to your mom's place for the week?"

My bag thumps on the floor when I shove it aside and take a seat on the bed. "My mother's place is out. I still can't get her to answer my calls. But I'm taking my car in case I need to ditch for a while."

Zayden knows of the tension between my father and me, so my warning comes as no surprise.

"If you need to, you know you can come to my dad's place for a day or so. Dani would love having you around."

Danielle, Zayden's little sister, had a lung transplant a few months ago. Fucking emphysema took hers out. The girl's sweet and deserves so much more than life has given her. It was touch and go for a while because her insurance wouldn't approve the transplant. My father offered to pay for the procedure, but Zayden and his dad, both being pridefully stubborn, refused. Thankfully, the insurance company got off their ass in time and Dani got a new set of lungs.

"I could do with some Dani time," I say, tossing a box of Red Hots on top of my duffle and pulling open another box. I drop a few in my mouth and chew. "You staying at home or your dad's place?"

Zayden snorts. "You know damn good and well your dad won't let me stay with Rylee in the house. Not to mention, her mom may cut off my junk in the middle of the night to make sure I can't touch her daughter under her roof. She's terrified I'll get her pregnant."

At one time, it would have pissed me off to hear my house referred as Evelyn's, and while I still may internally bristle a little on behalf of my mother, I've come to realize it's my father who I'm really angry with.

"With the way you two go at it like jack rabbits, it wouldn't surprise me either."

"Fuck you. I keep my shit wrapped and she's on the pill. Besides, Rylee's already threatened to castrate me if I get her pregnant before she has her degree. I like my balls just where they are."

"I bet you do. You'd be useless to Rylee if you no longer had them," I jest good-naturedly.

"I'd still have my mouth and hands," he boasts. "She wouldn't be going anywhere."

I laugh, the tight knot in my chest loosening. It's damn good to be able to joke around with Zayden again. I damn near irreparably fucked things up between us in my quest to break up my father and Evelyn. Zayden's a better man than me. It took a while, but things are getting back to normal. I have Rylee to thank for that. I have no doubt had she wanted to hold onto her grudge against me, Zayden would have stood by her side.

"There's another reason I called."

I tense at Zayden's quiet tone. "What?"

"Savannah's going home with Rylee this week."

A whole slew of curses fly through my head. This is not what I fucking need. Now I not only have to deal with my father, but Savannah on top of it. For a whole fucking week.

Instead of outwardly showing my irritation by the news, I bottle that shit inside.

"That's great," I say calmly. "And you're telling me this why?"

"Come on, man. You aren't fooling anyone. You've got some kind of beef with her. I, being the good friend that I am, was giving you a heads up."

"I'd have to care enough about the girl to have anything against her. She's the one who's always on my ass anytime I'm around."

"You keep telling yourself that. One day you might believe it."

"Whatever, Z. I appreciate it, but the warning wasn't necessary." The lie slips easily from my lips.

Someone hollers in the background on his end. "Be there in a minute, baby," Zayden yells back. "Listen, I gotta go. Just do me a favor and help make my life easier by being nice to Savannah."

I grunt. "Maybe you should be having this conversation with her." I toss another Red Hot in my mouth. "I've tried being the nice guy. She shoots me down any time I do."

"Just ignore her."

"Kinda hard to do when she'll be staying in my house."

"Shit, Oliver, throw me a fucking bone here. You and her get into it, I'll have Rylee bitching about it in my ear."

I laugh. "That's bullshit and you know it. Rylee has no qualms about coming to me when I've somehow pissed Savannah off."

"Just stay away from her as much as you can," he grunts with aggravation.

"Trust me, I plan on it. Looks like I'll have even more of a reason to visit little Dani."

"I'll give Dad a heads up. If I'm lucky, I'll manage to sneak into Rylee's room a couple of nights, so you'll have my room at home to yourself."

I shove my feet into my shoes and get up from the bed. "You're a ballsy fucker. My father will have your ass if he catches you."

"It'll be worth it. It's gonna suck not having Rylee in my bed at night."

Rylee and Savannah have an apartment together off campus, while Zayden chose to utilize the free housing that came with his scholarship. Even so, ninety percent of the time, one is at the other's place. It won't be long before they both say fuck it and Zayden moves into her apartment. Which is really going to be a bitch, because if I want to hang out with him, I'll be forced to be around Savannah even more. But then again, pissing her off has sort of become a sport for me.

"I'll catch you tomorrow evening," I say, hearing Rylee in the background asking Zayden what's taking so long.

"Yep. See you then."

I hang up and shove my phone in my pocket.

After throwing a few more Red Hots into my mouth, I toss the box on the table and snatch up my wallet and keys. I shrug on my coat next. Daffany's is a couple of blocks away, and it's a hell of a lot better than what this school offers. Another reason dorms are a bad idea is because of the crappy cafeteria food.

The hall is mostly clear when I leave my room. Almost everyone has already left for the holiday, with the exception of a few stragglers who've decided to stay here instead of going home or are leaving tomorrow.

I ignore the chill of the cold wind as I make my way across the quad to the parking lot. As soon as I'm close enough, I press my key fob to start my car. Thank Christ my car warms up fast. I slide inside and sigh when my ass hits the already warm seat.

As I pull out of the parking lot, my thoughts wander back to the hell my life's about to be for the next week.

Six days.

I can last six days.

two

SAVANNAH

I shift in the backseat of Rylee's Audi, staring out of the window as we make the relatively short trip to her mom's house. I hadn't planned to spend Thanksgiving break at the Conley's, but after my parents announced they were spending the holiday with my mom's sister in Iowa, I knew it was either this or stay home alone, which I seriously considered. Of course, there was no way Rylee was going to allow me to be alone.

"So, V." Rylee clears her throat from the passenger seat, her hotter than sin boyfriend, Zayden, behind the wheel. Moments later, she turns and by the look on her face, I can tell I'm not going to like what she has to say. "There's something I've been meaning to tell you." She kneads her bottom lip nervously between her teeth. "Don't get mad, okay?"

"You know, when you start a sentence with don't get mad, I'm already gearing up to be mad. You get that, right?" Rylee knows me better than anyone. Whatever she's about to say has a high probability of pissing me off, otherwise she wouldn't be trying to brace me for the impact.

"Oliver's going to be there this week," she says, almost too quickly for me to process her words. I stare at her for a full ten seconds before I've grasped what she said.

"Come again?" I blurt, hoping that maybe I heard her wrong. Oliver Conley is the absolute last person I want to spend the holiday with, or any other day for that matter. After everything he put Rylee through last spring, he's lucky I haven't stabbed him. He may be her stepbrother, but that doesn't mean I have to forgive him for what he did, even if Rylee has.

"I had no idea when I insisted you come. I guess his plans changed last night. He was supposed to spend the week at his mom's. Not really sure what changed." She shrugs.

"And this is something you couldn't have shared before we left?"

"No, because I knew if I did, you would use it as an excuse not to come, and I'm not leaving my best friend all alone on Thanksgiving."

"So you purposely withheld the information to get me to do what you wanted me to do?" I bite back in frustration.

"Yes." Her face scrunches in apology. "Listen, I know you don't like him, but over the last few months he's really been trying. Do you think *maybe* you could cut him some slack? For me." She pops her bottom lip out, giving a slight pout.

"You are the only reason I don't knee him in the nuts every time I see him," I point out. "That's about as tolerant as I get when he's involved. Honestly, Rylee, I don't know why you think a person who did all the things he did is even remotely redeemable."

"He had his reasons." Her defense of him causes my blood to boil.

"The fact that he's a spoiled, entitled prick who thinks he can throw a tantrum every time something doesn't go his way being one of them," I grumble loud enough for both of them to hear me.

I should tread a fine line where Oliver is concerned. He's not only my best friend's stepbrother, but her boyfriend's best friend. Yet, I can't seem to hold my tongue whenever his name comes up. I blame my mother. I inherited her inability to keep my mouth shut.

"V." Rylee sighs. "Please just *try* to be nice. Besides dinner, you probably won't even see him."

"He plans to hang at my house some of the time. He wants to spend some time with Dani while we're home," Zayden adds in after listening to us. "I get why you don't like him." He meets my gaze in the rearview mirror. "Hell, somedays I wonder why I do.

But he's a good guy at his core. He just does some really fucked up things on occasion."

"Good people don't do what he did."

"People make mistakes," Rylee cuts in. "The point is that we learn from them. And maybe this is naïve of me, but I really think he has seen the error of his ways and is trying to make things right," she offers with her annoying optimism. She's always been a glass half full kind of girl, but ever since her and Zayden have been seeing each other, it's like she sees the world through rose-colored lenses. Sometimes I want to shake her.

"I know Oliver better than anyone," Zayden cuts in before I have a chance to respond, his focus on the road. "Yes, he can be an asshole. Yes, sometimes he behaves like a spoiled little bitch. But he's been there for me in ways I will never be able to put into words. I promise you, he's not all bad. And if I didn't think he was sorry for what he did, there's no way I would let him within a hundred feet of Rylee."

"If I remember right, you were more pissed at him than anyone," I retort.

"Still am." He chuckles. "Just because I've chosen to forgive him doesn't mean I'm not still pissed about what he did. He knows one wrong move and he'll have me to answer to, and this time I won't hold back. Fuck a lifetime of friendship. If he hurts Rylee again, there's no going back and he knows it."

"I'm sorry, but I just don't see it. He's rude. Crass. Full of himself. He seriously doesn't even have one redeeming quality." I huff, but that's not entirely true.

Oliver Conley may be the scum of the earth, but he's scum that looks like he just stepped out of a GQ magazine. Tall, athletic build. Sandy blond hair that's always styled to perfection. And don't even get me started on his eyes—a mixture of blue and gray that makes it hard to pinpoint what color they actually are. He's gorgeous, though I'd never in a million years admit that out loud. But my hatred of him doesn't blind me from what he looks like. Truthfully, I think I dislike him more because of it.

"Look," Rylee turns deeper into her seat, "I'm not asking you to be his friend. Hell, I'm not even asking you to like him. I just need you to tolerate him. Do you think you can do that?"

"What the hell do you think I've been doing the last six months?"

"Giving him dirty looks. Throwing insults at him every time you're forced to cross paths. Or my favorite, when you hide in your bedroom and pretend like you're not home when he stops by."

"Well, which is it? Would you prefer the dirty looks and insults, or me hiding in your room all week, because those are really your only options?"

"V," Rylee groans.

"Don't V, me. You're the one who waited until we were almost at your house before telling me he would be there."

"Fine, if you won't do it for me, do it for my mom. You know how much she's looking forward to having everyone together."

"That's dirty. Even for you, Rylee Harper. Using Evelyn against me."

"Well, you leave me with no other choice. If you can't be nice for me, then you have to be nice for her."

"You do realize it's not in my nature to bite my tongue?"

"I do. But I also know how much you love my mom, and there isn't a chance in hell you would let that mouth of yours ruin the holiday she's been looking forward to."

She's right, of course. Evelyn has been like a second mom to me for years. I love her like she *is* my own and there isn't a thing I wouldn't do for her. And I know the same goes for her. She's shown me time and time again that she views me as part of her family. As much as I loathe Oliver, I love Evelyn more. And in my book, that means something.

"Fine," I concede. "I'll try," I grumble. "But if he comes at me wrong, I make no promises."

"He won't." Zayden's gaze once again meets mine in the mirror. "If he does, he'll have me to answer to."

"It's going to be fine. You'll see." Rylee reaches across the console into the backseat and pats my knee. "Who knows, maybe if you two don't spend the whole week insulting each other, you might actually find that you have some things in common."

"Now you've gone off the rails. Just because I said I would play nice doesn't mean I have any intention of actually talking to the douche canoe. My playing nice is not stabbing him with my fork at the dinner table."

In the beginning, my anger toward him was solely based on what he had done to my best friend. And while that's still a large part of why I don't like him, it's no longer just about Rylee. He's made it personal now. Hell, he made it personal a long time ago when he attacked my appearance and called me overweight. As if not being a hundred-pound bean pole automatically makes me fat. And while I've tried not to put a lot of stock into anything that comes out of his mouth, for some reason that's one comment I haven't been able to shake. I know that it has more to do with me than it does him, but I still want to gouge his eyes out for his little snide comments every time he makes one.

"I don't know. I think I might actually like to see that." Zayden chuckles. "I say we let her do her thing, babe." His head tilts in Rylee's direction. "Might make for one hell of a fucking show."

"Shut up." She playfully swats his arm. "Though, it certainly would be a Thanksgiving none of us would ever forget," she agrees.

"Are you two trying to talk me into it? Say the word, and I'm game." I don't try to hide my enthusiasm over the idea.

"You two." Rylee shakes her head. "There will be no stabbing."

"I don't have to stab him. I mean, there are plenty of ways I could...."

"Would you look at what you started?" Rylee cuts me off as she scolds Zayden, who laughs. I swear, these two are so freaking cute it's nauseating. "No bodily harm." Her gaze swings back to me.

"Fine." I sulk, crossing my arms in front of my chest.

"Now that that's settled, do you want to stop and get something to eat before we get to the house? My mom works until later, so I doubt she's going to want to do dinner tonight."

The mention of food makes my stomach groan loudly. I'm so hungry I feel like my insides have resorted to eating itself, and yet, the thought of actually eating food makes me feel sick.

"Yeah, that sounds good," Zayden is the first to answer.

"Yeah," I agree, even though I really don't want to.

"Let's wait until we get to town and go for pizza. I've been dying for some Perogi's," Rylee suggests.

"That sounds great. But you know if we go there, I'm going to have to get some to take to my dad's. Dani would likely murder me if she knew I went to her favorite pizza place and didn't bring her anything."

"Maybe we can wait and just order in. We can get one for Dani and your dad too."

"Sounds like a plan." He snags her hand, lifting it to his lips before laying a light kiss to it.

I can't help but smile at Zayden. For being kind of rough around the edges, he probably has the softest heart of anyone I know. You wouldn't know that from talking to him, but spend enough time around him and it's apparent. I don't think I could have asked for a better man for my best friend. I know there isn't one thing he wouldn't do for her, and I love him for that. I love that she has that. But I'd be lying if I said a part of me wasn't a little envious.

I know I'm still young, and have plenty of time to meet someone, but when I watch Rylee and Zayden together, I can't help but think that I'll never share that type of connection with another person. At least not on the same level. I'm fairly certain what Zayden and Rylee share is something that stands all on its own and isn't something many people are lucky enough to find.

I turn my gaze back out the window, not really paying attention to Rylee's response or what Zayden says after. My mind drifts back to Oliver and what the next six days will likely entail for me. Even if I promise to be on my best behavior, that doesn't mean he will be. And I'm not one to let someone walk all over me and not defend myself.

Maybe I'm just thinking the worst. I've been around Oliver a few times over the last couple of months, and while we almost always take shots at each other, it's not like we get into screaming matches or anything. It's nothing I can't get through. Then again, that's when I only have to endure him for a couple of hours, not six days. I'll be lucky if I haven't stabbed him in his sleep by day three.

I know *my* problem with him, but I've never fully understood *his* problem with me. Unless his problem with me is that I have a problem with him, which is what I originally assumed. But now, I don't know. It seems like his issue with me runs deeper than that. You would almost think *I* did something to him. Then again, maybe I did. I've taken quite a few shots at him over the last few months. Maybe I've bruised his ego a little.

Poor baby....

He's lucky I haven't bruised more than that.

At the end of the day, I know Oliver and I are going to have to reach some kind of common ground. As much as I hate it, he *is* my best friend's stepbrother and it doesn't look like that's something that is likely to change, given how happy Paul and Evelyn are. We're in each other's lives whether we like it or not.

Maybe these six days will be good for us. Or maybe one of us will end up killing the other before we make it that far.

I guess only time will tell....

three

OLIVER

I pocket my keys as I walk through the front door, dropping my bag in the entryway. Tension leaves my body stiff. It's been months since I've been home, and I already regret coming. The day I left for Seattle University, my father and I got into a huge argument. As the norm for the last year, it was about my mother. There were some things I wanted to know, and he refused to talk.

Fucking typical.

Feminine laughter comes from the kitchen, so that's where I head. It isn't Evelyn, because her car wasn't in the garage, so it's either Rylee or Savannah's. By the male laughter that follows, my guess is on Rylee.

I push open the door and come to a stop. A grin tugs at my lips as I lean against the wall and cross my arms over my chest. Zayden has Rylee pinned to the table, one of his hands keeping her arms locked around his waist by gripping her wrists, while he uses the other hand to tickle her side. A loud burst of giggles breaks from her as she squirms unsuccessfully in his arms.

"Oh, my God, Zayden, stop!" she squeals, throwing her head back. "You're gonna make me pee my pants!"

"Then give me what I want," he demands, moving his fingers up her ribs.

"No! Savannah could walk in at any minute."

I chuckle lightly because it's not Savanah they need to worry about.

Rylee lifts her head and peers at me around Zayden. Her eyes go wide. "Or maybe Oliver."

Zayden looks over his shoulder at me. "You've got shitty fucking timing."

I shrug and move from my perch. "It's my house." Walking to the fridge, I pull out a bottle of water. "How long have you been here?"

"Not long."

I uncap the bottle and take a pull. "Your mom at work?" I ask Rylee.

"Yeah. She called a bit ago. She's going to have a late night. We're ordering some pizza and watching a movie. You in?"

I take a moment to think about it. I was originally planning to be at home as little as possible to avoid my father as much as I could, but going out right now doesn't really appeal to me. He won't be home for another few hours anyway, so I can stick around for a bit.

"Sure." I recap my bottle and hop up on the counter. "You been home yet?"

Zayden leans back against the counter and tugs Rylee to his front. "Dad's at work and it's Danielle's last day before the holiday, so she's still in school. I plan to stop by and drop off a pizza for them later."

Movement to my left pulls my attention toward the door as Savannah walks in. We all look over at her. She gives me the scowl she reserves just for me, and I return it in kind.

"Your mom and dad make it to Iowa okay?" Rylee asks, pulling Savannah's attention to her.

As she answers, I take a minute to look at her. Thick blonde hair swept up on top of her head with a few pieces hanging loose. Slender but graceful neck. Sea-green eyes—slightly slanted. Boobs just big enough to fill a man's hand. And hips the perfect size for holding onto as you fuck her from behind. She's a damn fine package—one my dick has taken notice of. Too bad as soon as she opens her mouth, it takes her appeal down a couple or a hundred notches.

"I see the asshole's made it," she remarks, as if to prove my inner thoughts.

"And it looks like the bitch did too," I retort.

"You both knock it off," Rylee says, looking from one of us to the other with narrow eyes. "You're both adults. Now act like it."

"She started it," I grumble.

Rylee's lips twitch, but she holds back her smile. "Well, I'm finishing it." She pulls away from Zayden and grabs her phone from her back pocket. "I'm calling Perogi's. What does everyone want?"

"White pizza for me."

"What in the fuck is a white pizza?" I ask Savannah.

She doesn't even have to describe it, the name alone sounds disgusting.

With a huff and an eyeroll, she faces me. "It's made with ranch instead of red sauce, and mozz cheese, chicken—"

I cut her off, "Wait. You can't have a pizza without marinara sauce."

Crossing her arms over her chest, she asks with irritation in her tone, "Says who?"

"Says me."

"And you're the God of all things pizza?" She arches a brow.

"No, but everyone knows it's the sauce that makes the pizza. Especially from Perogi's."

"Not my pizza."

"What you get is not pizza. It's an abomination trying to mimic pizza."

A small growl slips past her lips, and I fight back a laugh when it looks like she wants to stomp her foot like a five-year old.

So much for Rylee's statement about us being adults.

Shooting me a glare, she turns back to Rylee. "A large white pizza for me."

Just to piss her off, because I know it will, I ask innocently, "Don't they offer personal pans at Perogi's?"

For a moment, it almost looks like there's pain in her expression, but it's gone before I can analyze it. Her glare turns murderous. "The better question is, do you have to special order extra small condoms, or can they be found on the shelf?"

Before Rylee can interrupt our bickering—and from the look on her face, she's about to jump all over my ass—I hop down from the counter.

"The better person to ask would be your last boyfriend." She opens her mouth to respond, but I give her my back and face a pissed off Rylee. "Meat lovers for me, with extra pepperoni and add mushrooms." I turn on my heel and stalk out of the room.

I PLANT my ass down in the only available seat and settle my plate of pizza on my lap. Zayden and Rylee are laying down huddled under a blanket on the couch and Savannah has taken up both cushions on the loveseat—also with a blanket over her—which happens to be my favorite place to sit.

I shoot the back of her head a glare and hope she can feel the heat of it. I'd demand she move, but by the look Rylee keeps sending me, I'm not sure my balls would stay attached to my body if I did.

I pick up a slice of pizza and take a big bite. "What are we watching?" I ask around the food in my mouth.

"Not telling," Rylee answers with her eyes still glued to the TV. "You'll have to wait and see."

"Don't feel left out. She's not telling me either," Zayden inserts.

"And this doesn't concern you? There's no telling what they're going to make us watch."

"You could always leave."

I look at Savannah with a sneer. "And you'd just love that, wouldn't you?"

"I'd love nothing more."

"And that's exactly why I won't be leaving."

Rylee yanks the covers off her in a fit of madness, leans away from Zayden to sit on the edge of the seat, and points one finger on each hand at me and Savannah.

"I've had enough," she growls. "This is ridiculous. It's Thanksgiving, for Christ sake. The time for being thankful, not *hateful*. If you two don't stop this shit right now, I'm going to tie you both to a chair, lock you in a room, and force you to talk about whatever the hell your issues are. Got it?"

She glares at Savannah until she gives her a muttered "got it" before aiming it at me. I jerk my chin up in agreement.

With a huff, she spins around and settles back against Zayden. He pulls the covers back over them and murmurs something in her ear that has her body relaxing.

I glance at Savannah to find her looking at me over her shoulder with hate-filled eyes, her mouth moving as she chews on her God-awful pizza. Using my middle finger, I scratch the side of my nose. Her eyes roll before she directs them back to the TV.

A moment later, the room fills with a beat, giving away that whatever we're watching is a Universal Studios movie. Stormy clouds appear next on the screen. I take a bite of my pizza, and nearly choke when I see the title of the movie.

"We are not watching *Fifty Shades of Grey*," Zayden and I both yell at the same time.

"Oh, yes, we are," Rylee demands. She snatches the remote from the back of the couch before Zayden can grab it.

"Damn it, Rylee. I'm not watching porn with our best friends in the room."

"It's not porn," Rylee argues, shooting daggers at him over her shoulder.

"The hell it's not."

"It's about a guy and a girl who like to have a bunch of raunchy sex. The whole premise of the story is based on his need to dominate and his issues with sex. Sounds like porn to me."

Savannah spins on the cushion until she's fully facing me. "Oh, my God. Stop being the typical male. There's so much more to the story than that. Of course, I wouldn't expect you to understand. Your head up here," she taps the side of her head, "isn't much bigger than the one down below." Her eyes point to my dick, and what do you know, it twitches.

I ignore her comment and tip up one corner of my mouth. "You really want me in the same room with you as boobs and bush are flashing on the screen? I'm a guy, it'll probably turn me on."

Her lip curls up into a sneer. "Sounds like your problem, not mine."

"Rylee," Zayden sighs. "Let's find something else to watch."

"Come on, babe. I promise if you give it a chance, you might actually find it interesting."

I snort, which earns me another glare from Rylee.

"Fine," he grumbles. "But I'm picking the next movie, and I guarantee there will be killing and gory shit involved."

She smiles and leans up to place a kiss against his cheek. "Deal."

"I also reserve the right to turn it off if I hear any grunts or groans coming from Oliver."

"Fuck you," I toss out.

"He'll behave." Rylee's tone brooks no argument, like she's telling me instead of requesting.

I shrug.

She presses play, and I recline back in my chair. I finish my pizza and toss my plate on the table beside me. The room is quiet, the only sound coming from the TV. With the lights down low, the light from the TV flickers on the walls.

A movement off to the side catches my attention, and I look to Savannah. She's leaning back against the arm of the loveseat. The blanket she's under has been shoved down to her waist and one of her bare legs, bent at the knee, is sticking out of it. It almost looks like she's naked from the waist down, but I know that's stupid. I can't help but stare at her leg and wonder how it would feel under my palm. Does she shave everyday so the skin would be soft and smooth? Does she shave *everywhere*?

I reach down and adjust my jeans when my dick begins to harden. It's sick, my fascination with this girl. She hates me, and I'm damn sure not fond of her either. Does my dick care? Fuck no. Because I can't seem to get him under control whenever she's around. Even when she pisses me off so much I want to wrap my hands around her tender neck and squeeze so she shuts her trap.

All of a sudden, she drops her empty plate to the floor and jackknifes off of the loveseat. With her hand to her stomach, she darts out of the room down the hallway, no doubt heading for the bathroom.

I look to Rylee and Zayden at the same time they look at me. Rylee nibbles on her bottom lip and she gets up from the couch.

"I'm going to go check on her."

Zayden looks concerned as Rylee dashes out of the room. It's probably from all the fucking pizza she consumed. She had more on her plate than I did, and I eat *a lot*.

"You need to lay off her," Zayden says, directing his eyes to me.

"I think you need to be telling her that. I only react when she starts in on me."

"Or you could ignore it," he suggests with a raised brow.

I pull a small box of Red Hots out of my pocket and dump some in my hand. "Not in my nature."

"Make it your nature."

"And if I don't?" I ask, chomping down on the cinnamon candies.

"Then we may have problems."

His words piss me off. I know what I did to Rylee was wrong, and I don't blame him for taking her side when shit went down. I had been out of line and took things too far. But I've apologized and worked my ass off in an attempt to make up for it. For him to insinuate that he'd side with Savannah—once again picking a girl over me—rankles me. I've tried being nice to her, but she wants none of it. I'll be damned if I'll lay down and be her whipping post.

Now you know what it feels like, my mind whispers.

I grit my teeth. Yeah, I guess I do know what it feels like. But unlike Savannah, what I did to Rylee was much worse. Even so, she didn't silently put up with my shit either.

"What do you expect me to do, Z?" I demand harshly. "Let the bitch say whatever the hell she wants without retaliation? If that's it, you can go fuck yourself."

He sighs and rubs the back of his neck. Swinging his legs around, he leans forward so his hands dangle between his knees.

"I'll talk to Rylee. Something's got to give between you and Savannah."

"Yeah, you do that," I grunt.

Not that it'll help. I've gotten on Savannah's bad side and apparently, she doesn't give second chances.

What-the-fuck-ever.

Four

SAVANNAH

"V, you okay?" Rylee calls through the closed door followed by a light knock.

I stare down at the remnants of my pizza now sitting in the bottom of the toilet and my stomach curls again.

"Yeah," I croak back. "The pizza didn't sit very well with me," I lie. "I'll be out in a minute."

"Okay. You sure you don't need anything? A water maybe?"

"No, I'm good."

"Okay," she murmurs seconds before I hear her feet pad back down the hallway.

I wasn't lying. The pizza really didn't sit well with me. Unfortunately, it seems like nothing does anymore. What started out as a small purge here and there has spiraled out of control. I know making myself throw up is stupid. And I know how harmful it can be, but over the last few years, my love of food and my desire to be smaller have been waging war on one another. I've tried to find a balance—eating less instead of gorging myself, but I still feel so guilty I have no choice but to expunge it from my body. As time has gone on, it's only gotten worse. It used to take me several minutes to make myself sick, but now it's like my body instantly rejects food the minute it enters my stomach.

Flushing the toilet, I straighten my posture, and wipe my mouth with the back of my hand. I take a deep breath in, feeling better by the second.

Crossing toward the sink, I wash my hands before blotting a

little water on my face. I'm delaying walking back into that living room because I know as soon as I do, Oliver is going to make some comment about me running to the bathroom, and I'm going to want to rip his throat out.

"You can do this," I whisper to my reflection. "No one knows." I take another deep pull of air in before spinning on my heel and exiting the bathroom.

When I re-enter the living room, Rylee has reclaimed her spot next to Zayden and Oliver doesn't look like he's moved. All three sets of eyes come to me as I settle back onto the loveseat and pull the blanket up to my chest.

"You okay?" Rylee asks over the too loud television.

"I'm good." I plaster on a smile and nod, my eyes sliding to Oliver when Rylee's attention goes back to the movie.

I tense when I realize he's watching me.

Does he know?

I crinkle my forehead and give him a look that can only be construed as 'fuck you' before turning my gaze toward the T.V. There's no way he knows. Getting sick one time because I ate too much pizza isn't something that automatically raises a red flag. People get sick all the time.

With this thought, I relax slightly and try to focus on the movie.

"Well, what did you think?" Rylee stretches her arms over her head as Zayden gets up to flip on the lights.

"It wasn't that bad," he says unconvincingly, garnering a snort from Oliver.

"Not that bad if you like soft porn with a mediocre storyline." Oliver reaches for the remote, turning the volume down.

"The storyline wasn't mediocre." Rylee seems personally offended, as if she were the one who wrote the damn thing.

Don't get me wrong, I love Fifty Shades as much as the next girl, but I never got into the series the way Rylee did. I'm more of a

Hunger Games or *Divergent* kind of girl. Dystopian has always been my jam.

"And seriously, who watches a movie like this with their brother in the room?" Oliver keeps going.

"Well for one, you're my stepbrother. And two, I thought my *adult* stepbrother was mature enough not to make it gross. It's not like I pulled out a porno and suggested we all watch it together."

"Might as well have."

"It wasn't that bad, Oliver." Zayden steps in to take Rylee's side. Something he does often. "I kind of liked how he's this fucked up guy with all these issues and she's this sweet, innocent girl who wants to show him there's more out there for him." He winks at Rylee as he reclaims the seat by her side.

I swear her smile nearly splits her face in half.

I guess it makes sense why Zayden would enjoy the storyline, given that he and Rylee shared similarly equal differences in the beginning. Not with the whole dom/sub aspect, but them as people. The two were definitely on opposite ends of the spectrum when they met, but look at them now. She's changed him, and he's changed her. But not in a way that makes them any less of who they are—if that makes any sense.

"You two make me sick." Oliver pushes to his feet. "Keep it up and I might upchuck in the bathroom like Savannah did earlier." He holds his stomach and forces a fake gag.

"Screw you." I flip him off. "It's not my fault the pizza upset my stomach."

"Maybe if you hadn't eaten so much it wouldn't have," he fires back, sending me from a simmer to a boil in one second flat.

"What the hell is that supposed to mean?" I'm on my feet before I even realize I've moved.

"Looks like maybe I struck a nerve." The smile on his face tells me he got the exact reaction he was hoping for.

Even though my instinct is to lash out, I decide to try to take the high road on this one—mainly because I don't want to draw any more attention to this matter. The last thing I need is for people to start connecting the dots. Not that they would, but the bigger deal I make of it, the more suspicious it will seem.

"You know what, Oliver? If insulting me helps you feel better about yourself," my eyes dart to his crotch to get my point across, "then you go right ahead. You've spent your whole life overcompensating for your shortcomings. Why stop now?"

Okay, so maybe that wasn't *exactly* the high road.

"Give me two minutes, and I'll show you I have nothing to overcompensate for."

"Only two?" I tilt my head to the side, my hands going to my hips. "I guess I shouldn't be surprised. Little and quick. You really are a winner."

If looks could kill, I'd be a melted heap of flesh on the floor right now, given the fire shooting out of Oliver's eyes.

"Alright." Zayden slaps his leg as he stands. "That's enough." He turns, grasping Oliver on the shoulder. He leans in and says something that only he can hear.

I watch Oliver's features relax slightly as Zayden steps past him, walking around the back of the couch where he leans over and kisses Rylee's temple.

"We're gonna head over to my dad's. I don't want to wait too late since I'm taking them dinner," he tells her.

"You want me to come?"

"Nah." He shakes his head. "Oliver's going to come with me. You stay here with Savannah, see your mom when she gets home."

"Okay." She turns her face upward to allow him to lay a kiss on her mouth. "Call me later?"

"I will. Love you." He kisses her again before straightening.

"Love you, too."

"Come on, Oliver, let's get out of here," he tells his best friend, who's anger filled gaze slides back to me.

"Let's." His nostrils flare moments before he spins on his heel and follows Zayden out of the room.

"What the hell?" Rylee blurts seconds later.

"What?" I plop back down on the loveseat, shoving the blanket to the side.

"I thought you said you'd try."

"This *is* me trying."

"Well, then I'd hate to see you not trying." She blows out a heavy breath and sinks further into the couch.

"I'm sorry, Ry. Truly. I know how badly you want me and your stepbrother to get along, but honestly, I don't see that happening. Not when he continuously makes little snide comments to purposely get a rise out of me."

"Get along? Hell, at this point I'd settle for not speaking. What is it with you two? It's like you just can't help yourselves."

"What can I say? He brings out the worst in me."

"And you in him apparently." She thinks on that for a minute. "I guess that's not entirely true." She laughs.

"Ya think?" I cross my arms and give her a pointed look.

"We've had this conversation before, and I know why you don't like Oliver. But V, I have to ask, are you sure that's all it is?"

"What do you mean?"

"I just mean, I've seen you not like people before, but I've never seen you act toward someone the way you act toward Oliver. I can't help but feel like maybe there's more to it that you're not telling me."

"Okay, now I'm confused. What more could there be?"

"I don't know." She shrugs innocently. "It's just…. Well…. I've seen the way you look at him when you think no one is watching."

"Come again?" I balk at her.

"If I didn't know any better, I'd think you were attracted to him."

"I'm sorry, what?" I shoot straight up in my seat.

"Look at you, V. Look at how extreme you reacted to me saying maybe you think he's hot. It's like you try too hard. Like you're trying to cover it up or something."

"Okay, now I think you've officially lost it."

"Have I? Or are you just too proud to admit that behind the constant bickering and arguing you actually kind of like him?"

"I'm going upstairs." I push to a stand.

"V."

"First, you don't tell me that he's going to be here. Then you accuse me of actually being attracted to that monster. What's next? You going to try to set us up?"

"V." She chuckles, standing. "It's not like that. I'm not saying you're in love with him or anything."

"No, just that I have the hots for him. As if that's any better." I step around the loveseat and head toward the foyer.

"Where are you going?" she calls after me.

"I'm going to take a long, hot shower and try to forget everything you just said," I tell her, pausing at the bottom of the stairs.

"I wasn't accusing you of anything. I was just asking."

"Well, as my best friend, I think you, better than anyone, know where I stand."

"You're right. I am your best friend. I know you, Savannah Reynolds. And I know what it means when the mere mention of you possibly being attracted to someone sends you running, even if you don't." She arches a brow from across the room.

"Oh my God," I groan loudly. "Let me know when my best friend comes back. Until then, I'm staying away from you." I stomp up the stairs, her laughter following after me as I go.

I push my way inside the guest bedroom next to Rylee's room, where I'm staying, and snag my bag off the floor. Dropping it on the bed, I pull out some lounge pants and a comfy tee before crossing the hallway to the bathroom.

Minutes later, I'm standing under a stream of hot water. Rylee's words continue to repeat in my head no matter how many times I try to shove them to the back.

Attracted to Oliver?

As if.

I wouldn't be attracted to that wretched man if he were the last male on Earth.

Sure, he's gorgeous. Not even I can deny that. But him being good looking and me being attracted to him are two vastly different things.

Sure, maybe the first time I met him I was a little taken aback. I don't know what I was expecting, but when I walked into that kitchen and laid eyes on him for the first time, it became clear that he wasn't it.

So, I guess if I'm being honest, maybe I *was* attracted to him for a millisecond. That is, until I'd remembered what he was doing to my best friend. Then he opened his mouth and sealed the deal. I've disliked him ever since.

But again, if I'm being completely honest with myself, I know that's not entirely true.

I think about his eyes—the way they burn hot with anger when he looks at me. The way the muscles in his arms flex like he's physically trying to restrain himself when I push him too far. I'd be lying if I said that doesn't do something funny to my insides.

I close my eyes and imagine him pressed against me. The tension between us exploding into something more than petty arguing. I picture his lips on my neck. His hands restraining me. It makes me sick to even think about, but I can't help it.

My hand travels south, and even though I feel disgusted by the thought, I whimper when my fingers glide against my wet core.

I'm wound so tight, my muscles ache against the tension in my body. I need a release. Something to take my mind off of everything. Something to make me feel good.

It's been months since I've been with someone. Months since I've had someone's hands on my body. Months since I've felt the sweet weight of another body on top of me. And I need it. God, do I need it. I feel like a starved animal in the woods searching for scraps—for something to curb the hunger I feel inside.

I use that as my justification for the turn my thoughts have taken. It's not that I want Oliver, I reason with myself. In fact, it has nothing to do with him. When you go this long without any relief, you'll feast on the most rotten of carcasses to survive. And that's what I'm doing. I'm using him. Using the thought of him to satisfy a need.

The build comes on fast and strong, my body trembling under the warm water that continues to pelt my shoulders and back. I grip the side of the shower with my free hand, my entire body tensing as my orgasm rips through me.

I bite my bottom lip to silence my cries of pleasure.

This. This is what I needed.

I slow the movement of my fingers as I slowly begin to come back down. And when the chase is over, when I've found the release I so desperately needed, my desire is replaced with disgust.

Disgust over what I just did—or rather *who* I was thinking about while I did it. Ashamed that I let the thought of someone so cruel and vile bring me such pleasure. And angry with myself for being so weak.

I imagine the look on his face if he knew. The smug, satisfied smirk on his lips, knowing that the mere thought of him nearly brought me to my knees, and my disgust only grows.

The water is almost cold by the time I exit the shower a few minutes later. While my body feels sated and relaxed, I can't seem to get my mind to shut off.

What if Rylee was right? What if me hating Oliver is a cover for something else? Something that up until this moment I refused to even entertain.

"No," I mutter to myself as I wrap a towel around my hair and another around my body. I won't let her get inside my head. I do *not* have a thing for Oliver Conley. I think I'd rather throw myself off a bridge than be with someone like him.

But no matter how much I try to convince myself of this fact, I also can't deny that the seed has been planted and try as I may, I can't seem to stop it from taking root.

But admitting you're physically attracted to someone doesn't really mean much. I'm attracted to tons of actors and musicians—it's not like that means I want to date them or anything.

I jump when a light knock sounds against the bathroom door.

"Hey, V, you about done? Mom's home," Rylee calls through the door.

"Yeah, let me get dressed, and I'll be down."

"Okay."

Drying off, I dress quickly, pushing Oliver to the back of my mind. I've got enough going on right now without adding him into the mix. I had a temporary lapse in judgement and now it's over. No reason to make something out of nothing.

With that thought taking hold, I exit the bathroom and go in search of Rylee and Evelyn.

Five

OLIVER

"Wow!" I say, smiling down at the little girl in front of me. "It looks like you've grown six inches since the last time I saw you." I look over at Zayden and wink. "Hey, Z. Are you sure this is really your sister? This girl looks too old."

Zayden chuckles as he plates a couple slices of pizza for Danielle. Once he finishes, he turns around, crosses his arms over his chest, and regards his sister. "You know, I was wondering the same thing when I walked in. There's only one way to find out."

Danielle rolls her eyes, but a smile plays on her lips. "Do *not* even think about it," she warns, casting Zayden and I both wary glances.

I grin, and before she knows it, I've gently got her tossed over my shoulder. She squeals. I turn around, presenting her feet to Z. "Come check. The Danielle we know is extremely ticklish on her feet."

She laughs hysterically and bounces around on my shoulder, her fists half-heartedly beating on my back as Zayden attacks her feet. After a couple of moments, I give mercy to the poor girl and flip her back down so she's standing.

"Yep, you're Danielle alright," I say with a grin and ruffle her hair.

She giggles and shakes her head. "You guys suck." She fixes the mess I've made of her hair and plops down at the table in front of the plate of pizza Zayden put down.

"You know you love us."

She takes a big bite then shrugs. "Maybe a little," she says around her food.

I chuckle as I make my way to the fridge and grab a bottle of water. Turning back to the room, I lean against the counter.

Although it's been months since Danielle had her lung transplant, and I've seen her several times since then, it's still amazing to see the color in her cheeks, full of energy, and her expression relaxed and not filled with misery. It was hard watching her slowly wither away. I can only imagine how tough it was on Zayden and his dad. It was a close call for a while, but thankfully, the insurance company came through before it was too late.

Allen, Zayden's dad, walks into the kitchen. After dropping a kiss on top of Danielle's head, he beelines it straight for the pizza. He takes a bite, then drops it back in the box before turning to Zayden.

"You see that? He notices the pizza before his own son," he says, giving his dad a one-arm hug.

"It's good to see you, son," Allen states, slapping Zayden on the back.

"Not as good as the pizza apparently."

"It's Perogi's. Need I say more?"

Laughing quietly, Zayden nods. "Point made."

I clap hands with him. "How have you been, Oliver?"

"Nothing to complain about."

He opens the cabinet in front of him and pulls out a glass. "How's school?" he asks Zayden.

Opening the fridge, Zayden hands him the pitcher of tea. "It's good."

"You keeping your grades up?"

"Yes, Dad," he grunts.

He looks to me next. "And you?"

"Yes, sir," I answer. "All A's and B's for me. I can show you my progress report if you'd like." I finish with a grin.

"Smartass," he mutters, and we all laugh.

Allen has never been much of a talker, but he's a damn good father to Zayden and Danielle. Hell, he's a better father to *me* than my own has ever been.

"How's your dad and Evelyn doing?"

I shrug. "Last I heard, they were doing fine. I haven't seen them since we got into town."

He eyes me for a moment. He may not know all of the details, but he knows there's tension between my father and me.

After he puts the tea back in the fridge, he dumps a couple slices on a plate and carries them to the table. "Grab a slice. Have a seat." He gestures to the two empty seats.

"We already ate. I just stopped by to drop off the pizza," Zayden says.

His brow raises. "You staying at the Conley's?"

"You know Paul would never let that happen. I'll be back later, after I drop Oliver off."

He nods and shoves a bite of pizza in his mouth. "When are you going to bring Rylee by? It's been too long since I've seen that pretty girl."

"Tomorrow."

Allen points his pizza at Zayden. "Not too late. I've got a shift tomorrow evening."

"They still putting you on nights?"

"Not often. Only here and there."

"Why don't you give Mrs. Hogan the next few days off? Rylee and I'll take Danielle while you're at work."

"Really?" Danielle asks excitedly. "Don't get me wrong, Mrs. Hogan is great, but it gets kinda boring there."

"You sure?" Allen asks.

"Yep. Danielle can hang out with me and Rylee."

Danielle fist pumps the air and hisses, "Yes!" She points her finger at him. "You're the best brother ever!"

He shoots her a wink. "You know it." He turns back to his dad. "I'm going to drop Oliver off and say goodnight to my girl. I'll be back in a bit."

"Do me a favor and stop and grab a gallon of milk while you're out."

"You got it."

I grab the sides of Danielle's head and force it forward to plant a kiss on the top. "I'll see you around, kid."

Zayden says his goodbyes and we leave.

"It's damn good to see her looking so healthy," I remark once we're on the road.

"Hell yeah, it is. She missed out on so much of a normal childhood. Things she'll never get back. I'll be damned if she misses more."

"I'm glad it all worked out."

"Me too."

It's quiet for a few minutes, just the low sound of the radio in the background. One of my favorite songs comes on, and right as I'm reaching to turn it up, Zayden starts speaking again.

"Look, man, there's something I gotta ask you."

I tense, not liking the hesitancy in his tone.

"What?"

His eyes move from the road to me, then back to the road.

"Is there something going on between you and Savannah?"

I jerk my head around, caught off guard by his ridiculous question.

"What the hell kind of question is that? Does it look like there's something going on between her and me? The girl can barely stand to be in the same room with me, let alone be close enough for me to touch her."

He nods. "That's true. But fuck, Oliver, the tension between you two is intense. Way more than just dislike."

"Try hatred," I mutter.

"Do you really hate her?"

I pause, because my first initial reaction is to say yes. But deep down, I know that's not true. I get Savannah's aversion to me, and to be honest, I don't blame her. What has my hackles rising anytime she's near is my body's reaction to her. The woman hates me with every fiber of her being, while I have to fight tooth and nail to keep my hands off her. She drives me bat shit crazy.

"No, I don't hate her," I admit reluctantly.

"But you want to," he observes.

"Fuck yes, I do."

"If it means anything to you, Rylee and I don't think Savannah really hates you either."

I bark out a laugh. "You're both delusional."

He pulls to a stop at a stop sign. "People don't react as strongly as she does without some hidden reason."

"They do when you fuck with their best friend the way I did Rylee."

His knuckles turn white on the steering wheel and his jaw ticks. Yeah, he's not totally over what I did.

"Rylee told Savannah that she's forgiven you. Lingering animosity is one thing, but her reaction to you is strong. I think she wants to hate you on her friend's behalf." He shrugs. "Maybe she feels like she *should* hate you. And it pisses her off that she actually feels something different."

I scowl at him. He's lost his damn mind. "Like what?"

Zayden wiggles his eyebrows. "Lust."

I grunt. "Even if she did, I wouldn't trust her around my dick."

He chuckles. "Come on, man. You can't tell me you haven't thought about sleeping with Savannah."

"Oh, I have." His brows shoot up at my easy admittance. "I've thought about it quite a bit. In detail. Then I remember she'd probably whack my junk off with a rusty knife."

He laughs, but I'm dead fucking serious. I can imagine her standing over my sleeping form, an evil smile in place and delighted anticipation in her eyes.

I shudder at the thought.

"Maybe you should try some of your infamous Oliver charm on her?" he suggests.

"She's immune. I've already tried," I grumble.

"When?" A horn goes off behind us and Zayden glares at the

rearview mirror. "Hold your fucking horses," he mutters and presses down on the gas.

"The first day we met."

"Well, try again."

"What the fuck do you want, Z?" I demand. "For Savannah and me to miraculously get along, have sex, get married, and have two-point-five kids?"

I glance at him, my jaw clenching when I find a contemplative look on his face. "It would sure make my and Rylee's lives a whole lot less stressful."

"And screw both of your best friends and what they feel. You're fucking crazy."

"You never know. You may find you actually like Savannah. Once you get to know her."

"You know what? I'm done with this pointless conversation. There's no way Savannah would ever give me the time of day. And even if by some miracle she did, I'm not sure I'd give it to her."

I reach over and turn the volume up on the radio before he can say anything more. Thankfully, he keeps his trap shut the rest of the way home.

The house is quiet when we walk inside. Zayden heads upstairs, no doubt to Rylee's room, and I go for the kitchen for my father's hidden stash of whiskey. All this talk of banging Savannah has my blood pressure rising. Unfortunately, I don't think it's because the thought of fucking her revolts me like it should.

Pushing open the kitchen door, I come to a stop when I find Evelyn at the counter drinking a glass of orange juice. Her eyes widen fractionally until she notices it's me.

"Hello, Oliver," she says demurely.

"Hey," I call as I head to the cabinet above the fridge. I open it and reach behind a couple of containers and grab the bottle of expensive whiskey.

She raises her brow when she sees the bottle but seems to decide not to make a comment on my underage choices. I grab a glass from the dishwasher and look over my shoulder at her. "Want a glass?"

She bites her lip as she ponders my question. She surprises the shit out of me when she nods. "Sure."

I grab another glass and put them both on the counter, standing on the opposite side of the bar from her. After pouring a couple inches in each, I slide one across the smooth surface. She picks it up, eyes it for a moment, before bringing it to her lips.

She sputters out a cough. "And now I remember why I don't imbibe."

I smile as I lift my glass and take a healthy swallow. "This is the smooth stuff. You should have tasted the shit Zayden and I used to get when we were younger."

She flinches at the curse word but doesn't reprimand me. Evelyn's always been careful on how she acts around me. She's a smart lady—she's a damn neurosurgeon—so she must know of my wariness of her in my home.

"You drank when you were younger?"

I lean my elbows on the bar. "Don't all teenagers?"

"Rylee doesn't," she defends.

"Okay," I say and hide my smile behind my glass, not willing to be the one to alter her perception of her perfect daughter.

She takes another tentative sip, then bristles. "I just can't do it."

"Try pouring it in with your orange juice. It'll help mask the flavor."

She does so and tries it again. "A little better," she murmurs. She sets her glass back down. "I wanted to thank you for coming for the holiday."

This isn't a subject I want to discuss with Rylee's mom, so with a simple chin lift, I look down and pour more whiskey in my glass.

"I know your father misses you."

I grunt as I drain the rest of my drink.

"I know he doesn't show it very well, but he really cares about you, Oliver."

"And you know this from being around less than a year?" I grind my molars when the words come out harsher than I'd intended.

"I can't begin to imagine everything you've been through or what your life was like before I came along. I may not know you that well, but I know Paul. Even before he and I got involved, I knew how deeply he cared about you."

I tense. My issues with my father marrying Evelyn may have cooled, but it's still a sore topic. Especially considering I knew he was seeing her before my parents divorced. It was this subject that led to our falling out the day I left for college. I wanted the details of his and my mother's divorce, and he refused to talk about it.

"Maybe you should send him a memo, because it sure as fuck doesn't feel like it to me."

She frowns and looks down at her glass as she spins it on the countertop. "I'm not excusing his behavior, but have you ever thought there may be a reason why he is the way he is?"

"I know why." She looks up. "My grandparents were rich assholes who never gave their kids the time of day. But it was my father's choice to follow in their footsteps. He is the way he is because he chooses to be."

She opens her mouth to say more, but I turn my back on her and walk to the sink, rinsing out my glass. I avoid her eyes when I turn back and head toward the door.

"I'm hitting the sack," I call over my shoulder. "I'll see you tomorrow."

I let out a breath when the door whooshes closed behind me. The stairs are silent as I ascend them. I come to a stop at one of the doors and stand there. Light filters through the inch of space at the bottom.

I ball my hands into fists when I feel a sudden urge to knock. The last thing I need right now is to see the contempt on Savannah's face. I'm still on edge from my conversation with Zayden and talking to Evelyn in the kitchen. There's no fucking telling what my reaction would be if she antagonized me. It would probably lean more toward tossing her on the bed and feasting on her too tempting body.

With a shake of my head, I turn away.

six

SAVANNAH

"So, Zayden, how are you liking school? Classes going okay?" Paul asks as he slides a forkful of potatoes into his mouth.

Thanksgiving thus far has been pretty uneventful, though I will say that the tension between Oliver and his father is so thick that I feel like I could reach out and physically touch it. No wonder he chose to spend the morning at Zayden's dad's house instead of staying here to help us cook. At first, I thought he was wanting to get out of helping, but now I'm realizing there may be more to it.

"It's been really good." Zayden nods, taking a drink of water. "I had to drop a class the first week because it wasn't a good fit, but other than that, I'm really liking all my courses."

"And by good fit, he means it wasn't what he thought it would be," Oliver interjects with a smirk.

I move some turkey around with my fork, unsure if I should eat more. I'm trying to find a good middle ground, hoping that if I don't eat too much my body won't revolt and force it all back up.

"I'll admit, I should have read the class description a little better." Zayden chuckles. "But I got it taken care of, so it wasn't an issue."

"That's good to hear. At least one of you boys actually takes school seriously." Paul's gaze slides to his son.

"What the hell is that supposed to mean?" Oliver drops his fork onto his plate, the sound echoing through the formal dining room.

"Maybe if you spent more time thinking about your studies and less time screwing off, your grades wouldn't be slipping."

This isn't the first time since we sat down where Paul has scolded Oliver about something. It seems to be a running theme in this household. If I didn't dislike him so much, I actually might feel bad for the guy.

"My grades?" He goes rigid in his seat. "I've got A's and B's."

"Exactly." Paul lifts a wine glass to his lips and takes a small drink. "If you actually applied yourself, you could be at the top of your class instead of floating somewhere in the middle."

"Paul," Evelyn cuts in, sliding her hand on top of his.

"I'm just saying, he could be doing better. Especially if he managed to show up to class everyday like he's supposed to. I'm not paying for him to be out gallivanting. I'm paying for him to get a good education."

"Maybe now isn't the time," Evelyn offers softly, her gaze sweeping around the table.

I glance at Rylee next to me, noticing she seems about as uncomfortable as I do.

"It's fine, Evelyn," Oliver cuts in. "Let him say what he wants to say. Go on, *father*, tell everyone what a fucking disappointment I am. You've never been one to hold back before."

"Do not use that kind of language at the table."

"Oh no!" Oliver covers his mouth dramatically. "Guess it's just another thing you can add to the long list of the ways I've let you down. And how the hell do you know about my attendance and grades? It's not like we've even talked about it."

"A friend of mine is a professor at the University. You know that."

"So, what, you're using him to spy on me now?"

"I'm not spying on you."

"No? Because it sure seems like that's exactly what you're doing. Looking into my grades, checking up on my attendance."

"I'm paying for your education, aren't I? I have a right to know if you're taking it seriously."

"I am taking it seriously," Oliver fires back, anger lacing his voice.

"Well, if you plan to attend law school in the future, you're going to have to do a hell of a lot better. Subpar grades won't get you very far."

"I'm not going to law school."

"Come again?" Paul seems taken aback by this news.

"Do you seriously think I plan on following in your footsteps?" He lets out an angry laugh. "Newsflash, *Dad*, I don't want to be anything like you."

"Because that would be so awful?"

"Actually, it would."

"Then what's your plan? Certainly, you have one considering the amount of money I'm shelling out for you to go to college."

"I'll figure something out. It's early. I have time."

"No, you don't. I swear, everything is a game to you. When are you going to grow up?"

"When are you going to stop being a dick?" Oliver fires back.

"Why can't you be more like Rylee? At least she's mature enough to have an actual goal. You, on the other hand, are doing the same thing you always do. Walking around like an entitled prick who thinks he can skate by. It's been the same story your entire life."

I bite the inside of my cheek. It's not fair for Paul to throw Rylee in the middle of this. And to do it in front of everyone in the middle of Thanksgiving dinner.

"Well, I'm sorry we can't all be fucking perfect like Rylee." Oliver shoves his chair backward as he stands—the legs scraping against the hardwood floor.

"Paul," Evelyn cuts in again, silencing her husband. "Oliver, please sit back down and eat your dinner."

"Actually, I'm good." Oliver tosses the napkin clenched in his hand onto the table. "I've lost my appetite." With that, he spins around and quickly exits the room.

"Why do you have to push him like that?" Evelyn scolds, clearly upset with her husband.

"The boy needs to understand."

"Then wait and talk to him in private. Don't embarrass him in front of his friends."

"Umm." Rylee slides her chair away from the table and stands. "I'm finished, so I'm going to go start cleaning up the kitchen."

"I'll help," I immediately offer, desperate to get out of this room.

"Me too," Zayden interjects, following after Rylee and me.

"Now see what you did," Evelyn says right as we exit the room.

I feel bad, because I know how much she was looking forward to having everyone together for her and Paul's first official Thanksgiving, but you couldn't pay me to continue to sit there. Awkward doesn't even begin to describe how that felt.

"Well, good to see Paul is still Paul." Zayden snorts.

"Is it always like that?" I ask, leaning my hip against the large island in the middle of the kitchen.

"Believe it or not, that was mild."

"Seriously?"

"It's been like this since we were kids," Zayden continues. "Paul has always pushed Oliver. And I do believe his heart is in the right place. It's just, I don't know. The two of them are like oil and water. Always have been."

"That's sad."

"I should probably go find him, make sure he's okay."

"Give him a few." Rylee stops him. "You know how he gets."

"Yeah, you're probably right," he agrees.

"Besides, you said you were going to help us clean up," she reminds him.

"Oh, I didn't actually mean that. I just wanted to get the fuck out of there." He chuckles when she shoves a dishrag into his hand.

"For that, you get to wash." She grins, her eyes coming to me. "V and I will start putting away the leftovers."

"But first, pie." Zayden tosses the rag onto the island.

"Pie? You ate at your dad's and again here. How could you possibly still be hungry? You know what? Scratch that. I forgot I'm talking to a bottomless pit."

"You know me so well, baby." He tugs her toward him, laying a kiss to her lips.

"On that note, I'm going to run upstairs and change into something a little more comfortable." I interrupt their sweet moment, drawing both of their eyes to me. "I feel like I'm about to explode out of this dress."

Lie. Lie. *All lies*. I feel like half the crap that comes out of my mouth anymore is a lie. The truth is, the instant Zayden mentioned pie, I about lost the contents of my stomach on the floor. I thought eating less would help me keep some food down, but even that doesn't seem to be working.

"I told you to wear your fat pants." Rylee giggles.

"And I told you that I wasn't wearing sweatpants to dinner," I fire back. "I'll be back in a minute." I turn and quickly exit the kitchen.

I try to steady my breathing as I climb the stairs. Maybe being away from all that food will help.

"Mother fucker," I hear seconds before something thuds against the wall right as I reach the second floor.

What the hell?

"Piece of shit." Another thud.

Everything inside of me is telling me to keep walking, but for some reason I stop in front of Oliver's bedroom door anyway.

"I'll show you a fucking disappointment," he yells, followed by the sound of various items hitting the floor.

Before I realize what I'm doing, my hand is reaching for the knob. Giving it a twist, I carefully push the door open.

"Oliver." I stop mid-motion when I see him standing in the middle of his bedroom floor, surrounded by clothes, books, blankets, and what appears to be the contents of a desk. It looks like he literally started tearing things out and throwing them all over the place.

His angry eyes snap to mine and his nostrils flare.

"What the fuck do you want?" he growls, not at all happy to see me standing in his doorway. Not that I can blame him. We aren't exactly *friendly*.

"I just…. Are you okay?"

I know we have our differences, but I'm not completely heartless.

"Why the fuck do you care?" He laughs, the sound wild and unhinged. "Or did you just come to see the show?"

"No, I just…."

"You like this, don't you?" He stalks toward me. "You like seeing me like this." He grabs my forearm and tugs me inside the room, slamming the door shut so hard that I jump. "Go ahead, get a good fucking look." He's so close that I can feel his hot breath dance across my face.

Seconds tick by as we stand here, staring at each other—our faces mere inches apart. The air is tight, making it impossible to pull in a real breath. I'm desperate to leave and yet too afraid to move.

The tension mounts, causing the little hairs on the back of my neck to stand up.

"Oliver, I…." Before I can finish the thought, Oliver's mouth slams down against mine, his tongue pushing its way past my lips before I have a chance to register the action. His hand tangles in the back of my hair, holding me in place.

My mind is screaming for him to stop, yet my body seems to have the opposite reaction. My arms go around his neck, and I pull him closer, desire flooding my lower belly. He kisses me hard, demanding, without apology, and I kiss him back just as forcefully.

I feel desperate. Crazed. Completely out of my fucking mind.

Oliver's body presses into mine, the heat of him wrapping me like a heavy blanket.

I can't think. Can't breathe.

All I want is to stop.

All I want is more.

My mind and body wage war on each other.

"Hey, V." We both go stiff at the sound of Rylee's voice.

As if this somehow snaps me back to reality, I push at Oliver's chest, relieved when he drops his hold on me.

I'm embarrassed.

No, I'm mortified.

And all I want to do is run away.

"V," I hear Rylee again and this time she sounds closer.

I turn toward the door.

Shit. Shit. *Shit.*

What do I do? How do I get out of this room without her seeing me?

I rack my brain for an excuse, for a plausible reason why I would be in Oliver's room, but I can't seem to come up with a single one.

Oliver brushes past me seconds before he reaches for the doorknob.

"What are you doing?" I whisper hiss, panic rising in my chest.

"Giving you a way out."

Before he can elaborate, he tugs open the door and slips into the hall, pulling it closed behind him.

I stand completely motionless, not sure what the hell is going on.

"Hey, have you seen V?" Rylee asks him seconds later.

"No. And I don't care to either."

I immediately want to punch him in the face, though I'm not entirely sure why. For pulling me into his room. For kissing me. For saying he doesn't care to see me.

He's covering for you—the realization comes on fast and leaves me feeling almost as off kilter as the kiss.

"I wonder where she went," she thinks aloud.

"Well, I'm sure she's around here somewhere. Maybe she stepped outside or something."

"Yeah, maybe." I hear her sigh. "Anyway, Zayden and I are getting ready to dig into my mom's famous pumpkin pie. You want to come down for a slice?"

"And have to deal with my father again? No thanks."

"It's just me and Z. Come on. You won't regret it. I promise."

"Fine," he concedes. I can't help but wonder if he actually wants pie or if he's doing it to get her to go back downstairs.

Moments later, I hear footsteps on the stairs and then silence.

I wait a few seconds to make sure the coast is clear before quietly slipping into the hall. I make a beeline for my room, quickly ducking inside before closing the door behind me. Pressing my back to the hard wood, I do my best to regulate my breathing and calm my erratic heartbeat.

I lift my hand and gently brush my fingertips across my lips, trying to wrap my head around what the hell just happened.

My stomach twists—only this time I'm not sure if it's because I'm going to be sick or because of the kiss I can still feel wreaking havoc over my entire body.

seven

OLIVER

The house is quiet when I leave my room and go downstairs. Evelyn is probably sitting on one of the comfortable chairs in front of the fireplace in the library reading a political thriller. I've noticed that's where she likes to go when she has free time around the house.

Zayden, Rylee, and Savannah left earlier to take Danielle to an indoor ice-skating rink. They invited me along, but I gave them a firm no. Who in the hell wants to slide on thin blades of steel across frozen water?

It would have been a good excuse to get out of the house and away from my father but taking breaks for holidays never mattered to him. I'm sure he's behind his desk at the office working on one case or another. I'm surprised he showed up on time for Thanksgiving dinner yesterday.

As a kid, I remember going to bed the night before Christmas and my father still wasn't home from work. He'd be present for birthdays, but only half-assed. His nose was always stuck in his computer with his phone pressed to his ear.

Yesterday may have been Thanksgiving, but the house still smells fucking amazing. Like apple pie or some shit. I have to hand it to Evelyn. She's a damn good cook. My mother never lifted a finger in the kitchen. Instead, we had a cook who came in each day and made our meals. One of the first things Evelyn did when she came to live here was let the cook go. I overheard her and my father talking one night that she refused to allow someone else to cook for her family.

My stomach growls, so I head in the direction of the kitchen for a plate of leftovers. Thanksgiving is one of my favorite holidays because of the plethora of food. What can I say, I love to eat. My dinner had been cut short yesterday because of the stunt my father pulled, so I didn't get to enjoy it as much as I would've liked. I'd left the house last night and only came back a couple of hours ago after having slept at Zayden's house. Now I can have a real dinner in peace.

Thinking of yesterday brings up an entirely different memory. One a hell of a lot more pleasing than my father being his usual asshole self.

My dick twitches when I think back to Savannah in my room. When she first appeared, all I wanted to do was take out my anger on her, and that's what I did. But for the first time ever, she actually looked… concerned for me, which really boggled my fucking mind. I've seen the way Savannah cares for Rylee, and she seems to care for Zayden by extension of Rylee, but when it comes to me, there's only ever been contempt. To see that look of worry in her eyes for *me*… I had no idea what to do with it.

So, I did the only thing I could do. I kissed her. It was both heaven and hell. Fuck, but she tasted good. Better than anything I could ever remember sampling before. But it was a mistake. There's no goddamn way I won't be able to *not* think about that kiss every time I see her now. Or want more from her. I've already been teetering on the edge of reason when it comes to her, and I'm afraid that kiss tipped the scale.

God help her if I ever get her alone again, because I seriously doubt my self-control will be strong enough to keep my hands off her.

My dick lengthens behind my zipper, and I shake my head to rid it of thoughts of Savannah. The woman is taking up too much space in my mind lately.

I'm passing my father's office when his voice surprises me, helping in my bid to forget Savannah.

"Oliver!" he booms. "Come in here. We need to talk."

I tense and grind my molars together, tempted to ignore his summons. I'm in no mood to put up with his shit right now. Deciding to get it over with, I roll my head around, loosening the tight muscles in my shoulders, and push his door the rest of the way open.

"I'm surprised you're here," I remark, striding across the room. I fold myself into the chair across from him.

He grunts as he slides a couple of folders to the side and flips the lid of his laptop closed. He folds his hands together in front of him and looks at me.

"I can't do that with Evelyn. I know how important the holidays are to her, so I'm making my best effort to be here when I can. At least for this week."

"God forbid if you go against her," I mutter.

"I care deeply for Evelyn. The last thing I want to do is upset her."

"But you didn't mind doing that to my mother and me?" I laugh bitterly. "No surprise there."

He pulls off his reading glasses and drops them on the desk. Using his pointer finger and thumb, he rubs his eyes.

"There's stuff between your mother and me that you don't understand, Oliver," he says tiredly.

"No shit. We've had this song and dance before. You say there's stuff I don't understand, but you refuse to tell me. Can I leave? This conversation is a waste of time."

"First, watch your language in this house. I'm tired of the lack of respect."

"Respect is earned, not given. And you haven't exactly *earned* mine."

"And you've lost all of mine," he fires back.

I laugh, but it's far from humorous. He's right. I'm sure I *have* lost his respect, but it's by his own doing. And I personally don't give a fuck.

He closes his eyes and blows out an audible breath. After a

moment, he opens them again and some of his anger is gone. Now he just looks weary.

"Look." He sighs. "I didn't bring you in here to argue." At my snort, he raises his brow. "I brought you in here to tell you why your mother hasn't been answering your phone calls."

"Yeah? And?"

His jaw clenches and the pulse in his temple throbs. It's the same look he gets any time my mother is brought up.

"She moved in with Benjamin."

It takes me a moment to recognize the name, and another to understand exactly what he's saying. "*Uncle* Benjamin?" I question, given that my father's brother is the only Benjamin I know.

He gives a clipped nod.

I stiffen in my chair and grip the arms so tight my knuckles protest. "You're joking," I accuse darkly.

"I wish I was, son."

I jackknife out of my chair and begin pacing the room, shooting him a glare as I pass in front of his desk.

"Are you telling me her and Uncle Benjamin are *together*?"

Another clipped nod.

I turn and face him, my body stiff with anger.

"This is bullshit. I thought you haven't talked to him in like twenty years or something, so how would you know? Besides, doesn't he live in Tennessee or some shit?"

The only reason I even know I *have* an uncle named Benjamin is because my grandparents mentioned him a couple times when I was younger, and I've seen pictures of him on their walls. I've never met the man and my father never talks about him. Anytime my grandparents brought him up, my father would flip his shit. Supposedly, he moved to Tennessee after he and my father had a huge falling out years ago, so I'm assuming this is where he still lives.

"Yes, he does. Your mother moved there. Her and Benjamin have been talking for some time now. As in, while she still lived here with us." His voice turns rough with anger.

I narrow my eyes and cross my arms over my chest. "What are you saying? They were having an affair while you were still married?"

He dips his chin. "Yes."

"There's no way my mother would do that. Especially with your estranged brother."

His eyes move past my shoulder and his nostrils flare. "This isn't the first affair she had with him," he says, looking back at me.

"What?" I spin away from him and rake my fingers through my hair. I was never stupid enough to think my mother was completely innocent in the ending of her marriage to my father. But her having an affair? No fucking way.

I turn back and face my father. As much as I don't want to think about my mother being capable of something like that, there's no denying the truth in his expression.

"When?" I grate out the question.

His eyes drop from mine for a moment before he glances back up. "Many years ago."

"Why the hell wasn't I ever told?"

"Because it wasn't your business. You were just a child, Oliver. You didn't deserve that kind of burden."

"That's why you and Uncle Benjamin had a falling out," I guess, putting the puzzle pieces together. It was never a conversation as to what happened. Only that he had done something unforgivable.

"Yes."

"Why would she do this? Could it have been because of the neglectful way you treated her?"

An affair is an affair. No matter how you look at it. There's no excuse for one. Even if a spouse treats the other like shit, you don't step out of the marriage. You dissolve it first. To not do so is selfish and cowardly.

Even so, my mind tries to come up with *why* my mother would do something like this. If what my father is saying is true, what she did was wrong no matter the reason, but maybe if I can justify it, to put some of the blame on my father, I can begin to understand.

"Your mother and my relationship wasn't always so... strained." He settles back in his chair and laces his fingers over his stomach. "Believe it or not, I loved your mother when we first met. I doted on her and gave her anything she wanted. All *I* wanted was for her to be happy. I thought we both were, but evidently, I was wrong."

Leaning forward, he pulls open the bottom drawer in his desk, grabs a bottle of expensive whiskey and two glasses, and sets them down on the smooth wooden surface. I raise a brow when he pours the amber liquid into both and offers me one.

He shrugs. "I know you sneak from my stash in the kitchen."

I grab the glass and retake my seat. The whiskey burns as it slides down my throat, but I need it.

"I was devastated when I found out. Devastated, but angry. Later when we argued about it, I also told her I wanted a divorce. She begged me to stay, swore until she was blue in the face that it was over and would never happen again. Love is fickle, Oliver." He tosses back the contents in his glass, baring his teeth. He pours himself another. "I loved her so much that I gave in. I believed her when she said it was over and it would never happen again. I also had you to think about. You were only a baby. I went to Benjamin's house the night I found out and we fought. I broke his nose and cracked his cheekbone. A week later, he was gone. I haven't spoken to him since. Well, until a few weeks ago."

I throw back the rest of my drink and snatch the bottle from his desk. He doesn't say anything as I pour myself another.

"I resented her because she caused a rift between my brother and me. I also resented her because a small part of me hated her." He looks down at his glass and swirls the liquid, appearing lost in thought. "No matter how much time had passed, I couldn't forget what she did," he murmurs. "Two years ago, I found out he was back in town to visit and they had resumed their affair. After that, there was no way I could continue being married to that woman. She's your mother, and I know you love her, Oliver, as you should, but I couldn't do it anymore."

I don't know what to think about all of this. This certainly explains the neglect and uncaring way he acted toward my mother over the years. I can't say I blame him. I wouldn't stay with a woman who had sex with another man. I've never understood it when adults stay married after an affair for the benefit of the child. The child *does not* benefit from a marriage as rotten as my parents'. A child may not understand the reasoning, but they feel the tension and animosity between their parents. It makes for a miserable childhood.

"That doesn't explain why she's not answering my calls," I tell him. "Or why she moved all the way to Tennessee without telling me."

"Because she doesn't want you to know."

"That's fucking stupid. She has to know I'd find out eventually."

He inclines his head. "That's true. You may not want to hear it, but your mother is manipulative. She'll keep you from hearing the truth for as long as possible, because it makes her seem guiltless. She thrives on you thinking she's perfect."

I grunt. "I never thought she was innocent in all this. No one ever is. I just never thought she cheated too."

"I never cheated on your mother, Oliver," he says quietly.

I give him a disbelieving look. "I beg to differ. The proof is in this house right now."

He shakes his head. "Technically, I guess you could say I did, but the divorce was already filed, and our lawyers were already in negotiation when I started seeing Evelyn in a sexual manner."

I frown. "Mom said you were already sleeping with Evelyn when you asked for a divorce."

"Your mother has said a lot of things that weren't true."

"Why would she lie?"

"Because it makes me the enemy and keeps her clean."

I get up from my chair and set my glass down on the desk. All of this new information is making my head throb. I walk over to the window and stare outside. Rylee and Savannah are back and are currently laughing as they walk toward the house. Zayden must be taking Danielle home.

They both look so happy and carefree, something I haven't felt in a long time. I don't think I've ever felt carefree like that in this house. I had Zayden growing up and we had some good times, but I've never felt peace like the two women do right now.

Once again, my thoughts move back to yesterday in my room, but instead of the carnal urges I felt before, longing takes its place. What would it be like to see a softer side of Savannah? To have that laughter and easy-going attitude directed toward me. It's a fruitless thought because it'll never happen. That bridge was burned the first moment we met.

I turn back to my father and give him a chin lift before heading toward the door, ready for this night to be over with and wishing I could forget it ever happened.

"Oliver," my father calls.

I'm at the doorway when I look back at him. "Thank you for being honest with me." Without another word, I leave his office, closing the door behind me.

eight

SAVANNAH

"God, it feels good to be home." Rylee plops down on the plush gray couch in our living room apartment and stretches out her legs. "I didn't realize how difficult it would be being back in that house after a few months away. I know things are different now, but I swear every time I step foot through that front door it feels like the first time I arrived there all over again."

"You're probably suffering from some sort of PTSD over what Oliver put you through." I snort, grabbing a water from the fridge before making my way back into the dining room where I abandoned my small suitcase next to the table.

"I don't think it's that serious." She shakes her head, her thick brown hair swaying as she does. "I guess I never really got used to being there. It never really felt like home, so going back there feels strange."

"It's just a house. Your home is where your family is." I shrug, taking a pull of water.

"Yeah, I know."

"Any word from your dad?" I broach the ever-growing sensitive topic of her *other* parent.

"Oh, I heard words, all right. Just not the right ones."

"Did he even apologize for canceling on you… again?"

"Please, that man doesn't know what an apology looks like. I'm at the point now where if he wants to see me, he'll reach out. And if he doesn't…."

"Well, then that's his loss," I finish her sentence.

"Exactly." She nods. "What about you? Did your parents make it back from Iowa okay?"

"They fly back tomorrow."

"Were they mad you didn't go with them?"

"I think they were a little disappointed, but they understood. Besides, I'll be home for Christmas in less than a month. Not to mention, I'll probably see them at least one weekend between now and then. You know if my mom goes more than two weeks without seeing me, she starts to crumble." I laugh.

"Oh, I know. That's because you're her baby."

"Yeah. Unfortunately for me, she doesn't seem to realize that I'm not actually a baby anymore." I roll my eyes.

"Well, for what it's worth, I'm glad you came home with me. I know you weren't looking forward to dealing with Oliver, but you have to admit, besides the first day we were there, he behaved himself quite nicely."

The mention of Oliver causes my stomach to knot. I've replayed the events of Thanksgiving Day over and over in my head during the last few days and for the life of me, I still don't think I've fully grasped what happened.

I want to regret it. I want to be disgusted by the memory of his lips on mine. Only I'm not. Quite the opposite actually. Because no matter how much I dislike him, that kiss did something to me. Something I'm not sure I'm ready to admit to myself just yet.

"Well, it doesn't hurt that he avoided us like the plague," I respond, feigning disinterest.

"He did seem a little off, didn't he?"

I bite the inside of my cheek.

Obviously, I didn't tell Rylee about the kiss, and I have no intention of doing so. It's not like it meant anything anyway…. Right?

"And then him up and leaving a day early without telling us," she continues. "Something is *definitely* up with him."

"Probably just more bullshit with his dad." I sigh audibly, like I couldn't be less interested.

"Yeah, probably. I'm going to call him later and make sure he's okay."

"He doesn't deserve you," I tell her, grabbing the handle of my suitcase. "I'm gonna take my stuff to my room and get unpacked," I say, desperate to get away from the topic of her stepbrother.

"Yeah, I probably should too. Are you going to hop in the shower?"

"I was planning on it."

"Okay, I'll wait until you're done so I'll have better water pressure. Do me a favor and save me some hot water."

"I make no promises," I playfully tease as I head down the hallway toward my bedroom.

Slipping inside, I shut the door behind me before dropping my suitcase onto the bed. Unzipping it, I toss open the lid and start to sort through my things—throwing dirty clothes in the hamper and setting some of my toiletries on top of the dresser.

Rylee's right, it does feel good to be home.

Stripping out of my sweater and leggings, I flip on the light in my attached bathroom. As much as I love that Rylee and I have separate bathrooms, I hate that mine is shared with guests—having two doors—one that opens up to my room and one that opens to the hallway.

I would have preferred the private bath, but I opted for the bigger bedroom. I'm not really sure if the tradeoff was worth it, but alas, what's done is done. It's not like we have many guests. Well, other than Zayden, but he usually uses Rylee's bathroom. Hell, when he's here, I barely see either of them.

Turning on the shower, I grab a towel from under the sink before dropping it on the floor next to the tub, catching my reflection in the floor length mirror attached to the back of the door. I instantly cringe.

Every time I look at my body, all I can see are the imperfections. The little skin rolls on my back. The way my thighs are too close together. How my hips bump out, making me look even fatter than I already am. It's disgusting. I'm disgusting.

I quickly turn away, thinking I should probably remove that mirror as soon as possible. Shedding my bra and panties, I slip into the shower, the hot water instantly soothing the tension in my shoulders.

I shoot upright in bed, a loud banging noise startling me from sleep. Glancing at the clock on my bedside table, I see that it's just after one in the morning. Rubbing my eyes with the back of my hands, I almost think I dreamt the noise, until seconds later, it starts again.

What the hell?

Throwing back the covers, I grab my thin, knee-length robe and quickly slide it over my shoulders before peeking out into the hallway.

Bang. Bang. Bang.

I realize the sound is from someone pounding on our front door.

Rylee appears from her room moments later, looking about as confused as I feel.

"Rylee," a male voice comes from the hallway, barely audible.

She turns wide eyes to me.

"Is that…." She heads to the front door and peers out the peephole. "It's Oliver," she calls back toward me before unlocking the door and pulling it open. "Oliver…. What the…?" She isn't able to finish her sentence before Oliver comes stumbling through the door, a brown bag clenched in his right hand.

"Oh, good. You're up," he slurs, nearly losing his balance when he moves to close the door behind him.

"Oliver, what the hell?" Rylee shakes her head. "It's one o'clock in the morning."

"It is?" He laughs to himself. "Well, hell." He stumbles forward a couple of steps before he catches sight of me standing in the mouth of the hallway. "Well, if it isn't Savannah." He hiccups. "Turns out, you're not the only one in this world who hates me." He lifts the brown bag and takes a long drink of whatever liquor is hidden beneath the paper. "Turns out my own mother does too!" he announces, spreading his arms wide.

"Okay now, that's enough." Rylee snags the bottle from his hand and turns, handing it to me before he can take it back.

"What the hell?" he slurs, looking down at Rylee like she just shot his dog. "I thought we were tight."

"We are. Which is why I'm cutting you off." She nudges her head toward the kitchen, and I head that way without any further explanation.

I slip past Oliver, and without a word, dump the contents of the bottle into the sink.

"Cutting me off." He rolls his lips like he's giving raspberries to the air, completely oblivious to what just became of his whiskey.

Dropping the bag and bottle into the trash, I re-enter the room, getting my first good look at Oliver since he arrived.

He's a mess. Wild hair. Red rings under his bloodshot eyes. Wrinkled shirt. And is he wearing flip flops... in late November? I shake off the thought and refocus on his face. Even staggering drunk, he's still so good looking it pisses me off.

It would be so much easier to hate him. So much easier to pretend that what happened on Thanksgiving never happened—if my heart didn't pick up speed every time I've looked at him since then. Stupid Oliver with his stupid perfect face and his stupid gorgeous eyes and his stupid breathtaking smile.

Stupid. Stupid. Stupid.

"Yes, cutting you off," Rylee says, cutting into my thoughts. She grabs Oliver by the arm before trying to lead him to the couch. He trips and falls into her, nearly taking them both to the ground, but somehow Rylee is able to keep her balance.

Realizing she's not going to get him there on her own, I slide to his other side and wrap my arm around his waist, attempting to help her get him to the couch. Oliver is a pretty lean guy, but he's also tall and solid, which makes it near impossible to balance his weight.

It takes more effort than it should with him swaying like he's in the middle of a restless ocean, but we finally manage to get him there, though once we do, he immediately tries to stand up again.

"Oliver, why don't you stay here, and I'll get you some water." Rylee tries to reason with him.

"I don't want any fucking water." He tries to get up again. "Where the fuck is my whiskey?" At this point, he's slurring so bad that his words are all running together, making it difficult to understand what he's saying.

"Your whiskey is gone. You drank it all," she tells him, making sure he's going to stay sitting before straightening her posture. She turns toward me, cheeks flushed and eyes full of concern. "Can you stay with him for a minute? I need to get my phone and call Zayden."

The last thing I want to say is yes, but knowing I can't say no, I nod, watching her leave the room moments later.

When I glance down at Oliver, his hazy eyes are looking up at me, a drunken smirk tugging at his mouth.

"You're really pretty." He laughs to himself.

"And you're really drunk," I state the obvious, cursing myself for letting his compliment have any effect on me whatsoever.

"That may be, but you're still pretty." He reaches up and grabs my hand. He tugs, and I fall into his lap.

"Oliver." I attempt to stand, but he holds me in place—surprisingly strong for how inebriated he is. Honestly, it's a wonder he's not puking or passed out. Or both.

"And you taste really good, too." He nuzzles his nose against my ear, causing little tiny bumps to break out over my skin.

I will not let this man get to me. I will not let this man get to me. I will not let this man get to me.

"Oliver." I try to get up again, but to no avail.

"I wish you didn't hate me. Why do you have to hate me so much?" He wraps his arms around my middle and hugs me to him. It's awkward and uncomfortable, but I also can't deny the warmth that spreads through me.

"I don't hate you." I give up fighting, sitting board stiff in his lap.

"You do. Everyone hates me." He drops his head to my chest, a half laugh, half sob sounding from his throat.

No matter our bad blood, I can't help but feel sorry for the guy.

"I'm sure that's not true." I pat his head like a dog I'm scared to touch.

"It is. And they should. I'm a fucking piece of shit," he grunts, the words barely audible.

"You're not a piece of shit." The words feel like sandpaper in my throat. They're definitely not words I ever thought I'd be saying to him. But it's clear he's really drunk and upset about something, and I'm not one to kick someone when they're down. No matter who they are.

"You're just saying that. You hate me more than anyone."

"That's not true. I don't hate you." I look up when Rylee enters the room, her cell phone pressed to her ear. "Help me," I mouth to her, not sure what the hell to do.

"Yeah, it's bad," she says into the phone, no doubt to Zayden. "And I'm pretty sure he's holding V hostage now." A hint of a smile graces her face.

"Did you know my mother is fucking my uncle?" Oliver's head pops up abruptly, his half-cocked eyes meeting mine. "She's an uncle fucker." He snorts. "Oh, and she moved all the way to Tennessee without telling her only son." He laughs loudly like it's the funniest thing he's ever heard—but there's also anger there. Anger that he's trying really hard not to show.

I look up at Rylee, who only shrugs, clearly having no idea what he's talking about. "He's talking about his mom leaving," she says into the phone. "Yeah, I think you should." She pauses for a long moment. "Okay, see you soon. I love you." Moments later, she ends the call. "Zayden is on his way," she tells me, looking from my face to my body that's currently being held captive in Oliver's lap, back up to my face. "Um?" She gives me a confused look.

"Your guess is as good as mine." I huff. "Maybe you could help me," I mutter to my best friend.

She covers her mouth to muffle her laugh before nodding.

Taking a seat next to Oliver, she tries to pull his arm from around me, telling him that Zayden is on his way. Unfortunately, Oliver has other plans, because as she tries to loosen his grip on me, he tightens it significantly, nearly squeezing the breath right out of me.

"Oliver, you have to let go of Savannah now," she coaxes him gently.

"I was wrong." His gaze swings to her. "Everything I did. To you. To Z. It was all fucking wrong."

"It's okay. We've been over this. It's in the past," she reassures him.

"I blamed him. I blamed your mom. I blamed *you*. And the whole fucking time it was her. It was fucking her."

"What was her, Oliver? What happened?" Rylee asks, handling him with kid gloves. Not that I blame her. His behavior is bizarre to say the least. Who knows what might set him off at this point.

"I just want to forget, you know? I want to take it all back."

"Forget what? What are you talking about, Oliver?"

"Fuck." His hold on me releases, and I waste no time clamoring to my feet. When I glance back down at Oliver, his head is resting against the back of the couch, his arms slumped at his sides. "I'm sorry," he grumbles, his head bobbing as he looks over at Rylee and then up to me. "I'm sorry for everything." He holds my gaze for a long moment before his head drops back and his eyes slide closed.

nine

OLIVER

"Time to wake up, sleeping beauty."

I crack my eyelids open, intending to shoot my best friend a glare, but slam them closed before I can. With a groan, I throw my arm over my eyes for added protection against the head killing bright light.

"Fuck off," I growl. I smack my lips together. Why the hell does it feel like I ate cotton? "And close the fucking curtains while you're at it."

"No can do, brother. It's past eleven, and it's time for you to vacate my girlfriend's couch."

I manage to slit one eye open just enough to see Zayden standing at my feet. Right before he plops down on my legs, I bend them.

At the mention of Rylee's couch, memories of last night slam into me like pins being hit by a bowling ball.

Getting drunk off my ass in hopes of forgetting my mother's betrayal.

Showing up at Savannah and Rylee's place.

Seeing the pitying look on Savannah's face as I held her on my lap and sang my woes to her.

Apologizing again for the things I did to Rylee and Z.

Shoving my hands against the cushion beneath me, I hoist myself around so I can throw my feet to the floor. I groan when my stomach churns and a sharp pain hits my head.

"Fuck me," I grumble and lean my head against the back of the couch. My eyes slide closed, but it only marginally helps my queasiness.

"Here." I roll my head and peek open my eyes. Zayden's holding out a bottle of pills and a glass of orange juice. "Figured you might need this."

Over Zayden's shoulder, I spot Savannah and Rylee in the kitchen. Rylee has her back to me as she cooks something on the stove. Savannah's at the bar and her eyes keep darting in my direction.

I grab the bottle and glass, and clumsily open the former. Half of the tablets dump into my palm when I tip it to my cupped hand. I toss back two and chug the orange juice before I put the rest back in the bottle. When I lean forward, I notice the blanket that's still over my lap. What a fool I must have looked like sleeping under a pink flowery blanket.

"What's going on with you, Oliver?" Zayden asks, leaning over with his elbows propped on his knees, turning his head to look at me.

I grit my teeth at the reminder of my fucked-up life.

"Apparently, it wasn't my father who couldn't keep his dick in his pants while he was married. My mother was the one, spreading her legs for my uncle. And to top it off, it wasn't the first time she's had an affair with him."

"Wait, what?" His brows dip in confusion. "You don't...." He tilts his head slightly. "You mean the uncle you've never met?"

I nod, then wince as the pounding in my head gets worse. "The one and only."

"Damn. That's some fucked up shit there," Zayden states the obvious.

"Yeah, well, it appears the reason she hasn't been answering my calls is because she moved in with Uncle Benjamin in Tennessee. She couldn't even tell me she was moving across the continent."

"I won't ask how your dad's taking it. I could tell by the way he'd acted over break that he's pretty pissed."

"I can't say I blame him," I mutter, rubbing my temples to help ease the ache. "He's taking it better than I would have in his shoes."

There's a loud bang in the kitchen, and I grimace when I feel the repercussion in my temples. I tilt my head and look across the room. Savannah's glaring down at the floor, and I read her lips as she mumbles, "Shit".

"What are you going to do?" Zayden asks, and I pull my eyes away from Savannah.

"Not a damn thing. Fuck her and her secrets." She's my mother and I still love her, but I don't like her at the moment. I scrub a hand over my face then stare ahead. "I'm sorry about crashing at your girl's place. I have no fucking clue what I was thinking last night."

"Don't worry about it." He slaps my back and gets up. I shoot him a glare because the bastard knows jostling me like that jolts my head. He chuckles at my irate look. "There's a spare toothbrush in the bathroom. Come get something to eat when you're done."

He walks into the kitchen and snags Rylee around the waist, landing a kiss against her lips so loud even I can hear it. I flick my gaze to Savannah and see her eyes dart away from me.

Tossing the blanket off my lap, I get up and stumble to the bathroom, my hand going to the wall to catch myself before I face plant against the drywall. The pills I took have lessened the pain in my head, but my stomach still rumbles uneasily. Standing in front of the toilet, I lean my arm on the cabinet above it and rest my forehead against my arm. I sigh as I relieve myself.

After I wash my hands, I grab the packaged toothbrush and squirt on some toothpaste. As I stand there and scrub my teeth, I let my eyes wander. If memory serves correctly, this is the bathroom Savannah uses. I open the medicine cabinet and survey the contents inside. Deodorant, several bottles of vitamins, a small first aid kit, and a nail kit.

I close the door and spit into the sink, then swish water around my mouth before spitting that out as well. After splashing water on my face, I grab the towel from the back of the door. Inhaling deeply, I groan when Savannah's unique sent fills my nose. I pull back and look at the towel. An image of her running it all over her body, in places I wouldn't mind exploring with my hands and mouth, has blood rushing to my dick. Without an ounce of guilt, I take another whiff of the towel before hanging it back in place.

Leaving the bathroom feeling slightly better, I walk down the hallway. Stopping at the door I know is Savannah's bedroom, I look down the hallway and notice that no one can see me from the kitchen or living room. It would be so easy to slip inside and snoop around. I pull my hand back before it touches the doorknob, deciding sniffing her towel is probably enough pervertedness for one day.

Zayden and Rylee are on the couch watching TV, plates of food on their laps. Rylee offers me a small smile as I pass by them. Savannah's in the kitchen, her phone on the counter in front of her as she slides her finger across the screen. She doesn't acknowledge me as I walk to the cabinet beside the stove, but I still feel her eyes on me.

I wasn't in the bathroom long, so I know she hasn't eaten yet. Deciding to play the nice guy in light of my shitty behavior last night, I grab two plates and start loading them with bacon, sausage, eggs, grits, and toast. Taking down two glasses, I pour orange juice in one and use the tap to fill the other with water. I need to hydrate, stat.

Carrying both plates to the bar, I put them down and look at Savannah. "Come eat with me."

She eyes the plate like it's a snake about to strike, and I'm not sure if she's hesitant because of the food or me.

"I'm not gonna bite." I grin cockily at her. "Unless you want me to, of course."

Rolling her eyes, she looks back down at her phone. "Thanks, but I'm not hungry."

I've jabbed her before about eating, but it was only because I know girls are sensitive about their image, so I knew it would get to her. To be honest, looking at her, she could do with some meat on her bones. Her collarbones protrude from her shoulders and her face and arms are a bit too slim.

Noticing a dark tinge beneath her eyes has guilt hitting me in the solar plexus. I'm sure she didn't get much sleep due to my late-night visit.

I let out a low breath and take my own seat. "Come on, Savannah. I'm trying to make up for my behavior last night. Could you make it a tad bit easier on me?"

Her eyes are wary when she lifts them to me. Her bottom lip rolls between her white teeth as she contemplates my words. After a moment, she presses the button on the side of her phone, and the screen goes dark. Walking around the bar, she takes the stool beside me. She pays me no attention as I continue to watch her for another moment before picking up my fork and diving in. The silence around us is surprisingly comfortable.

I moan when I bite into a crispy piece of bacon. "Damn, that's good. All bacon should come this crispy."

Her spoonful of grits pauses halfway to her mouth and she slides her eyes to me. "You like crispy bacon?"

I shove another piece in my mouth before I answer. "It's the only way to eat it. The half-ass chewy way a lot of people cook it is disgusting."

"Hmm…." She hums, her expression perplexed. "I actually agree with you. When Zayden stays here with Rylee, we play rock, paper, scissors to see who makes the bacon because he likes his gummy, and Rylee and I like ours almost burnt."

"Fuck that. The crunchier, the better."

She's quiet as she continues to eat, and again, I can't help but watch her. She takes small measured bites, chews slowly, and her throat bobs when she swallows. Looking at her neck, I can't help but wonder what she tastes like there.

I shake my head to rid itself of the thought.

It's weird having a casual conversation with Savannah after the way we've both antagonized each other. But it's kinda nice.

"I wanted to apologize for the way I acted last night," I tell her quietly. I need to apologize to Rylee too, but I'll do that after I finish eating.

She shrugs, like it's no big deal. "Don't worry about it. No harm, no foul."

I look down at my food and scoop up some eggs. "Maybe not, but I shouldn't have acted the way I did."

She pushes her plate away, even though she's barely touched any of it. "It's okay. I get you're going through some stuff right now."

I shouldn't care, but I fucking hate that she saw me the way I was last night. I hate even more that she saw what happened between my father and me. Savannah's opinion of me is already low enough, and I've never cared before what she thought of me, but something's changed after that night in my room. I no longer want her to look at me with loathing. I want her to see me as more than the asshole stepbrother who tried to ruin her best friend's life. I want her to see *me*. I want that as much as I want to get to know her better.

"You should eat more." I use my fork to point at her plate.

She snorts and shoots me an incredulous look. "Yeah, right."

I slowly roam my gaze from her face, to her chest, then to her waist before lifting my eyes back to her face. She's lost weight since the beginning of the school year, and for some reason that bothers me.

Her eyes narrow into slits at my assessment.

"I'm serious."

"So, at first you say I eat too much, and now you're saying I'm not eating enough?" she asks, leaning back in her chair and crossing her arms over her chest. "Can you make up your mind?"

Shame isn't something I'm accustomed to feeling, but at the moment, I'm slammed with it. As much as I want to look away from her incensed stare, I hold her gaze, hoping she hears the truth in my next words.

"I was wrong to say those things to you. I was pissed the first time I said something. When I saw your reaction, I knew it angered you, so I used it against you again. The last thing you need is to lose weight, Savannah."

She gets up from her stool and carries her plate to the trash, casting me a doubtful sideways glance. I want to clock my own jaw for making her question her appearance. The woman is sex on legs, every fucking inch of her. I've never understood why girls get so bent out of shape over their self-images, but I get it now. It's guys like me, ones who make them feel self-conscious about themselves, who doubt their weight and looks.

You're such a fuck-up, Oliver.

Finding only one way to prove to her that my words are true, I get up and follow her. She's at the trashcan dumping her food, having not noticed my approach, when I come up behind her. She startles when she spins around and finds me so close.

"What are you…?"

I grab the plate and gently set it down on the counter. The last thing I want is to alert Zayden and Rylee that something is going on and for them to investigate.

Grabbing her hips, I maneuver her out of view of the living room and press her back against the counter. I set my hands on the edge on either side of her.

"Oliver—" she starts, but it ends on a gasp when I set my lips against her neck.

Lazily, I lick along the smooth column of skin. My earlier thought of what she would taste like is answered. Fucking phenomenal. And addicting. I could easily become addicted to licking her neck.

"Oliver, what are you doing?" she asks breathlessly. I smile against her neck when she tilts her head to the side. I half expected her to push me back and slap me by now, but I'm damn glad she hasn't.

"Proving what an asshole I am and showing you exactly how perfect I think your body is."

Her hands move to my waist, and for a moment I worry she's going to shove me away, but instead, her fingers curl into the material. "And you couldn't do that with words?"

"Tried that. It wasn't working." I move my lips up to her ear and nibble at the lobe. My dick punches against my zipper when she releases a little moan. I cup the side of her face and level mine over hers so I can see her eyes. "When one thing doesn't work, you try another. As if you can't already tell…." I press my hips against her so she can feel my hardening shaft. Her eyes widen. "Your body feels pretty fucking fantastic against mine."

"Oh, uhh…."

I cut her off by pressing my lips against hers. I've thought about our first kiss many times over the last few days, wondering if my mind played tricks on me and the kiss wasn't as good as I remembered.

It did play tricks on me. It's so much better than memory serves. I could kiss her for hours and still beg for more.

My hand on her cheek moves to the back of her neck. Using her hair, I tilt her head to the side, gaining better access to her perfect mouth. Her tongue dances alongside mine. Grabbing the back of one of her thighs, I bring her leg up and over my hip so I can press my shaft against her center. She moans, nails digging into my side and her heel pushing against my ass to get me closer.

What I wouldn't give to strip her bare right here and take her against the counter. If Zayden and Rylee weren't in the living room, I might even try. She'd feel so fucking good wrapped around my dick.

A low growl leaves my lips when her fingers dip beneath my t-shirt to rake along my abs.

"Fuck, woman. You're driving me crazy," I groan against her lips.

I hike her leg up higher and grind against her harder. My dick pulses, and I feel the wetness of pre-cum against the jean material.

"Oh!" a squeak comes from behind us.

One minute I've got my tongue down Savannah's throat, and the next I'm being shoved away. Without looking, I know Rylee is behind us. Savannah's shocked eyes dart from mine to over my shoulder.

"Shit!" Rylee says, her voice high-pitched. "I'm so sorry!"

"Not sorry enough if you're still standing there," I growl, my asshole side showing once again. But goddamn it, why the hell did she have to come into the kitchen right this minute?

"Oliver!" Savannah says loudly, her eyes blazing with familiar anger. "Asshole alert!"

"Sorry." I rake my hands through my hair before spinning and facing a wide-eyed Rylee. "Sorry, Rylee. It's just your timing is shit."

"Apparently so," she mutters. Her gaze flickers back and forth between me and Savannah before a slow smile appears on her face.

"This isn't what it looks like," Savannah defends.

"It was exactly what it looked like." I shoot her a *what the fuck* look.

Rylee ignores my comment and faces her friend with a cheeky grin. "And what was it supposed to look like?"

"I don't know." She blows some hair out of her face. "Just not what you're thinking."

Rylee laughs. "To me it looked like you two were seconds away from doing the nasty on our kitchen counter."

"Rylee!" Savannah screeches. "Jesus."

"What?" She shrugs. "I'm just calling it like I see it."

I chuckle and shove my hands in my pockets. Savannah looks at me like she's imagining bashing my head in with a frying pan. Not one of those cheap steel ones, but a heavy cast iron frying pan. I just grin at her.

"That's the last time that will ever happen."

My grin grows. "We'll see."

Her eyes squint and her tongue darts out to lick her bottom lip. As if she remembered my lips were just on hers and she's essentially tasting me, her pert little nose wrinkles and she scrubs her mouth with the back of her hand.

It only makes me chuckle again.

"Whatever," she huffs. After shooting both Rylee and me a glare, she storms out of the kitchen. It's cute. She looks like a middle schooler when she doesn't get her way.

"Well, that was enlightening," Rylee remarks quietly, directing her questioning gaze back at me.

"Don't ask," I warn.

Her mouth moves, like she wants to do just that, but thinks better of it and walks out of the kitchen.

I stay behind and stew over what happened between Savannah and me, again.

Savannah claims it'll never happen again, but I've got news for her. If I have my way, it'll not only happen many more times, but I'll also have her naked in my bed, screaming my name.

ten

SAVANNAH

"V, can I come in?" Rylee's soft voice filters in through my closed bedroom door.

"I don't want to talk about it," I call back, my gaze locked on the ceiling above me as I lay sprawled out on top of my unmade bed.

"The boys are gone," she informs me, a hint of a smile in her voice. "I'm coming in, so if you're naked I suggest you cover yourself." With that, the door swings open and Rylee comes strolling in—her thick, dark hair tied in a messy knot on top of her head.

I purposely avoid looking at her and press my eyes closed. Maybe if I pretend like I'm trying to nap she won't force me into a conversation I don't want to have.

I still haven't wrapped my head around what happened with Oliver in the kitchen this morning. One minute I'm irritated that he continues to comment on my eating habits—whether good or bad—and the next he's got me pressed into the counter with his tongue down my throat. And then of course, to add insult to injury, Rylee had to walk in right in the thick of it. And as if I wasn't mortified enough, Oliver pretty much guaranteed that what Rylee had interrupted was far from over. Well, not if I have anything to say about it.

Sure, he's gorgeous. And hands down, the best kisser. But he's also crude and mean and tends to act like a spoiled child when things don't go his way.

So, then why have I been unable to think of anything but his lips on mine since the moment we were interrupted?

"Hey." The mattress dips as Rylee takes a seat on the edge of my bed.

"I said I don't want to talk about it," I grumble, throwing my arm over my face.

"Considering what I walked in on a little bit ago, you have some explaining to do whether you want to or not." She chuckles. "So, are you going to tell me what's going on?"

"Nothing. There's nothing going on."

"V." Her fingers close around my forearm seconds before she pulls my arm away from my face. "That wasn't nothing."

"I hate him," I grind out. "Him kissing me doesn't change that."

"And the fact that you were kissing him back?"

"I plead temporary insanity."

Rylee laughs, the sound rumbling from deep in her chest.

"And the first time you kissed?" My eyes pop open and my gaze slides to hers, the shock I feel likely displayed all over my face. "Oliver told Zayden. Zayden told me," she says in way of explanation.

"And you didn't say anything?" I question, finding it hard to believe that she had knowledge of me and Oliver sharing a kiss and refrained from saying anything about it.

"Well, in all fairness, I just found out a few minutes ago. The real question is, why didn't you tell me?"

"Because it was stupid and it meant nothing. I didn't want you thinking something was going on."

"It's too late for that. You two practically swallowing each other's faces this morning kind of solidified that." She shifts. "You know, it's okay to like him."

"That's just it. I don't like him."

"Then why kiss him?"

"I didn't kiss him. He kissed me," I argue.

"From where I was standing, you were kissing each other," she points out. "Listen, I know you and Oliver haven't really gotten along in the past, but he's not a bad guy."

"Not a bad guy?" I snort, shooting upright in bed. "Not a bad guy?" I repeat. "Are you forgetting everything he put you through?"

"That's in the past. I don't agree with what he did, but in a way, I kind of understand. Not that I could ever hurt someone like that, but still, he's made it his mission to do right by me since then, and so far he has. I'd even go as far as to say that I now consider him a friend."

"You've always been more forgiving than me. If he had done that shit to me, he would be lacking the parts that make him a man. I would have made sure of that."

"V." Rylee laughs.

"I'm serious, Ry. What he did goes way past punishing you for something you had no control over to begin with. Normal people, good people, don't do shit like that."

"Even the best people can make horrible decisions when they're in pain." She gives me a soft smile. "All I'm saying is that if you like him, there's nothing wrong with that. I wouldn't think less of you. Honestly, I kind of like the idea of you two together."

"Now you're getting ahead of yourself."

"Am I?" She quirks a brow.

"Look, we kissed. That's all it was, a kiss. It shouldn't have happened, and it won't be happening again."

"I hear you. Doesn't mean I believe you."

"Ugh. Can we be done now? Because I really don't want to talk about this anymore."

"Fine. I won't push," she concedes. "All I will say is that if you and Oliver decide it's easier to like each other than hate each other, you have my full support. Maybe just keep it behind closed doors next time. As much as I love you both, I'd rather not have that mental picture burned into my brain."

"You can leave now." I gesture toward the door.

"Actually, there's something else I've been meaning to talk to you about," Rylee pauses, hesitation in her expression.

"Okay," I interject after a few long moments have passed.

"Are you feeling okay?"

"Huh?"

"Well, it's just.... I've noticed you've been getting sick a lot recently. And well, you've lost a bit of weight too. I just want to make sure there's not something going on with you."

"I've been having some digestive issues. Nothing to be worried about. I'm actually thinking about going to the doctor to be tested for food sensitivities." It's the first thing I can think of.

It's true. I have lost weight. Probably more than is healthy for my height and build. When this all started, I only wanted to shed a few pounds. Now, I honestly don't know how to stop it. Even though every time I look in the mirror all I see are imperfections, I have still tried to stop. But it's like my body doesn't compute with my brain. I eat and ninety percent of the time I get sick, even though I don't want to.

"You've never had any issues in the past, have you?"

"No, but I've been doing some research, and they say that you can develop certain sensitivities and allergies with age. Sarah got diagnosed with Celiac Disease last year after eating gluten her entire life."

I'm grasping. I know I am. I just hope she doesn't see through me.

"I guess that's true." She nods. "Well, whatever it is, you should probably make a doctor's appointment soon. If you lose any more weight there won't be any of you left."

"Yeah. Right." I roll my eyes.

"I'm serious, V. Look at you. You're tiny."

"And you're delusional," I fire back.

"I am not. And I'm not the only one who has noticed how small you're getting. Zayden said something to me over Thanksgiving. And he's a guy. Guys don't typically notice things like that."

"I'm so glad you two have taken to discussing my weight behind my back," I snip, aggravation clear in my tone.

First Oliver, now Rylee and Zayden. Geez, what is it with these people? I get that I've lost weight, but with the way she's acting you would think I was nothing but skin and bones. I have half a mind to pull up my shirt and show her the roll currently curled over the top of my pants.

"It's not like we're sitting around having conversations about it. Zayden mentioned it, and truthfully, I had noticed the same thing."

"I'm not anorexic if that's what you're implying. I eat. You know I eat."

"I wasn't accusing you of anything. I just want to make sure you're okay."

"Well, I am. I'm perfect." I force a smile. "And like I said, I'm going to make a doctor's appointment to figure out what's going on with my stomach issues."

"I think that sounds like a good idea." She pats my knee as she stands. "And if you want anyone to go with you, I'd be happy to tag along."

"Ry, I'm not five. I don't need my mommy to take me to the doctor."

She rolls her eyes. "I know that. I just want you to know the offer is there in case you don't want to go alone."

"Thank you for the offer, but I think I can manage."

"Okay then." She turns toward the door, making it all of two steps before turning back toward me. "By the way, Zayden wants us to go to a party with him this Friday. I told him I didn't think you were on the schedule at work, but that I'd double check and see if you were free."

Rylee and I landed part time jobs at the small coffee shop around the corner shortly after we moved here. It isn't much, and we're lucky if we get thirty hours a week between the two of us, but it gives us a little money of our own. Considering that our parents are paying for our tuitions, as well as halving our apartment, we figure the least we can do is buy our own food and necessities.

"A party? What party?" My ears perk up.

When I imagined college, I imagined frat parties and bars with fake I.D.s. I envisioned crazy adventures and wild nights where I wouldn't make it home until after the sun had come up. But it hasn't been like that at all. Maybe it's because we're still freshmen and new to the scene, or maybe it's because we live off campus and aren't really on the *in* when it comes to what's happening and where, but so far this whole college experience has been a lot less exciting than I thought it would be.

"Just some college party at the WSU campus. I guess Zayden's roommate and another friend of his are going and have been hounding him about going out with them."

"I'm pretty sure Levi only has me on the schedule Thursday and Sunday this week, so yeah, a party sounds fun. I don't know about you, but I need a night to let loose."

I don't bother to ask if Oliver will be there. Truth be told, I don't really want to know. If he shows up, I'll avoid him. If he doesn't, even better. Either way, I'm not going to let him, of all people, keep me from attending my very first college party.

"Great. I'll let him know we're in." She smiles, exiting my room seconds later.

I flop back down onto my bed, my thoughts drifting back to what Rylee said about my weight and taking notice to how frequently I've been getting sick. I thought I was being careful to hide it, other than the pizza debacle last week in which hiding it was impossible, considering I almost yacked all over the Conley's living room floor. But obviously, I haven't been careful enough.

My stomach twists.

I have a problem. I know I do. But I also know that it's something I can fix on my own. I don't need Rylee or anyone else worrying about me. It's just going to take some time to get my body back on the right track.

I'm getting really good at lying to myself….

I shake the thought away, turning my focus to my cell phone as it buzzes to life on my nightstand. Rolling, I snag it off the table before holding it up in front of my face. My stomach twists again, only this time for an entirely different reason.

It's a text message… from Oliver.

Oliver: *I can't stop thinking about that kiss and how much I want to do it again.*

I smile in spite of myself.

And even though I tell myself not to answer, it doesn't stop my fingers from flying across the screen just the same. I type a message, delete it, and then type another before finally hitting send.

Me: *Well I guess it's too bad for you that it won't be happening again.*

His reply is almost instant.

Oliver: *Guess we'll see.*

Me: *Guess we will.*

I knead my bottom lip between my teeth trying to keep my smile at bay.

What the hell is wrong with me?

Oliver: *You can't keep pretending you hate me. Not when you kiss me the way you did this morning.*

Me: *Correction, you kissed me.*

Oliver: *Didn't stop you from kissing me back.*

Me: *Lapse in judgement. Won't happen again.*

Oliver: *Keep telling yourself that. We both know you want me.*

I put my hand over my mouth to stifle my laugh, not sure if I'm more amused or repulsed by his off-putting cockiness.

Me: *Keep telling yourself that. Won't make it any more true.*

I use his own words against him.

Oliver: *Have dinner with me tonight.*

His request catches me completely off guard. Not sure what to say, I wait a full two minutes before texting him back.

Me: *Sorry, can't.*

Oliver: *Can't or won't?*

Me: *Does it really matter?*

Oliver: *Matters to me.*

Me: *Fine. Won't.*

Oliver: *Has anyone ever told you that you're mean?*

Me: *Pot meet kettle.*

Oliver: *Fair enough. Guess I deserve that.*

I'm still reading his most recent message when another one comes in.

Oliver: *Have dinner with me.*

I shake my head, indecision weighing heavily in my chest. On one hand, the thought of sitting across a dinner table from him trying to fake my way through conversation seems laughable. On the other, I can't deny the flurry of excitement that swarms my stomach at the thought.

Me: I already said no.

Oliver: Come on. One meal.

Me: And why would I want to do that?

Oliver: I'll make it worth your while. I promise.

I take a deep breath in and let it out slowly.

Am I actually considering this? Am I *actually* considering going out to dinner with Oliver freaking Conley? Have I officially lost my mind? I hate the guy. Or at least, I *did* hate him. Now I'm not so sure what I feel.

Before I have time to talk myself out of it, I type out a response and immediately hit send without thinking it all the way through.

Me: Fine. One meal. But that's it.

Oliver: I'll pick you up at 7. Wear something sexy.

I drop my phone face down onto the bed, my mind reeling.

Wear something sexy?

A nervous knot forms in the pit of my stomach.

What the hell did I just get myself into?

eleven

OLIVER

"You look beautiful," I tell the stunning woman in front of me, barely able to get the words out of my suddenly dry mouth. Beautiful doesn't cut it, but it's the best I can come up with since my brain has short-circuited.

With her eyes rolling and a scoff coming from her lips, she turns to lock the door. I let my eyes slowly slide down her body. Even while I've wanted to strangle her—multiple times—I've never been able to deny how goddamn magnificent she looks. Tonight even more so with her hair swept up off her neck, the black sheer shirt over a white camisole, and tight black skirt. My gaze drifts to her feet, and I barely suppress a groan at her black fuck-me heels. The image of her digging those heels into my back as I pound into her is so strong I can almost feel it.

The woman is clearly trying to kill me.

"Hey!" The snap of her fingers in front of my face pulls me from my fantasies. "Eyes up here, buddy."

My lips tip up into a smirk. "Fine, but I ain't promising they'll stay up there. Have you fucking seen what you're wearing? No man in their right mind couldn't help but look."

She huffs, blowing a few pieces of hair from her face. "Don't make me regret this, Oliver."

I crowd her against the door, not touching her, but close enough that I can feel the heat radiating from her body. Her intoxicating scent invades my senses. "The only regret either of us will have is if I don't fuck you mindless at the end of this date."

"You know what?" She puts her hands on my chest and tries to shove me back. I don't budge. "What the hell was I thinking when I agreed to go out with you. This was a mistake."

When she shoves me again, I grab both of her hands and flatten them against my pecs. "Relax, Savannah," I say gently. "I'm joking, okay? Well, only half joking. You may not regret me not fucking you, but I damn sure will. Sorry, baby, but I'm only human."

"Whatever," she mutters. Is it my imagination or did her fingers curl a fraction against my chest? "Just step back so we can go."

Not wanting to give her another reason to cancel our date, I step back. She eyes me warily for a moment before she tosses her keys into her little black purse and begins sashaying her ass toward the elevator. Shaking my head, I follow behind her like a pathetic dog, my eyes glued to her delectable backside.

Unsurprisingly, she's quiet in the elevator and on our walk to my car. Being the gentleman that I am, I open the door for her. "My lady." And because I wouldn't be Oliver Conley without the dramatics, I add a little flourish with my hand when I gesture to her seat.

She does her eye-roll thing again, but if I'm not mistaken, her lips twitch as she slides into the car. My own lips tip up at the corners as I shut the door and make my way around the car before taking my spot behind the wheel.

I have no idea why I'm trying so hard with Savannah. This afternoon, when I asked her to go out with me, it was an impulse I didn't realize I followed through with until after I typed out the message and hit send. Though, once the words were out, I wasn't even the slightest bit tempted to take them back. In fact, when she initially rejected my offer, something heavy like a sledgehammer hit me square in the chest. I really, *really* wanted her to say yes. It was dumb, given the way she detests me, but after kissing her in my room Thanksgiving night and having her pressed against me in the kitchen earlier today, an uncontrollable need to see her again gripped me. It was like this invisible force was pulling me toward her.

After giving her a sideways glance, I start my car and pull away from the curb.

"I take it Z and Rylee aren't home?" I ask, just to fill the silence in the small space.

She keeps her eyes pointed at the windshield when she answers. "No, they decided to spend the night at Zayden's dorm. Thank goodness," she mutters the last.

"Why 'thank goodness'?"

"Because the last thing I need is for Rylee to hound me with questions about you and I going out tonight." She looks over at me, her eyes narrowed. "Speaking of, this date stays between us. I already had to explain the kiss in your room to Rylee because you couldn't keep your mouth shut. Thanks for that, by the way."

Her words irritate me, when really, they shouldn't. I can't blame her for not wanting Rylee to know about our date. Especially since Rylee's not the type to hold her tongue when it comes to things she cares deeply about. And if there's one thing I know, Rylee cares a lot for Savannah. I can imagine the inquisition Savannah would go through if Rylee were to know about our date.

Even so, it pisses me off that she wants to keep it a secret, but I keep my feelings to myself. I'll allow it for now.

The restaurant isn't far from Savannah's apartment, so I pull up to the valet only moments later. I toss the keys to the kid parking cars and once again open her door. When I hold out my hand to help her from her seat, she eyes it for a moment like it's a snake ready to attack before slowly placing her palm in mine. I want to keep hold of her, to lace our fingers together, but once she's on the sidewalk, she pulls away.

I shrug the rejection off, accepting that it's going to take time to expunge Savannah's misgivings toward me. Hey, just having her agree to go out with me is a step in the right direction.

The place I chose to bring her to isn't super fancy, but it's not a hole in the wall either. I overheard some of the girls at school talking about a small Italian place with delicious food that gives off a relaxing and ambient vibe. The place is new and has become quite popular.

"Hi, welcome to Angelo's," the hostess states when we approach a small podium. "Will it be just the two of you dining tonight?"

"Yes," I answer.

"Perfect. If you'll follow me, we'll get you seated."

Sliding my hand to the small of Savannah's back, her eyes move to me. I lift a brow at her questioning look, but she doesn't say anything, and instead follows the hostess to our booth. Once the hostess walks away, the heat of Savannah's gaze hits me. She drops her purse on the table with a clunk.

"Okay. What's up with you?" she demands, her tone no nonsense.

Leaning back with an arm stretched out along the back of the booth, I ask, "What do you mean?"

"Don't play stupid with me, Oliver. We both know you can't stand me any more than I can stand you. So, why are you acting like I'm one of your favorite people all of a sudden?"

Before I can answer, the waitress walks up asking for our drink order. I request a bottle of their house wine. She then turns to Savannah. "And for you?"

"I'll be sharing what he's having."

"Could I see your ID, please?"

I snicker quietly at the request. Sensing my amusement, Savannah's eyes flicker to me and turn to slits. With jerky movements, she snatches her ID out of her purse. A fake one, of course, since I know she's not twenty-one.

While the waitress looks over the fake driver's license, Savannah keeps her glare directly at me. I can't keep the smile from forming on my lips.

"Where'd you get the fake from?" I ask once the waitress walks off.

"I'm sure from the same place you got yours," she answers.

"How do you know I have one?"

"Doesn't half the school population?"

I nod. "If not more."

She slips the ID back in her purse. "Are you going to answer my question from before?"

"Depends."

"On what?"

"On if you'll answer my question on why you agreed to go out with me."

She takes a moment, but nods tightly.

I sigh and relax in my seat. "Contrary to what you believe, Savannah, I don't *not* like you. I only react when you act like a bitch to me." I hold up my hand when she opens her mouth to speak. "I get it. I know you hate me, and I don't blame you for it. What I did to Rylee was repulsive, to say the least. You know my reasoning behind my actions, and while it doesn't excuse the things I did to Rylee, I genuinely thought they were at the time. I was an asshole, and I truly regret what I did. As much as I wish I could take them back, I can't."

She doesn't say anything for several long moments as she fiddles with the white cloth wrapped around her silverware. She's quiet for so long that the waitress comes back with the wine, and I pour us both a glass. We both pick random things from the menu for our order.

"To be honest, I don't know why I agreed to go out with you," she begins, her voice quiet and contemplative. "Call it self-punishment or maybe curiosity. I don't know what it is. All I know is, and I'm being frank here because you already know this, I don't like you." I flinch, but she doesn't see it because her eyes are still on the napkin. "It's hard for me to look past what you did to Rylee. You not only hurt her, and while my pain wasn't anything compared to hers, you hurt me too. I love Rylee like a sister. And because of that, I feel her pain when she's hurt."

"Savannah," I start, but stop when she lifts her eyes. Anger heats their green depths, but there's more there. Something close to vulnerability. That can't be right, though. In the short time I've known Savannah, she's never given off the vibe that she's capable of being vulnerable. She's one of the strongest women I've ever met. Or at least that's what she exudes.

"That's only one reason why I hate being around you. As much as seeing your face irritates me, I can't help the way my body reacts to yours."

My brows shoot up with her admission. I've felt how soft her body becomes when I have her lips against mine and our bodies pressed together, but I never expected her to admit it.

"I abhor that," she continues, further shocking me. "I hate that you smell good. I hate that you taste good. And I especially hate that no matter how much I try to ignore it and turn it into more hate, I can't help but wonder what it would be like to be with you."

I'm sure I look like a fish out of water with my mouth opening and closing, but I'm stunned speechless. What the fuck can I say? I've felt what she's felt. Hated her for the way she constantly spewed nasty comments my way. Wanted to strangle her just to shut her up. But at the same time, wanted to throw her on my bed and fuck every hole she has. The only difference is, her hatred has merit, whereas mine really doesn't.

The waitress picks that moment to bring our food. I'm thankful for the interruption because it gives me another moment to process. All too soon though, we're left alone again.

"I never thought I'd see the day where the great Oliver Conley didn't have something to say," she comments. Seeing her lips twitching as she fights back a smile has my own lifting at the corners.

"Well, you did kinda surprise me. I mean, I already knew you wanted me," I toss her a wink, "but I didn't expect you to admit it so easily."

She harrumphs. "Don't expect it to happen again. And don't think anything will come of it. My body may be interested in yours, but my head screams to stay the fuck away. I'm giving in a little by being here because Rylee wants us to get along, so I'm willing to give it a try."

I nod, conceding for the moment. I'll allow her to think our relationship will stay platonic for right now, but make no mistake, we will end up in my bed at some point.

I look down at her food and frown. "What the hell did you order?"

She looks at her plate and her nose wrinkles. "I have no clue, but there's no way I'm eating that. Just looking at it turns my stomach."

I take in her features and notice her complexion has gone a shade whiter. Not that I blame her. The shit on her plate looks like green slimy hair. My own stomach flips looking at it.

Unraveling my silverware, I use my napkin and toss it over her food. Picking up her plate, I move it out of the way and push my own to the center of the table.

"We'll share mine."

She eyes my food like it isn't much better than hers. It's chicken marsala. What's not to like?

"That's okay. Suddenly, I'm not very hungry." Her eyes slide to her covered dish.

I cut off a piece of chicken. "Come on. At least give it a try. I bet you'll love it."

Instead of giving her the fork, I hold it up in front of her. Her body language is stiff as her eyes flicker from the chicken, to me, and back again. After a moment, she opens her mouth and leans forward, gingerly taking the meat from my fork. I watch as she chews.

Her eyes close and she lets out a little moan that goes straight to my dick.

"Wow. That *is* good," she says, licking the residue from her lips.

"Told you you'd love it."

I cut another piece and pop it into my mouth, letting the flavors roll around before swallowing. I hold up another piece for Savannah and she accepts it.

"Tell me about your family," I request after several moments.

"Why?"

"Because I figure since we're trying this getting along thing, maybe we should get to know each other better."

She props an elbow on the table and drops her chin in her hand. "Umm…okay. Let's see. Mom and Dad own a realty company. They've had the business since not long after they married. They were high school sweethearts. Got married right after college and had me a couple of years later. Great parents and a wonderful childhood."

I fork one of the roasted green beans and lift it to Savannah's lips.

"That must have been nice. Are you close with them?"

"Pretty close. Mom freaks if she doesn't hear from me at least every other day, so to avoid any meltdowns, I make sure to call often."

"And your dad?"

A smile lights her face. "I'm a daddy's girl all the way."

A pang hits my chest. Growing up, I tried everything I could to get my father to notice me. To love me like all other fathers love their sons. But no matter what I did, it wasn't good enough. *I* was never good enough. I stopped trying once I hit high school and realized there was nothing I could do. I'd always be a fucked-up failure in Paul Conley's eyes.

Forcing those thoughts from my mind, I stab a piece of meat and hold it up for Savannah. She shakes her head. I want to force her to eat more, but I don't want to piss her off, so I drop the fork to my plate and pick up my glass of wine.

"What about you?"

I raise my brow.

"It's obvious there's tension between you and your dad. Has it always been that way?"

I drain the rest of my glass and pour more before I answer.

"My whole life."

Her brows knit. "That must have been hard."

I shrug. "When I was younger it was, but I've grown not to care what he thinks of me anymore."

"It's still a shame. No child should feel unwanted or unloved by a parent." She runs her finger through the condensation on her glass. "What about your mom?"

I release a sigh and prop my elbows on the table. "My mother was better." I frown. "Or so I thought." I lift my eyes to hers. "I've thought about her a lot over the last few days, since I found out she cheated on my father—not once, but twice—and I realized something. When my father told me about her cheating, he claimed she was a manipulator, and I can see it now. They were subtle, but I remember the little jabs aimed at my father. She'd tell me things about him, things a boy wouldn't recognize as influences to turn me against him."

"I'm sorry."

I look down at my hand when Savannah places hers on top of mine. This is the first time she's willingly touched me tonight, and I have to admit, it's nice.

"It is what it is. She's gone and didn't think it was necessary to tell me. So I say fuck her. And fuck my father. I really don't give a shit anymore."

I decide to change the subject, because this shit is depressing, and I really don't want to think about it anymore. Especially while out with Savannah. We talk about school and Savannah's job at the coffee shop for about thirty minutes before I hand over my credit card to the waitress.

Way too soon for my liking, I'm parking in front of Savannah's apartment. It's been strange, this date. I've taken girls out before, but I've never dreaded a date ending as much as I'm dreading Savannah walking away from me. Especially since she's acted the complete opposite of how she normally acts around me.

Milking every second I can with her, I open my door and walk around to open hers.

"I'm not inviting you in, you know," she states, her eyes sliding to me as we ride the elevator up to the fourth floor.

"I'm not asking you to," I retort. "I'm just walking you to your door like a gentleman would."

She snorts. "Have you ever acted like a gentleman a day in your life?"

"There's a first time for everything, isn't there?" I grin.

"Seems like there's a lot of firsts coming from you tonight."

I hold my arm out for her to walk off the elevator first. "I could say the same about you."

She sucks her teeth and shakes her head but doesn't say anything further. Her keys are already in her hand when we stop outside her door. Before she opens it, she turns to face me.

"As surprised as I am to say this, I actually had a good time tonight."

"I did too."

My gaze gets stuck on her lips when her tongue peeks out to lick the bottom one.

"Well, I'm going to head in." She tosses her thumb over her shoulder to the door. I glance up when I note the nervousness in her words. "I'll see you around."

I take a step closer, boxing her in against the door.

"Oliver," she starts, her voice quivering. "I already told you I'm—"

"Not inviting me in," I finish for her. Resting my hands on the door beside her head, I lean closer. "But I never agreed not to take another kiss. Aren't dates supposed to at least end with a kiss?"

I don't give her time to answer before I slant my head and take her lips with my own. A groan rumbles from my throat at my first taste of her since this morning. Fuck, she tastes good.

It takes a moment and a few swipes of my tongue before she allows me entrance. Her fingers dig into my sides, and I'm not sure if she's trying to push me away or hold onto me. I get my answer when a little mewling sound vibrates against my lips. I'm rock hard behind the zipper of my jeans, and I'd give damn near anything to thrust my hips forward to show her exactly what she's doing to me. I hold myself still, though, not wanting to break the spell our kiss has wrapped around us.

After several moments of drinking her in, I nip her bottom lip and reluctantly pull back. I grin cockily at her when she stares up at me with dazed eyes.

"Goodnight, Savannah." I tuck a piece of hair behind her ear and step back. "Sweet dreams."

I turn on my heel and walk away, afraid if I stay longer I'll beg her to let me inside.

twelve

SAVANNAH

"Are you ready?" Rylee pops her head into the open bathroom door, her gaze doing a full sweep of me when she does.

I'm dressed a little risqué compared to my usual style. Black halter dress that hits me about mid-thigh, four-inch black heels, and my lips painted fire engine red.

"Wow. V, you look incredible." She whistles loudly.

"I think maybe the dress is too tight." I tug at the material, feeling self-conscious. Sure, it fits me great, but every time I look in the mirror all I see is the bulge of my belly and the curve of my love handles.

"I think it looks incredible."

"It's our first college party, and I've been waiting for a reason to wear this dress. You don't think it's too much?"

"Too much? Um, no. I think you look smoking hot."

I pull my gaze away from my reflection and look toward Rylee. She's dressed a bit more modestly than me, but still looks incredible. She has on a black flair skirt, a white tank top with a long silver necklace draped down the front, and her long hair is curled, falling around her shoulders in perfect waves.

"Speaking of looking hot." I gesture toward my best friend.

"I was going for sexy, but trendy."

"Well, you've accomplished that. What shoes are you going to wear?" I look down at her bare feet.

"I'm stuck between my knee-high boots or my black, strappy heels."

"Heels," I advise her.

"Yeah, that's what I was leaning toward." She smiles. "Anyway, we should probably get going soon. I ordered an Uber ten minutes ago; I can't imagine it will be too much longer before it gets here."

Even though I told Rylee I wouldn't drink and would drive us there and back, she still insisted we get an Uber. I guess she knows once we get there, I'll probably end up wanting to drink. Zayden had offered to come pick us up, but Rylee didn't see the sense in him driving all the way over here when we could just as easily order a ride.

"Okay, I'll be done in just a minute," I tell her, watching her disappear from the doorway moments later.

I turn my gaze back toward my reflection, once again tugging on the material of the dress. It's unforgiving. I might as well be naked at this point considering you can see every ounce of flab I have.

"This is stupid." I shake my head, turning to head into my bedroom, fully prepared to change. I no more than reach my closet when Rylee hollers that the car is here. "Shit," I mutter, glancing down at my outfit. "Well, looks like this is it." I turn and head out into the living room.

"So, you don't go to WSU?" The guy I've been talking to for the last couple of minutes leans in closer, having to raise his voice over the music blaring through the house.

While I've been with Rylee and Zayden since we got here, I excused myself a few minutes ago to get another drink and decided to hang out in the kitchen for a minute—given that it's the least crowded room in the house. Which, when you think about it, really doesn't make that much sense considering it's where all the alcohol is.

I had no sooner leaned against the counter after refilling my drink when one of the fraternity brothers slid up to me, giving me the type of smolder that's probably worked for him a hundred times in the past, but did nothing for me. Don't get me wrong, he's cute.

In a very jock kind of way. Big arms, broad shoulders, sandy-colored hair that's short on the sides and longer on top. But when you slide up next to a girl and boast about how this is *your* party and how lucky *she* should feel to be here, it doesn't really set the mood.

"Seattle University," I answer, tipping my drink to my lips. Thank God for the buzz swimming in my veins, otherwise I probably would have abandoned this conversation the second it started.

I'm not sure that I have a *type*, per se, but cocky frat boy who thinks he's the best thing since sliced bread has never been my cup of tea.

Oliver's face flashes through my mind at the thought, and I quickly go for another drink.

I have no idea where we stand. At dinner the other night we decided to be friends…. I think. But then the way he kissed me—there was nothing friendly about it. It was raw and carnal—definitely not the way friends should kiss—if friends made a habit of kissing, that is, which I'm pretty sure most don't.

"So what brings you out here?" Brad interrupts my thoughts. Or was it Chad? Shit, I can't remember.

"A friend of mine goes to school here," I say in way of explanation.

"Well, that's a lucky break for me." His eyes slide down my body, making me feel like a juicy slab of meat, rather than an actual person.

"Is it?" I arch a brow, deciding to humor him rather than telling him to fuck off like I want to.

"It is." He turns, caging me against the counter.

"I should probably go find my friend," I blurt when his face dips close to mine. Talking is one thing, but if he thinks this is going past that, he's got another think coming.

"Why? When we're having so much fun right here?"

My eyes dart to the doorway as I try to figure out how I can ease my way out of this situation without ruffling this guy's feathers. But when my gaze locks with a pair of familiar blue eyes, my mind literally goes blank.

Oliver....

His eyes narrow, and I take in the flare of his nostrils and the way his shoulders go tight. But before I have time to process what I'm seeing, I feel rough lips press to mine. I jump, my drink sloshing all over the place as I push what's his name away.

"What the fuck?" he grumbles as I dip underneath his arm.

"Sorry, Brad, but I gotta go." I set my cup on the counter and turn to the doorway that's now empty.

"It's Chad," he hollers after me, but I really couldn't care less at this point.

I veer down the hallway and head toward the living room. The music is so loud I can barely hear myself think. I press up, looking over the crowd of people all smooshed together like sardines, spotting Rylee and Zayden off to the far side, grinding on each other like there's not a single other person in the room.

Shaking my head, I turn and head in the opposite direction.

I have no idea what Oliver is doing here. Last I heard, he wasn't coming. And while I shouldn't be excited that he showed up, a part of me is—as much as I hate to admit it.

I scour the rest of the house—the dining room, the game room, the back yard, but I can't find Oliver anywhere. *Did I imagine him standing there?* Heading back into the kitchen, I'm relieved to see Brad/Chad is gone. Crossing toward the counter, I quickly mix another drink, adding extra tequila this time, before heading back toward the living room.

I no more than get both feet into the room when my steps falter. Not even three feet in front of me is Oliver, dancing with a girl so provocatively that it makes what Rylee and Zayden were doing earlier look like child's play.

Well, that certainly didn't take him long. It couldn't have been more than fifteen minutes since I saw him in the kitchen.

His hands are everywhere. Across her chest, gripping her ass as he grinds himself into her, in her hair as he tugs her head back and trails his tongue across her throat.

Anger slams into me like a semi-truck, knocking me backward a step.

I don't understand the emotion. All I know is that right now I have half a mind to walk over and grab Goldilocks by her fake extensions and drag her out of the room.

What the hell?

I look down at my glass, thinking maybe I'm drunker than I originally thought. What else could explain this sudden flash of anger making me feel like my skin is literally on fire?

Oliver's mouth continues to work across the girl's neck. He works his way upward, sucking her earlobe into his mouth before dragging his teeth across it as he releases.

I need to get out of here—it's the only thought I have. But right then Oliver's eyes pop open and his gaze meets mine, and I'm frozen in place. He smiles, but not in the way you would smile at someone you're happy to see. Without breaking eye contact with me, he leans down, dipping the girl so that her head and shoulders fall backward, giving him access to the swell of her breast. Gaze locked on me, his tongue slides under the material of her revealing top, no doubt sweeping across her nipple.

It's like watching a car crash. I don't want to see it, but I can't look away either.

I grind my teeth, anger and confusion seeping out of every pore.

I don't understand my reaction. I shouldn't give a shit who or what he does. He's nothing to me. But if that's true, then why do I feel so hurt by the little show he's clearly putting on just for me?

I think I'm going to be sick.

I turn and quickly exit the room, barely making it into the front yard before dropping my cup in the grass and losing the contents of my stomach in a cluster of bushes that line the porch.

Tears slide past my lashes as dry heaves continue to rocket through my body long after I've expelled all the alcohol from my system.

"Are you okay?" I go ramrod straight at the sound of Oliver's voice behind me.

Wiping my mouth with the back of my hand, I turn, my intense glare locking on Oliver's face.

"Why the hell do you care?" I bite.

"Savannah," he starts, looking almost remorseful. For some reason, that only pisses me off more.

"I'm fine. You can go back inside now." I angrily gesture toward the house.

"You're not fine." He takes a step closer. "Come on, I'll take you home." He reaches for me.

I pull back, looking down at his hand in disgust.

"Thanks, but no thanks." I wipe my fingers under my eyes where my mascara has no doubt started to run. "I'm sure your little bimbo is missing you. Perhaps you should go back inside and finish what you started."

A trace of a smile tugs at his lips, and he cocks his head to the side.

"What?" I snap, feeling irritated by the way he's looking at me.

"You're jealous." It's a statement, not a question.

"Jealous?" I snort out a laugh. "That would imply I give a shit about what you do. Which, I don't."

"Your actions would suggest otherwise."

"What my actions would suggest is that I've had a little too much to drink."

"Is that why you were getting all cozy in the kitchen with that meathead? Because you had too much to drink?"

Suddenly, something hits me. The way he looked at me from the doorway. The way his posture was tight and his brows were knitted together. Was *he* jealous? Is that what that little show was about? His way of getting back at me for something he thought he walked in on.

I stare at him for a long moment, taking in the messy way his hair lays across his forehead. The way his shoulders rise and fall under the material of his black tee as he breathes, slow and controlled.

My heart flips in spite of myself.

God, why does he have to be so good looking?

Why does he have to stand there looking impossibly handsome and yet equally as irritating.

"What was going on in the kitchen is none of your business. Last time I checked, I'm a single woman who can do whatever the hell she pleases."

"The same can be said for me," he counters. "Well, not the woman part, but the single part. And yet you seem pretty pissed at me at the moment."

"I'm not pissed. I don't feel good," I lie, the words catching in my throat.

"You sure that's it?" He takes another step toward me. "Or is it that you didn't like seeing me with another woman—just like I didn't like seeing you with another man?"

"For your information, I wasn't *with* another man. We were just talking."

"Looked like there was a hell of a lot more than talking going on." He grinds his teeth together.

"Well, it wasn't. He made a move, I rejected him. But you didn't stick around long enough to see that part. Either way, it took you what, five minutes before you had your tongue all over some random girl?"

"And you claim you aren't jealous."

"I'm not." I stomp my foot like a temperamental child.

"Let me remind you that you were the one who said you didn't want anything from this." He gestures between the two of us.

"I don't." I take a deep inhale through my nose.

"And yet, you're standing here looking at me like I just ripped the head off your favorite doll."

"Maybe because you proved me right."

"What's that supposed to mean?"

"You can't help yourself, can you? Something doesn't go your way and your first instinct is to lash out like a spoiled child and make a show of doing so." My hands go to my hips. "You think I'm stupid? You think I didn't know that little performance in there was for me? Of course I did. Because that's who you are, Oliver. The kind of guy who purposely hurts people when things don't go his way."

He opens his mouth to speak, but snaps it closed again, contemplating my words.

"For a moment, I thought maybe there was more to you. That maybe I had judged you too harshly. But now, I know that I had you pegged right all along. You are *exactly* the person I thought you were and tonight solidified that fact."

"Like you're so innocent." His nostrils flare.

"I was talking to someone in the kitchen, and then he tried to kiss me. I had no idea that you were even here tonight. I wasn't putting on a show. You just happened to walk in on a situation you didn't fully understand. The two are completely different."

"You're right." He blows out a heavy breath. "I saw you with that guy, and I lost it. I won't deny that it pissed me off. Fuck, it more than pissed me off. I wanted to grab that guy and bounce his fucking head off the countertop."

"So *you* were jealous."

"Fuck yes, I was jealous!" His voice echoes around me, the intensity of his words damn near knocking the wind out of me. "I came here tonight for you. I thought...*fuck*, I don't know what I thought. But then I walked in and saw you with that guy..."

I won't lie and say that his admission doesn't affect me—it does. But it doesn't change anything. Because if tonight has taught me anything—it's that Oliver is who he is, and that's never going to change.

"So what, you thought you'd even the playing field?" I scuff my heel in the ground.

"Savannah." He once again reaches for me.

"No." I take a step back.

"I'm sorry, okay? Is that what you want to hear?"

"I don't want anything from you, Oliver. Not even an apology."

"You're right. Okay? I acted like a fucking spoiled child. I saw you with that guy and instead of doing what I should have done, which was talk to you, I ran off like a little pussy and purposely tried to hurt you. I've been doing shit like this my entire life. Deflecting, trying to hurt people before they have a chance to hurt me. You just…fuck!" he yells to the sky, tugging on his hair. "You drive me fucking crazy." His eyes come back to mine. "I have never been so infuriated with someone yet so consumed by them at the same time."

"Well, I'll make it simple for you, there is no us. There will never be an us. And as far as I'm concerned, you can go lick all over as many sweaty whores as you want. Because whatever this was," I gesture between the two of us, "it's over."

"Over?" he balks. "Fuck, you were too chicken shit to even let it get started."

"Why wouldn't I be? You just admitted that you purposely hurt people before they can hurt you. Why would I want to get involved with you when even you, yourself, can see how fucked up that is?"

"You're right. I am fucked up. I'm just a fucked up, unlovable piece of shit." He tries to hold the angry façade in place, but I can see the hurt that builds behind his expression. "Glad we could get that out of the way."

Before I can reply, Oliver spins around and takes off back into the house, making me feel like maybe he's not the only monster between the two of us. Because if this guilt pressing on my chest is any indication, I might be just as bad as him.

He acted out of jealousy and purposely hurt me. But isn't that what I did with the things I said? Is how I just behaved any better?

I'm tempted to go back inside. To go after him and apologize, but my pride stops me.

This was never going to work anyway. Better that I cut ties now and save both of us a lot of heartache in the future. While physically we seem completely compatible, I think it's pretty clear that emotionally we are on opposite ends of the planet.

Yet, even though I know I'm right, it doesn't stop the small ache in my chest from forming. Because deep down, even though I hate to admit it, I think a part of me was actually starting to really like him.

thirteen

OLIVER

I slam my fist against the punching bag so hard that vibrations radiate up my arm to my shoulder. I'm sweaty and out of breath, but the pain feels good, so I do it again and again and again. The Stone Temple Pilots blast in my ears, drowning out the noise of the gym.

I don't know how much time passes before I'm forced to hunch over with my hands on my knees before I pass the fuck out. I've been working my body for the last two hours, and it's still not enough to take my mind off the shit show my life is at the moment.

Grabbing my towel off a nearby bench, I swipe it across my forehead before snatching up my water bottle and chugging half of it. I shoot a couple of guys who are watching me warily a *fuck-off* glare as I head toward the showers. I chose to come to the gym here at school instead of the one across town because it was closer, but now I regret that shit. At least there, my chances of running into someone I know are slim. Here, I'm surrounded by pansy ass fuck faces who are too afraid to approach me. But then again, that's a good thing, because I'm in no mood to deal with anyone.

I don't know who I'm pissed at more. My father for all the shit he's put me through. My mother for cheating and all of the lies. Savannah for making me feel things for her I have no right to feel. Or myself for the stupid mistake I made last Friday at the party. All I saw was red when I walked into that room and saw the douche so close to Savannah. It was pure luck that I didn't go over there and rip his goddamn head off. I came close, even took several steps toward them before I veered away and grabbed the arm of the first girl I came across.

I won't admit this shit out loud but seeing Savannah with that guy hurt. Really fucking hurt. My first instinct was to hurt her back. And I did. I saw it in her eyes when she said that whatever is, or was, going on between us was over. *That* was the reason I walked away from her. I couldn't stand to see the pain on her face. Pain that *I* caused.

I haven't seen her since. I've purposely stayed away. Because I'm a pussy and don't want to see that pain again. My jaw clenches. Or take the chance of seeing her with someone else.

Using my fist, I slam through the doors to the locker room. A guy sitting on a bench glances over at me before turning back to whatever's on his phone. After grabbing my bottle of shampoo from a locker, I reach back and tug my shirt over my head as I walk to the showers. Once I'm naked, I don't wait for the water to warm before I step under the spray. The shock of cold water feels good, so I hang my head for a few moments. Dumping some shampoo in my palm, I wash my hair and use the extra suds to lather my body.

I've finished washing up and have a towel wrapped around my hips, digging through my bag when a couple of guys walk in.

"Did you see the rack on her?" one guy boasts, holding his hands out in front of his chest as if holding a pair of tits.

"Only reason her tits are so big is because she had no meat on her bones," the other guy snorts. "There's not an inch to grab on to for support."

"True that." The first guy opens a locker and stuffs a bag inside. He turns to his friend and laughs. "But all that hair will do just fine. Wrap that shit around my hand and hold her still while I plow her from behind." He thrusts his hips.

Fucking idiots.

The second guy punches his friend on the shoulder. "You're such an asshole, dude."

"Asshole or not, I bet you fifty bucks I'll have her underneath me by the end of the night."

They turn from the locker and head back toward the door. The first guy catches my eye and offers a chin lift. I don't offer one back.

Guys like him make me sick. I may be an asshole, but the girls I sleep with know exactly what they're getting when I fuck them. No strings attached fun. That's it. The dick who just left no doubt plays on the feelings of girls just to get them in bed, only to hightail it out of there once he's had them.

After I'm dressed and my gym clothes are stuffed in my bag, I shoulder it and head out of the locker room. Next stop is one of the campus cafes for an extra-large coffee. I have an exam tomorrow I've been putting off studying for, so it's going to be an all-nighter. Despite my father's beliefs that I'm fucking around in college and don't care about my grades, I actually do. I'll be damned if I fuck up my only way to get out from under him. I still don't know what the fuck I plan to do with my life, other than getting far away from him. It's the reason why I'm taking his money to attend college in the first place. I figured with all the shit he's put me through, he damn well owes it to me.

I pull my phone from my pocket to check the time when something has me jerking my head to the side. The dickheads from the locker room are at the weight benches. But instead of lifting weights, they are both on the benches and have their eyes hungrily pinned a few feet away from them. I'm just about to dismiss them and whatever poor girl they have their sights set on when I realize *who* they are looking at.

Savannah and Rylee don't even see the fuckers leering at them. Both have earbuds in as they jog on treadmills.

My blood boils and my first instinct is to go over to the guys, pluck out their eyeballs, and stuff them up their asses. I drop my bag with a thump and stalk their way. Like the girls, they don't see me approach.

I'm so focused on getting to the guys and beating the shit out of them that I don't see Savannah until she grabs my arm—having no idea how she got off the treadmill so damn fast. I stop, keeping my eyes on the pair of assholes, who are now looking at me. After a moment, I pull my eyes away from them and look at Savannah.

"What are you doing?" she hisses, out of breath, her eyes darting back and forth between me and the two dead fuckers.

"It's none of your concern."

"You've got murder in your eyes, Oliver. So yes, I'd say it is my concern."

"Fine," I bite out. "Let me rephrase. It's none of your business."

Her lips tighten and her fingers dig into my forearm. "Again. It is my business when it looks like you're going to do serious harm to those two guys who were just looking at Rylee and me."

My gaze sharpens on her. "They were doing more than looking. They were talking stupid shit in the locker room."

"So?" She huffs and throws her other hand on her hip. "That gives you the right to beat the crap out of them?"

I glare over at the guys and see them warily watching me as they gather their shit together. Irritation has my heart pounding when I realize they're leaving. I glance back down at Savannah.

"Yes, it does."

"That's stupid, Oliver. They can say whatever they want to say."

"Not the shit that was leaving their mouths."

"Why are you so butt hurt over what some guys were saying?"

I lean down and get in her face. "Because no one says shit about my girl. Not where I can hear it."

Her eyes widen and she releases my arm to take a step back. I clench my teeth and stuff my hands in my pockets before I reach out and yank her to me.

"Hey. What's going on over here?" Rylee asks, walking up to us. "Everything okay?"

"Everything's fine," I answer Rylee, but keep my eyes on Savannah.

"Okaaay," she says slowly, bouncing her eyes between Savannah and me. "Umm… Savannah and I were just finishing up here before I drop her back off at the apartment. I'm headed to Zayden's for the night."

"I'll take her home," I say before I can stop myself because I'm apparently into self-torture.

"There's no need for that," Savannah states. "Rylee can take me home."

"Actually, that would be great, Oliver. Zayden has to get to bed early because he has a big test tomorrow, so the earlier I get there, the more time I get to spend with him."

Savannah's eyes narrow as she swings her head around to glare at Rylee. "You told me earlier that he had an easy day tomorrow."

She shrugs. "Sorry. Must have forgotten about the test."

She's lying. It's written all over her fake innocent expression.

"Yeah. Right," Savannah mutters. "You know what? It doesn't matter. I'll call an Uber."

She turns to walk away, but I grab her arm and pull her back to me. "Don't be stupid, Savannah. It's just a car ride home."

"Fine." She releases a long breath and her shoulders sag. "Let me grab my stuff."

I watch as she walks away, my eyes glued to her ass in her tight as hell yoga pants. I slide my gaze up, and it zeroes in on the dimples in her shoulders. Ones I'd love nothing more than to dip my tongue in as she writhes beneath me.

I yank my eyes away and look at Rylee. "I don't like the two of you coming to the gym at night. And I'm surprised Zayden lets you."

She laughs and pats my chest. "He's already tried stopping us, but like you're going to have to do, he got over it." Her smile drops some. "We aren't stupid, you know. We carry mace in our bags."

"I still don't like it." My eyes move past her to where the guys were. They've either moved somewhere out of sight or were pussies and left. "Mace can't always save you."

"And that's why we're also taking krav maga classes a couple nights a week."

My brows jump up. This is news to me. "Since when?"

"Since the beginning of the school year. It was Savannah's idea.

She had a cousin who was attacked on campus in Georgia a few years ago."

I nod tightly. I still hate the idea of her and Savannah walking around campus at night, but there's only so much I can do. And knowing they're taking precautions lessens some of my anxiety.

Savannah walks up carrying her gym bag.

"You ready?"

She nods.

I grab her bag from her shoulder and lift a brow when she opens her mouth to protest. With an eyeroll, she turns away from me. After I pick up my own bag, the girls and I leave the gym. Rylee rolls her eyes when I insist on walking her to her car.

It's dark out with only a few people milling about, and even though it's not that late, there's no way in hell I'm letting her walk to her car alone. People don't realize how often people are attacked on college campuses. Especially ones this size.

Once Savannah and I are in my car, I glance at her.

"Have you eaten yet?"

"I really don't think—"

"Jesus," I groan, cutting her off. "Would you fucking relax? I asked in case you wanted me to stop somewhere so you could grab yourself something." I jam the key in the ignition. "I have no plans to force you to stay in my company any longer than necessary."

I speed out of the parking lot, more frustrated at myself for caring about Savannah's wellbeing than her abhorrence of being near me. Why in the hell should I care if she's taking care of herself when the woman couldn't give two fucks about me?

"I'm sorry," she says in the quiet car. "I didn't mean to be rude. I ate before Rylee and I went to the gym."

All I can manage to give her is a jerky nod. She turns quiet after that and stares out the windshield. I toy with the idea of turning on the radio to block out the uncomfortable silence, but I decide not to. If I have to be uncomfortable, so can she.

A few minutes later, I pull into the parking lot of her apartment building, and park in a close spot. Reaching back, I grab her bag from the backseat and drop it in her lap. Feeling the intensity of her eyes on me, I keep mine pointed forward.

"Thanks for the ride home."

"Welcome," I grunt.

Another minute goes by. "I really am sorry. I've just had—"

"Don't worry about it."

She sighs, and a pang hits my chest at the dejected sound. I open my mouth to apologize for being a dick, but she slings the passenger door open and climbs out before I can. I grip the steering wheel in an effort to keep from going after her. Even so, I can't help but watch her walk across the parking lot.

She takes the first step leading to the door and my heart fucking drops when her foot slips. Her arms go out in front of her to catch herself right before her face cracks against the concrete steps, but she goes down hard on her knees.

I'm out of my car and across the lot seconds later.

"Shit. Are you okay?" I ask, kneeling down beside her.

She spins around to sit on the step and brushes her hands off. There are a few small surface scratches.

"Yeah," she grumbles. "Just a bruised ego."

I notice a rip in her leggings and grimace at the blood darkening the material. "Looks like you got your knee pretty good."

She looks at the scrape. "Crap. And these are my favorite yoga pants."

I chuckle and grab her bag from the bottom step. After shouldering it, I reach down and help her up. "Need me to carry you?"

Her eyes dart up to mine in amusement. "It's a skinned knee, Oliver. Not a broken ankle. I think I can manage to walk up a few stairs."

I glance back down to her knee and lift a brow. "That's debatable."

She raps the back of her hand against my stomach. "Smartass."

I chuckle again and follow behind her as she ascends the stairs, keeping a careful eye on her. She turns back around when she reaches the door.

"What are you doing?"

Crossing my arms over my chest, I shoot her a *duh* look. "Making sure you get to your apartment okay and checking on your knee."

She stares a me a moment before she shakes her head with an audible grumble and grabs the handle. Once we're inside her apartment, I drop her bag by the door.

"First aid kit?"

I already know she has one in her bathroom from my morning here a week ago, but I don't think her knowing I snooped in her medicine cabinet would go over well with her.

"You don't have to doctor me, Oliver."

"First aid kit?" I ask again.

With a huff, she points to the hallway. "Medicine cabinet in the bathroom."

"Why don't you get changed into some shorts while I grab it."

She follows me down the hallway, going into the bedroom beside the bathroom and closing the door behind her. I grab the kit out of the medicine cabinet and go to leave when I stop. Stepping closer to the second door in the bathroom—which I thought was a closet—I press my ear against the wood. Muttered curses and shuffling of clothes greets my ear.

Fuck me.

Savannah's on the other side, probably naked. I stifle a groan at the images bombarding my mind. Before my hardening dick gets me into trouble by tempting me to open the door, I leave the bathroom. I drop the kit on the couch and go to the kitchen. After filling a glass with water from the tap, I chug it down.

The light pad of feet has me spinning around as Savannah steps into the kitchen. My mouth goes dry when I take in what she's wearing. A fitted black t-shirt that molds across her ample chest and a pair of dark shorts that fit entirely too well. She shifts from one bare foot to the other, as if my assessment of her makes her nervous.

I clear my throat before I attempt to speak.

"You ready?"

"Yeah."

She turns, and I follow her back into the living room. Once she's situated on the couch, I take a seat on the coffee table directly in front of her. Looking at the scrape on her knee, I realize it's really not that bad. She could have taken care of it herself, but I'm secretly glad I insisted on looking myself. It gives me more time with her.

With the location of the scrape, it's hard to see with her leg bent, so I grab the back of her knee and carefully bring her leg up so it's laying across my thighs. Her skin feels so fucking soft. Would she slap me if I grazed my hand further up her thigh?

Hell yeah, she would.

Mentally shaking myself, I grab some gauze and the small bottle of peroxide. Holding the gauze close to the scrape, I pour some of the liquid over the scrape. It fizzes on the open wound.

"How have you been?" Savannah's quiet voice has me looking up at her.

I shrug as I pour more liquid on the scrape. "Fine. Busy with school."

"Have you been able to get in touch with your mom?" She attempts to make small talk.

"No, and I've stopped trying."

Savannah shifts over on the couch and something catches my eye. A small red box is wedged between two cushions. Noticing my attention has been drawn away from her knee, Savannah looks down beside her. Her head jerks up, her eyes wide when they meet mine. Reaching out, I snag the box of Red Hots.

"Those are Rylee's," she blurts quickly.

I smirk. "Try again. I know for a fact that Rylee hates Red Hots."

"Zayden?" She poses it like a question, as if asking if that suggestion is more plausible.

My smirk turns into a full-fledge grin as I shake my head.

"Fine," she grumbles. "They're mine, okay?"

Laughing, I open the box and tip it to my lips, letting a few of the hot candies fall into my mouth.

"Gimme those," she growls, snatching the box from me. I watch in amusement as she dumps some candy into her hand before popping them in her mouth.

It's cute as fuck. Did she buy them because she really likes them? Or because they remind her of me?

"Why do you eat so many of these anyway?" she asks.

I rifle through the kit, looking for some antibiotic ointment.

"No clue. I've just always liked them. Even as a kid, they were what I always chose off the candy shelf."

"It's a weird choice for a kid."

I shrug. "Maybe."

I apply the ointment to her knee and place a bandage over the area. My hand lingers on the underside of her knee, enjoying the sensation of her warm and smooth skin against my palm. I slowly rub my thumb back and forth.

Looking up at her, I find her green eyes pinned on me. The box of candy is sitting in her lap, forgotten. Her chest rises and falls faster than it should, and her lips are parted as she takes in shallow breaths.

The look in her eyes as her tongue darts out to lick her bottom lip is too much for me to handle. Gently, I set her foot on the floor, then drop to my knees in front of her. Wedging my hips between her legs, I scoot closer to her. I can practically feel the heat coming off her, and it only manages to raise my own body temperature by several degrees.

Sliding my hands up her thighs until my fingers curl around her waist, I slowly slide her to the edge of the couch. A hiss leaves my lips when her hot core meets my shaft.

I have never, in my entire fucking life, wanted someone as much as I want Savannah.

I keep waiting for her to push me away, but she doesn't. I'm surprised when her legs lock around my waist and she grips the front of my shirt, tugging me forward.

One minute I'm gauging her reaction, the next I'm slamming my mouth against hers. She tastes like cinnamon and sin. A heady combination.

I groan and deepen the kiss, thrusting my hips against her. My dick is so hard it feels like it's going to break off.

"I need you, Oliver," she moans breathily, sending my need skyrocketing. "I need you," she repeats, the look in her eyes telling me exactly what she means by *need*.

Never have I loved words more than the ones she just uttered. I pull back just enough so I can see her face. "I need you to be sure. Really fucking sure. Because once I get started, baby, I don't know if I'll be able to stop."

She licks my bottom lip before biting down on it gently. "I'm sure."

"What happened to whatever this is, is over?" I question, wanting to punch myself in the face for even bringing that shit up.

"I changed my mind." There's something desperate in her tone. Something that tells me that this isn't just about me. I shouldn't oblige. I should force her to talk to me. But fuck me if I'm not a selfish bastard who can't resist the opportunity to have her beneath me.

Gripping her ass, I get to my feet with her still wrapped around me.

With determined strides, I carry her to her room.

Fourteen

SAVANNAH

I don't know what I'm doing or why. All I know is that I need this. I need to feel something, anything. I've had this pit in my stomach for days, this ache that has solidified itself and refuses to go away.

I refuse to think too much about this. Right now, I only want to lose myself in the man who has more than gotten under my skin. A man, who in a lot of ways, I don't even like. And yet here I am, kissing him, begging for what I need.

Him.

"Oliver," I pant against his lips as he deposits me on the bed, crawling up the mattress in a way that forces me to move with him.

"Fuck, Savannah." He runs his hand down my side. "Do you have any idea how badly I want this?"

Just hearing him say it causes my already heated skin to erupt into an inferno.

His lips are everywhere. My jaw. My neck. Across my collarbone. Trailing a path of heat everywhere they touch. When he tugs my shirt down and sucks one of my nipples into his mouth, I gasp. He's not gentle, but right now gentle is not what I want.

He moves to the other side, repeating the process, swirling his tongue around the hard bud. My fingers dig into the sheets as my back arches, silently begging for more.

He shifts upward, pulling me with him, and removes my shirt and sports bra in one swift movement. I wish I had thought to shower at the gym, but I'm too lost to the sensation of his hands on my body to care too much at the moment.

The room is completely dark, with the exception of the small glow from the hallway light peeking through the door. But Oliver's touch makes the whole room feel alive. Like the sun is blaring down on us inside the four walls of this room.

Guiding me back down, he starts at my neck and slowly, torturously, makes his way all the way down to the waistband of my pants—nipping and tasting my skin as he descends.

I'm a ball of nerves as he grabs the stretchy waistband and tugs down, raising up just enough to remove them and my panties before tossing them somewhere on the floor. And then his mouth is on me, teasing me, tasting me. I writhe against him as his tongue laps against my core, sliding between my folds.

I've never felt anything like it before. Sure, I've had guys go down on me, but never like this. Never with so much skill and determination. He works my body so expertly, as if it was a road map that he's studied a million times. He knows every turn, every back road, every winding street like he's committed it all to memory.

My orgasm comes on so fast and strong that I cry out in both surprise and pleasure. It rockets through me with so much intensity that I grind down on his face, never wanting the feeling to end.

Oliver growls, slowing his movements as he eases me down.

"Fuck. I could do that forever." He brushes the tip of his nose against my clit and inhales deeply. I want to tell him to stop, and normally I probably would, but with Oliver, I don't know, it's hard to explain. Maybe it's because I've convinced myself that I don't care what he thinks. Or maybe it's because he does it with such appreciation for my body that I don't hear the usual voice of self-doubt in the back of my head.

Oliver lifts his head and begins working his way up my body like a predator about to devour his prey. I anticipate his every move, yet every slip of his tongue and press of his lips makes me jump slightly.

When he reaches my jaw, he nips at the flesh before sitting up just enough to tug his shirt over his head. I can't see the smile on his face, but I can feel it the instant his lips touch mine. He slides his tongue into my mouth, swirling it against mine. I can taste myself on him, and it's hands down one of the most erotic things I've ever experienced.

"Now, Oliver," I breathe against his mouth, the ache in my belly not satisfied. I need more. So much more.

"Condom?" He sucks my bottom lip into his mouth and bites down gently. I can feel the sensation all the way to my toes.

"Top drawer of the nightstand." My voice is breathy.

He shifts, tugging open the drawer before he rustles through the contents, trying to find the small box of condoms I keep in there, just in case. Of course, when I bought them I never in a million years dreamed it would be Oliver in my bed.

He locates the box and quickly tears it open, pulling one of the condoms out. Working down his shorts, he rips the packet with his teeth and rolls the condom on.

I'm a ball of nerves as I wait.

A part of me is screaming to stop this before it goes too far. The other part of me wants nothing more than to feel him inside of me. It's a push and pull. A back and forth. My mind and my heart waging war on one another.

Only this isn't about my heart. This is about my body. And right now, all it wants is something only this man can give me.

Oliver settles back down on top of me, lining himself at my entrance before hesitating. Pushing my hair away from my face, he looks down at me for a long moment.

"What are you waiting for?" I groan impatiently.

"Just taking it all in," he says, jolting forward abruptly.

He fills me so suddenly and completely that I'm not sure which is greater, the pleasure or the pain. I cry out, his mouth swallowing up the sound seconds later.

And then he's moving, thrusting into me with so much force that I'm sliding up the bed, the sheets bunching beneath me. I claw at his back, pull at his hair, buck my hips upward, meeting him thrust for thrust.

I feel him everywhere. From the top of my head to the tips of my toes. There isn't a single part of my body unaffected.

I wouldn't say I'm promiscuous by any means, but having been with three guys before Oliver, I know that what I feel, what he's making me feel, is not the norm. I shudder to think how much practice he's had to make him this good, and quickly push the thought away.

Oliver slides his hand around the back of my knee and arches my leg up, giving him the ability to hit me in just the right spot. His other hand is firmly on my hip, his fingers biting into my skin. I moan and writhe, mumbling incoherently about how good he feels and how I never want him to stop.

And then it's back. The build. The tingling sensation that starts at the back of my neck and slowly spreads down my spine. My skin prickles. Sweat beads across my forehead. And if not for Oliver's weight holding me down, I'd swear I was moments from floating away.

My second orgasm hits a thousand times harder than the first. It feels like I'm being torn open from the inside out, the build so slow that by the time it finally peaks, I'm not sure if I can take anymore.

I explode around Oliver's thick length, crying out so loudly that all I hear is my voice reverberating off of the walls back to me.

I vaguely catch the deep rumble of a groan from Oliver through the fog that has encompassed me. I feel the tenseness in his legs, feel the force of his thrusts, and then seconds later, he collapses down on top of me.

"That was…." He drops his face into the crook of my neck, forcing me to take the full weight of his body, his chest rising and falling in quick succession as he works to catch his breath. "Fucking incredible," he finally finishes his thought, his voice vibrating against my damp skin.

Seconds bleed into minutes as the heat of the moment passes.

And when I finally find my way back down to Earth, I don't regret it the way I'd expected to. Hell, if anything, I think I want to do it again.

It wasn't what I'd expected.... None of this has been what I'd expected. Then again, I'd never actually expected this to happen... ever.

"I need to go to the bathroom," I tell Oliver, who's still planted inside me after several minutes.

"Don't make me move." He smiles against my neck. "I've decided I'm going to stay here forever, buried inside your warm pussy."

"You realize most girls don't like that word." I giggle when his head pops up and his eyes meet mine.

"What? Pussy?"

"Yeah." I nod, crinkling my nose.

"And why the hell not?"

"Because it's crude and ungentlemanly."

"I hate to break it to you, V, but I am not a gentleman."

The use of my nickname sounds unfamiliar coming off his lips, yet I can't deny that I like how it sounds.

"Bathroom. Now." I pat on his shoulder.

"Fine," he grumbles, sliding out of me. My body objects to the loss of him.

He rolls to the side, the absence of his weight hitting me like a blast of cold air.

I quickly sit up and climb out of bed, disappearing into the bathroom seconds later.

When the door is closed and locked behind me, I flip on the light and turn toward my reflection. My cheeks are flushed. There's some red spots on my neck and chest from Oliver's mouth. And I'm fairly certain I can already see a bruise forming on my hip from his fingers.

I smile, shoving little strands of hair stuck to my forehead out of my face. I think this might be the first time in a long time I've looked at myself naked and not felt absolutely disgusted with what I see. Maybe it's the buzz of the orgasm high still sifting through my veins. Or maybe it's that I feel so deliriously happy that the imperfections of my body don't seem as important.

Happy? I find myself questioning the thought. Is that what I feel?

I think on it for a moment, realizing that's exactly what it is. I feel happy.

I want to regret it. I want to be mad at myself for giving into Oliver Conley, but I can't seem to muster even an ounce of remorse.

Pulling my bottom lip between my teeth, I close my eyes and relish in the sweet soreness of my lips—knowing Oliver's kiss is what caused it.

"You okay in there?" Oliver knocks on the door, startling me out of the dreamy daze that seems to have settled over me.

"Yeah." I turn, pulling back the shower curtain before flipping on the water.

"Are you showering?" he asks, humor in his voice.

"I didn't shower after I worked out," I say in way of explanation, grabbing a towel from underneath the sink.

"And it made you taste that much sweeter."

My gut instinct is to balk at his comment, or at the very least, be disgusted by it. Only I'm not. In fact, the statement has me ready to tear open the door and go for round two.

But knowing myself, and knowing I need a minute to process, I refrain, stepping under the spray of the hot water instead.

I've only just gotten my hair wet when the shower curtain moves. My eyes open right in time to see Oliver step into the shower with me, a mischievous look on his face.

"What the hell do you think you're doing?" I try to act appalled but fail miserably.

"Taking a shower." He shrugs, the grin on his face so adorable. I swear I feel my insides melt a little.

Wait.... Did I just refer to Oliver as adorable?

What the hell kind of drugs am I on right now?

This is Oliver Conley we're talking about.

The man who grates on me so badly sometimes I want to claw his eyeballs out.

The man who's so infuriating that I've actually daydreamed about running him over with my car.

The man who only days ago I could barely stand the sight of.

It's like I've entered some sort of alternate reality and everything that should be, isn't, and everything that shouldn't be, is.

"How did you even get in here?" I question, wiping the water from under my eyes.

"It's a pretty simple lock. You can pick it with just about anything. A butter knife. A screwdriver. The end part of a pair of fingernail clippers." He smiles, telling me this is the method he used.

"So in other words, I need to get a better lock."

"Hmm." He taps his chin. "I'm going to say no to that one." He steps closer, sliding one hand around the small of my back and the other across the side of my neck.

With one quick tug, I'm in his arms.

He stares down at me for a long moment, his eyes sweeping across my face.

"You're beautiful," he tells me, his voice so soft that I barely catch his words over the sound of the water.

I'm not sure what to say. The way he's looking at me. The way he's talking to me. It's like he's someone completely different. Where's the vile, self-serving asshole that I'm used to seeing? The one who has an insult at the ready every time I speak? The one who makes me want to throw myself off a cliff every time he opens his mouth.

There is no trace of that man right now.

It's as if, standing here, we're two completely different people.

Before I can think of any kind of response that wouldn't sound completely ridiculous, Oliver leans forward, kissing me slow and deep.

It doesn't take long for the leisurely kiss to heat up, and before I realize it, Oliver has me pinned against the shower wall, his fingers inside of me.

If I thought for one second that this was only going to be a one-time thing, I was wrong. Dead wrong. Because as I come apart on his hand, all I can think is how badly I want to do this over and over again.

fifteen

OLIVER

I wake to the best fucking feeling in the world. A warm body pressed against me, my face buried in her luscious hair, and my dick wedged between two warm ass cheeks. Taking a deep breath in, I inhale Savannah's delicious scent. I never knew actually sleeping with someone could be so pleasurable. Something tells me it's the person, not so much the action.

Opening my lips, I lick a spot in the crook of her shoulder then suck a piece of skin into my mouth.

Savannah moans and presses her ass back against me.

"If you leave a hicky on me, I'm going to kick your ass."

Her sleepy voice is sexy as hell.

Releasing the suction I have on her, I lean back and look at the mark I left, along with the few others I left last night.

"Too late."

She growls, but I hear the smile she's fighting. Does she like the thought of me marking her? I know I really like seeing them.

"What time is it?"

"Don't know," I mumble as I kiss a path from her shoulder up her neck. "Don't care."

She grabs her phone from the nightstand, and a moment later, she jerks up in bed.

"Shit!" she nearly shouts. "You've got to go! Rylee will be home soon!"

Grabbing her by the back of her head, I yank her back down. "Fuck that. I'm not going anywhere. And neither are you." To punctuate this, I settle myself between her legs, effectively keeping her exactly where I want her.

"Oliv— Oh, God," she moans when I press my hardness against her. Too bad she put her panties back on before we went to sleep last night. "You don't play fair."

"Never said I did, baby."

She pants and tilts her head to the side. "I don't want Rylee to see you here."

"Why?" I kiss down her neck until I reach the valley between her breasts. Her nails dig into my sides so hard I let out a hiss.

"Because I don't want her to get the wrong idea."

I take little nibbles across the top of her breasts before I zero in on a nipple. She tastes so fucking sweet in my mouth.

"And what idea is that?"

I feel her eyes on me, so I look up.

"That we're actually together."

Smiling, because she's so fucking cute, I lick her nipple. "We are."

Her eyebrows slant and she presses her lips together. "No, we aren't."

Climbing back up her body so my face is right in front of her, I stare down into her beautiful green eyes. She needs to hear me and hear me well.

"I don't know where your head's at right now, Savannah, but this isn't a one-time deal for me. I'm not here because I want to fuck you once and be done with you. I've never been tempted before to have more than casual sex with a girl, but I damn sure want more with you. Don't ask me why because I have no fucking clue. I just don't like the thought of walking away from you."

The expression on her face softens, and the knot that was forming in my chest loosens. No way was I taking no for an answer, but it makes my life a hell of a lot easier with her acceptance.

"I'm actually glad you feel that way, because I was seriously contemplating chaining you to my bed so you couldn't leave."

I open my mouth to tell her she can still chain me to her bed when a door outside of her room slams shut. My eyes fall to Savannah's. "You wanna get this over with now or later?"

She bites her lip contemplatively. "Might as well do it now." Her eyes roll around. "She's never going to let me live this down," she grumbles.

Chuckling, I lean down for a quick kiss. "You're a big girl. You can handle it."

"Says the guy who doesn't live with Rylee."

Using my fists, I hoist myself up and off her, then hold my hand out to help her up. As soon as she's on her feet, I yank her against my chest.

"Just tell her what I did with my tongue last night. That'll shut her up."

"Yeah." She giggles. "I *won't* be doing that."

Grabbing our shirts off the floor, I hand her hers and tug mine over my head. Once we're both suitably dressed, I grab her hand and we walk to the door. Just as I grip the knob, there's a thump against the wall right outside the door, followed by a quiet giggle.

"Oh, my God, Zayden, we have to be careful or we'll wake Savannah," Rylee's muffled voice comes through the door.

"She sleeps like the dead." Zayden's voice sounds more muffled, like his lips are pressed against something. "If my dick isn't buried in your pussy within the next few minutes, I'm going to lose my shit."

"You are not fucking me outside my best friend's bedroom door."

"Then I suggest you let go of my dick so I can carry us to your room."

There are a few more mumbled words before Z apparently has enough and stumbles his way into Rylee's room. Another door slams shut seconds later. I look down at Savannah and find her wide eyes on me. There's a cute blush on her cheeks and her bottom lip is being abused by her teeth.

"So, I guess telling Rylee about us will have to wait."

"Yep." I turn to face her fully and gently tug her to me. "Wonder what we should do in the meantime."

"I'll make us some coffee."

When she tries to pull back from me, I tighten my hold around her waist.

Slowly shaking my head, I grin at her. "I have better plans."

Her eyes go big again. "Not happening."

Moans seep through the walls, no doubt coming from Rylee's room. Savannah's eyes dart to the wall before coming back to me.

"I bet we could be louder." I'd laugh at her expression if I wasn't afraid she'd slap me.

"We won't be finding out."

"Come on, baby." I take a couple of steps, forcing her backward toward the bed. "Let's show them how it's done." Another couple of steps.

More muffled sounds filter into the room.

Slipping my hands inside her shorts, I squeeze her ass cheeks, making sure my fingertips are low enough to graze the outside of her pussy. She's already dripping, so as appalling as the idea of fucking to the sounds of Z and Rylee may be to her, it's also making her hot and bothered.

Fuck knows it has me hard as stone.

"We are not doing this, Oliver." But the way her eyes are glazing over and the little pants leaving her mouth says something else.

"Fuck me harder, Zayden," comes Rylee's muffled voice.

One more step and the back of her knees touch the bed. Dipping lower, I push my middle finger inside her tight pussy. It slides in easily and her eyes fall closed on a soft moan.

"You're an asshole, you know that?" she murmurs.

Her lids flutter open and the look she gives me nearly has me falling to my knees to worship her. Blatant lust and carnal need blazes bright. She grips the waistband of my shorts and quickly pushes them down.

"Fuck me and fuck me quick," she all but growls. "And keep it quiet."

Grinning victoriously, I whip off my shirt and make quick work of hers. Her shorts come off next. As soon as we're both naked, I push her down onto the bed and crawl on top of her. After paying homage to her fantastic tits, I grab a condom from the nightstand and slip it over my rigid shaft.

"Fuck yeah, baby," Zayden grunts. "Grind that pussy all over me. Fuck, you feel so good."

At Zayden's words, I notch the tip of my dick at Savannah's entrance and without warning, thrust inside in one smooth motion. She cries out, her walls gripping me so tight it feels like she won't ever let me go.

So much for keeping it quiet. Not that I particularly wanted her to be.

I stare down at her, hypnotized at the stunning look on her face. Many men have said it about their women, but there's truly never been a more beautiful sight than watching Savannah come undone.

Her nails dig into my ass. "Harder, Oliver. I need it harder and faster."

Giving her exactly what she wants, I grab the back of her leg, lift it over my hip, and slam forward. I fuck her hard and sweet, giving her everything I have in me. Her moans mix with Rylee's, and I wonder if her and Zayden can hear her.

I've never been the typical guy who fantasizes about having two women at once. I wouldn't say no if the opportunity presented itself, but it hasn't been something I've necessarily wanted. I figured if a woman knows how to please a man, it's a waste to add another. But it's hot as fuck to hear Savannah and Rylee getting off at the same time.

I pick up speed and grunt when Savannah's walls clamp down on me. With her eyes half-closed and her mouth open as she lets out a loud moan, I let myself go. She milks me for everything I'm worth, wringing every drop of cum out of me.

Her arms fall lax beside her head, and she stares up at me dazedly. Brushing a few strands of hair from her face, I lean down and give her a lazy kiss.

"FYI, as soon as I have the energy, you're dead meat."

Chuckling, I fall to her side and throw an arm over my eyes. "It was worth it."

WITH A SMIRK, I follow behind Savannah as she begrudgingly leaves her bedroom. I barely hold back my laughter when we hit the living room and spot Rylee sitting on the couch, her eyes pointed straight at Savannah. She lifts a brow when she notices me behind her.

"Don't start with me," Savannah warns, moving around the couch to go to the kitchen.

Rylee jumps up to block her. "I don't think so. You," she says, pointing at me before throwing her thumb over her shoulder, "to the kitchen. And you," she looks at Savannah and points toward the hallway, "to my room."

Turning, Savannah shoots me a glare. "This is all your fault."

Lowering my head, I give her lips a peck. "And you don't regret a single second of it."

"I'm not so sure about that," she mutters grumpily, but still rises on her tippy toes to get at my lips better. I grin and give her what she wants.

Rylee clearing her throat a moment later has *me* turning grumpy. Tossing Rylee a disgruntled look, I walk past her into the kitchen. As the women walk in the opposite direction, I hear Rylee say right before the bedroom door closes, "Lucy, you've got some 'splaining to do."

Zayden is leaning back against the counter, his coffee mug hiding his smirk. I walk over to the coffee maker and grab a mug down from the cabinet.

"Thought you had some big test today."

"Nope."

So, Rylee *did* lie last night. I'll have to give her an extra-large hug when she gets done grilling Savannah.

I pour some of the bitter black brew into my mug and drop in a spoonful of sugar before giving it a good stir. Feeling his questioning gaze on me, I turn and face Zayden, leaning back against the opposite counter.

Before he has a chance to say anything—I know he's going to from the look in his eyes—I decide to be the first one to speak. "Are you two always so fucking loud?"

I chuckle when I catch him off guard, which doesn't happen often with Z. He chokes on his coffee and quickly sets the mug down before he spills it.

He clears his throat. "It's never been a problem before. And from the sound of it, it wasn't a problem today."

My grin is Cheshire big. "Hell no, it wasn't. It was almost like listening to porn."

"You're sick." He laughs, folding his arms over his chest.

"If I'm sick, then so are you and the girls. Don't fucking deny you and Rylee didn't get off listening to me and Savannah go at it. Lord knows it had both my and Savannah's motors running in high gear."

"Maybe so, but that shit isn't happening again."

I lift my shoulders. "Sure. So long as you and my stepsister keep it down, we will too."

"So, I guess you and Savannah worked things out? No more trying to kill each other?"

"For the time being."

"You know she's not someone you can play around with, right?"

His comment irritates me. My reputation as the love 'em and leave 'em type may be true, but every girl I've ever fucked knew the score. And it pisses me off that Zayden would think I'd dump Savannah at the first opportunity.

"Thanks for the harsh judgement, asshole. I have no plans to ditch Savannah. I actually really fucking like her."

"I wasn't implying that you would. I'm just saying she's not like the girls you usually pick."

"I know that." I chug the rest of my coffee and set the mug in the sink before facing him again. "She's a fuck of a lot different than the girls I usually go for. That's why I like her so much. All the other girls chased me. Savannah is the first girl I've had to chase. She's the first I've *wanted* to chase."

His brows jump up. "Sounds serious."

"It's still too early to tell, but for the first time, I want to find out where this goes. The woman drives me mad half of the time, but the other half... I don't know." I look down at my bare feet. "It's hard to explain."

"I get it. They burrow so far under your skin there's no way to get them out. You *don't want* to get them out."

That's actually a damn good assessment. I don't know what it is about Savannah, but she's got her claws in me deep, and I'm thinking I may never want her to release me.

I jut my chin toward the hallway. "How long do you think this is going to take?"

"There's no fucking telling. You're lucky Rylee didn't bust down the door when she realized it was *you* in the room with Savannah. She's been chomping at the bit for the last few minutes."

"Girls and their gossip. Whatcha want to bet they're in their comparing our dick sizes."

With a head shake, he walks to the fridge and grabs out the package of bacon and a carton of eggs. I snatch the bacon from his hand.

"You've got egg duty. I'll take care of the bacon. I'm not eating the rubbery shit you make."

Grabbing my phone, I find my hard rock playlist and blast some tunes while Z and I prepare breakfast for our women.

sixteen

SAVANNAH

"I knew it!" Rylee smacks her leg with a hard crack. "I knew it was only a matter of time." I can't tell if she's more surprised or amused at this point.

I've just spent the last ten minutes filling her in on everything that happened last night... and this morning. Truth be told, I still don't think I've fully processed any of it. On one hand, I feel like I'm over the moon. On the other, I'm a little hesitant to let this go any further.

After all, this is Oliver Conley we're talking about. The man has quite the reputation. What if this is all some sort of game to him? What if he's trying to get close to me for the sole purpose of hurting me? It sounds farfetched, I know, but he's proven he's capable of doing unspeakable things. My poor best friend is the perfect example of that.

"I knew there was something more to how much you two acted like you hated each other," she continues.

"Now, I wouldn't go that far." I stop her. "That wasn't an act. Honestly, I'm still not sure if I even like him."

"Uh huh." She gives me a disbelieving look. "You forget, I know you, Savannah Reynolds. You have tells that always give you away."

"I do not," I needlessly argue.

"Yeah. Okay." She rolls her eyes dramatically.

"It just kind of happened, okay?"

"Just kind of happened?" She laughs in the back of her throat.

"What I heard this morning was not 'just kind of happened'." She air quotes with her fingers. "Come on, V, this is me. You know you can tell me anything. No judgement."

I pull in a deep breath and let it out slowly.

"Fine," I finally concede. "I might like him."

"Might?" She arches a brow.

"Fine. I like him. There, are you happy now?"

"Oh, V." She gives me a sympathetic look. "If anyone understands what it's like to have feelings for someone you shouldn't, it's me. Or are you forgetting how the beginning of Zayden and my relationship started?"

"He's just...he's not a good guy, Ry."

"Who says?"

"His actions say."

"Everyone makes mistakes. It doesn't mean he's a bad person."

"I think the proof is kind of in the pudding."

"But it's not always so black and white. Take Zayden for example. When I first met him, he was horrible to me. Treated me like the dirt on the bottom of his shoe. And now look at us. Sometimes even the most volatile relationships can blossom into something more."

"I guess." I shrug. "I just.... I just don't want to get my hopes up. Ya know? I mean, the way he was last night. The way he was this morning. It's like he's not at all who I thought he was. Well, that's not entirely true, but it is at the same time. There's a softer side to him. A side I honestly never expected to see."

"That's because he likes you."

"How do you know that for sure?" I question.

"I can tell. I've known for a while now. Hell, maybe I knew before he did. And who can blame him? Look at you." I shrink a little under her gaze. I can't help it. Anytime my appearance comes to the forefront, it's my knee jerk reaction. "You're beautiful and funny and smart. Why wouldn't any guy want a chance to be with someone like you?"

"I can think of a lot of reasons," I grumble.

"Stop that," she chastises me. "You are an amazing person, V. Why do you always have to think the worst of yourself?"

"It's hardwired, I guess."

"Well, unwire it. It's time you start seeing yourself the way everyone else does."

I think on that for a moment. She's not wrong. I've always been my toughest critic, but it's hard to change your way of thinking when you've been at it for so long.

"Oliver isn't perfect. I'll give you that," she keeps going. "But I think if you give him a chance, he just might surprise you."

"Maybe." I wring my hands together.

"Just don't overthink it. Feel things out, see where they go. And if he hurts you, he'll have me to answer to."

"Because you're so scary," I tease.

"Maybe not, but my man sure as hell is." She grins. "And I know he'll kill Oliver if he does something to hurt you."

"I'm guessing you think that should make me feel better." I laugh.

"Hell yes, it should." Her voice goes up a few notches. "Like I said, see what happens. True, it might not work out. But, V," she pauses, "what if it does?"

"That's the very question I've been asking myself all night."

"Sometimes you have to take a risk. Now." She sticks her pointer finger out toward my face. "About this morning. I love you, but the last thing I want to do is hear my best friend and stepbrother going at it like wild animals."

"Pot meet kettle," I quip.

"Fair enough. But seriously, keep it down next time."

"I tried." A trace of a smile touches my lips. "He's just…." I stop, wondering if I should say this next part. "Well, let's just say he may talk a big game, but he definitely has the skills to back it up."

And boy does he ever. I've never experienced anything like it. Being with Oliver is like bumping up from the minor league to the majors. It's a whole different ball game.

"Eww." She curls her nose. "TMI, my dear friend. TMI." She shakes her head, her thick brown hair sweeping against her shoulders as she does.

"Just sayin'." I chuckle.

"On that note, maybe we should go out and see what the boys are up to."

"Is it weird that I'm nervous to go back out there?" I ask, hitching my thumb toward the door.

"Are you kidding? When I first started seeing Zayden, just the thought of passing him in the halls made me half sick to my stomach. That's how I knew I really liked him." She gives me a knowing look.

"Not sure that's much of a comfort," I whine.

"Oh, hush." She sweeps past me, tugging open the door moments later. "Come on. I smell bacon." She throws me a smile over her shoulder before sashaying out into the hallway.

I follow her, feeling all types of nerves pinging around inside my stomach.

When we reach the kitchen, Zayden is setting out plates while Oliver stands in front of the stove flipping bacon. I have to admit, the sight of him cooking in my kitchen after the most mind-blowing night of my life is quite nice. Maybe I could get used to this....

"Hey." Zayden leans over and kisses Rylee on the temple when she slides up next to him. "Everything good?"

"Yep." She pops her lips. "What are you guys making? It smells amazing."

"Cheesy scrambled eggs, toast, and Oliver is finishing up the bacon now. He wouldn't let me cook it."

"I knew I kept you around for a reason," she says to Oliver's back. I watch his head turn, a lopsided smile on his face.

"I told him his bacon making skills are seriously lacking." He chuckles when Zayden tosses up a middle finger in his direction.

"No offense, babe." Rylee turns back to Z.

"You say that, but with the way you two are dogging on my cooking skills, I gotta admit, I'm a little offended."

"There are other things you're good at. Really, really good at." She gives him a sexy little grin.

"Don't go stroking his ego, sis. He doesn't need that head of his getting any bigger," Oliver interjects, his gaze sliding to mine for a brief moment when I step into the doorway of the kitchen and lean my shoulder against the frame, watching the three of them. He gives me a sweet smile, one that has my heart doing funny things inside my chest.

"Yeah, because you're one to talk," Zayden bites back, jarring Oliver when he reaches out and punches him in the bicep.

"Why do you always resort to violence." Oliver rubs his arm dramatically. "Rylee, you need to get your man in check."

"Me?" She laughs. "He's your best friend. You get him in check."

"V, a little help here." Oliver looks back to me.

"Sorry, you three are on your own." I hold my hands up.

"Do you guys need any help?" Rylee chimes in, looking around the kitchen.

"Nope." Zayden shakes his head. "As soon as Oliver is done with the bacon, breakfast will be ready."

My stomach doubles over a little at the thought of eating. I know I need to. Hell, I even want to. But my body does not cooperate anymore. I eat. I feel sick. I usually end up puking. It's an endless cycle. One that I wish I could break. I'm just not sure how. I know I need help. I know that this whole thing has spiraled way out of control, but right now, I don't want to think about any of that. I just want to enjoy this. Laughing with my friends. Basking in the glow that Oliver has left me with. Embracing the giddiness I feel when his eyes lock with mine as he turns to deposit bacon onto the plates already filled with eggs and toast.

It's nothing that I expected, and yet oddly, it feels right.

And for now, that's enough.

"Finally, you answer." My mom's voice comes through the line seconds after I press the phone to my ear.

"Hi, Mom. Sorry. I meant to call you back last night after I left the gym, but I got, um, sidetracked."

"Too busy to call your poor mom and check in?" she asks. "It's been what, four days since I've heard from you?" The way she says it you would think it was more like four months.

"I know. I'm bogged down with schoolwork and have been picking up some extra shifts at work. I promise I'm not intentionally avoiding you."

"I was starting to think maybe you were." I can hear the teasing tone of her voice and know she's only giving me a hard time. "How's everything? How's school?"

"School is good. Work is good. Everything is really good." I smile when the thought of Oliver fills my mind.

I've thought of nothing but him since he left earlier today. I half expected him to stay, but shortly after breakfast he announced he needed to head back to his dorm to study for an exam he has in one of his afternoon classes. I'm surprised by how disappointed I felt in that moment.

Not that I could have spent the whole day with him anyway. I had two afternoon classes, and now I'm heading to the coffee shop for my shift. I'm glad I have things to do. The last thing I want is to sit around obsessing over a man who, up until a few short days ago, I couldn't stand the sight of.

"I'm actually heading to work right now." I slide on my jacket, balancing my phone between my shoulder and my ear.

I love that I can walk to work. It makes the whole commuting thing so much easier.

"Oh, well, I can let you go."

"No, that's okay. We can talk as I walk. It'll make the trip go faster," I tell her, locking the door of my apartment before heading down the empty hallway. "How's everything with you? Dad good?"

"Yep. We're both doing good. Dad has decided to tear up the flooring in the main room and redo it by himself. And right before

Christmas, no less." I can hear the aggravation in her tone. "You should see the house right now. I swear that man is like a tornado. Tools everywhere. Dust on everything. I can't even walk into the family room. It looks like a war zone."

"Uh oh." I laugh, knowing exactly what she's dealing with. Every so often my father gets a wild hair to do some kind of renovation and it never, and I mean *never*, goes according to plan. You would think that one of these days he'd get smart and hire someone to do the work, but no, he's way too stubborn for that.

"I told him if he didn't have it finished by Friday I was going to move in with you until he's done."

"And how did that go over?" I step out into the chilly air, snuggling further into my jacket.

"He told me to have fun."

I bark out a laugh.

"Of course he did."

"So, I was trying to figure out the schedule for the holidays this year. When is your school break again?"

"The seventeenth until January sixth, I think."

"That's perfect. I can't wait to have you home for two whole weeks."

"Uh, Mom. I wasn't planning on staying at the house my entire break," I tell her gently, hoping she doesn't lose her mind. Being her only child, she's been having a hard time since I moved out.

"Oh." I can hear the disappointment in her voice. "How long were you planning on staying?"

"Actually, I wasn't. I'll be there for Christmas dinner, and I'll probably stay the night Christmas Eve, but other than that, I was planning on staying home."

"Well, I can't say I'm happy to hear this, but I guess I understand. You're an adult now." She tries to mask her emotion with understanding. "What about Rylee? Do you think you can convince her to come for Christmas dinner? Dad and I would love to see her."

"Depending on when it is, I'm sure I can convince her to tag along."

"Wonderful." Her mood seems to improve slightly. My parents love Rylee. She's always been like a second daughter to them. Since we were kids, there's barely been a family function she hasn't been a part of, and the same for me with her family. "If there's anyone else you'd like to bring..." she trails off, dropping a not so subtle hint.

"There isn't," I tell her flatly.

"Well, if there is, you're welcome to bring them."

My mom has a bad habit of trying to pry into my love life, or lack thereof. And while normally I'm an open book, for the most part, I have absolutely no intention of telling her a single thing about Oliver until I know for sure what, if anything, this is.

He claims we're an *us* now, and while I like the sound of it, I'm not quite so sure yet.

"I'll keep that in mind." I appease her the best I can.

"Okay. Well, I won't keep you. You're probably at work already."

"Just walking in the front door." I push my way inside the warm, bustling coffee shop. Even though it's six in the evening, there's not one single table open. Product of being blocks from campus.

"Okay then. You'll call me tomorrow?"

"I'll try," I promise.

"I love you, my sweet girl."

"Love you too, Mom." I end the call, waving to Rylee, who's already behind the counter. Her shift started two hours ago, which means she'll get to leave about halfway through my shift. Lucky. I love working here, but I hate closing.

Shoving my phone into my bag, I head toward the back of the shop to get my apron and nametag, ready to get the next four hours over with so that I can go home and climb into my bed. I'm so exhausted I feel like I'm running on fumes.

I have Oliver to thank for that.

A smile touches my lips at the thought of him.

In fact, every time he crosses my mind, which has been a lot today, I find myself overtaken with childlike excitement. I honestly don't know what happened last night, but I'm starting to think he slipped me some kind of love potion or something.

That's the only thing that explains the way I feel. The only thing that makes me feel even remotely better. Because the alternative—that I'm actually falling for him—is too much for my mind to process right now.

Love potion…. Yep, we're going to go with that.

seventeen

OLIVER

My lips curl into a sneer as I swipe my finger across the screen and ignore the call. Pulling my key card from my wallet, I tap it against the black box and the outer door to my dorm building unlocks. I do the same to the inner door. The lobby is empty except for Tommy, one of the dorm monitors, who sits behind the visitor check-in desk.

"How's it going, Oliver?" he calls as I walk past him.

"Same shit."

"You going to the party this Friday?"

"Nah. Not this time."

Forgoing the elevators, I push open the door to the stairwell and climb four flights. My phone rings again as I enter my dorm, but once again, I ignore it. My mother's called several times since yesterday. I've got no desire to talk to the lying, cheating bitch. I will eventually, but for now, she can kiss my ass. I've got nothing to say to her. Or rather, I've got nothing *nice* to say to her.

Kicking my door closed behind me, I drop my phone, wallet, and keys on the nightstand then grab my Physics book. Fucking homework. I hate to do it, but it's a necessary evil if I want to get out from under my father's thumb.

I'd much rather study at Savannah's house, but she kicked me out. Claiming the only studying I'd get done was how to fuck her into the mattress. I left with the promise that I'd come back later tonight. Now I understand Z's need to be up Rylee's ass all the time. I never thought I'd admit this, but the woman has me wrapped around her pretty little finger.

Sitting in my desk chair, I kick my feet up on the mattress and crack open the book. I've read no more than one page before there's a knock on my door. With a sigh, I toss the book on the bed and go see what fucker is interrupting me.

I'm surprised when I pull it open and see my father on the other side. His hands are stuffed in his pockets and he's scowling at a couple of guys who have their heads together, talking quietly a few doors down.

"What are you doing here?"

I stand in the doorway, not bothering to invite him inside. It doesn't matter. He barrels his way past me.

"Does the Dean know there are kids dealing drugs in the fucking hallways of this place?" he asks angrily.

"I don't know, and I don't really give a fuck what the Dean knows. It's not my business to inform him." Crossing my arms over my chest, I glare at him. "Now, I'll ask again. What are you doing here?"

He assesses the pile of dirty clothes I have on the floor in the corner before he turns to face me.

"I had business close by and figured I'd come check in on you."

I snort. "Sure. And I'm Elvis fucking Presley. How about you try again, old man."

He glowers. "And how about you lose the attitude for one goddamn minute? Jesus Christ, Oliver." He rakes his fingers through his hair. "Can we not have a civilized conversation for once?"

I keep my mouth shut. Is it possible to have a civilized conversation with my father? For anyone else, yes, it is. With me? Fuck no. Because I no longer put up with his bullshit. I'm done being his mental punching bag. I have been for years. That's why we don't get along.

He sighs and kicks the desk chair around to take a seat. I don't move from my spot as he leans with his elbows on his knees. After a moment, he finally breaks the silence.

"Your mother called," he says quietly, staring off into space.

"What in the hell did she want?"

"Said she's been trying to call you. She got worried because you haven't been answering."

I grunt and plop down on my bed. "She sure as hell wasn't worried when she wasn't answering my calls. Nor was she worried when she moved across the country without telling me."

"I told her I'd check in with you."

"Well, you can tell her I'll call her when I damn well please. She can fucking stew for a while."

Leaning back in the chair, he laces his fingers over his stomach and regards me. "How have you been?"

"Just peachy."

"Rylee told Evelyn that you've been seeing her friend, Savannah." He lifts a brow. "How's that going?"

Rylee needs to learn to keep her big mouth shut. I don't tell my father shit about my life for a reason. Mainly because it's not his concern, and he's never been curious before.

"It's fine," I bite out. "Why the curiosity about my life now? You've never wanted to know before."

Two lines form between his eyes. "That's not true, Oliver."

Rolling my eyes, I look back at him with an eat shit look. "That's bullshit, and you and I both know it. You don't give two fucks about my life unless it directly affects you."

"Oli—"

I get up from the bed and stalk over to the door. Yanking it open, I glare at him. "I've got to study, so if that's all you wanted, it's time for you to go. Tell my mother to back off. I'll call her whenever."

He regards me for a moment, his frown still in place, before he slowly gets up from the chair and approaches me. He stops in the doorway.

"I know things haven't been good between us for years, Oliver, and I know some of it's my fault."

I snort.

"Fine," he sighs, "most of it's my fault. I'd like for that to change.

I've been a shitty father to you, and for that, I'm sorry. But I've *never* not cared."

I stare off, not acknowledging his request. He's going to have to work a hell of a lot harder than that to get past all of the shit he's done for the last eighteen years.

With a defeated sigh, he turns and leaves. I slam the door shut behind him so hard the walls rattle.

A COUPLE OF HOURS LATER, I rap my knuckles against the door and wait. When it's pulled open and Savannah appears, I waste no time yanking her to my chest. My mouth plunders hers in a heated kiss that I'd like to continue in the bedroom. Unfortunately, we're interrupted by someone clearing their throat. I glare at my stepsister over Savannah's shoulder.

"Aren't you supposed to be at Zayden's tonight?"

"Yep, but our plans changed. Zayden's coming here instead. So you're stuck with us." Her lips quirk up. "Sorry." She pauses. "Not sorry."

"Bitch," I mutter.

With a laugh, she walks off into the kitchen.

Savannah pinches my side. "Be nice."

Something jabs me in the back. "Move your ass," Z rumbles behind me.

Stepping out of his way, I turn and find him with his hands full of Chinese food containers and a six pack of beer. Before he can walk away, I snag a couple beers by their necks.

"Appreciate it, man."

"Thanks for the help, asshole," he says, stalking off toward the kitchen.

"So much for having a night to ourselves," I grumble.

Savannah laughs and grabs one of the beers. "Poor baby."

I palm her ass and bury my face in her neck. "We can always see who screams the loudest."

She steps back and pokes me in the chest. "We are not doing that. Get that shit out of your head." Her eyes narrow before she turns and walks away.

With a chuckle, I follow behind her. I was just joking.

Sort of.

In the kitchen, Zayden and Rylee are unloading cartons of Chinese food onto the counter.

"Thank fuck you got food," I remark, going to a cabinet and grabbing some paper plates for everyone. "I'm starving."

"You're always starving."

I flick the end of Rylee's ponytail as I pass by her to go to the counter where the food sits. "That's cause I'm a growing boy."

"You got the boy part right," Z jests.

I chuck a packet of soy sauce at his head.

Grabbing two plates, I set them down in front of me and glance at Savannah.

"You want Lo Mein or rice?"

"Actually." She sidles up next to me and presses a kiss to my cheek. "While you three eat, I'm going to grab a shower."

Before she can walk off, I grab her wrist. "You're not eating?"

"I already ate."

"When?" Rylee asks, snagging an eggroll and dropping it on her plate before facing her friend.

"While you were taking a shower."

"Why though?" Rylee frowns. "You knew Zayden was picking up Chinese. It's your favorite."

Savannah's eyes slide away from Rylee. "I'm just not in the mood for Chinese."

"V—"

"Can you stop grilling me?" Savannah erupts, her eyes flaring with anger. She takes a deep breath. "I ate while you were in the shower. It's not a big deal. Jesus," she mutters. "Now, if it's alright with you, I'm gonna go take a shower."

Before anyone can say anything else, she turns and stomps off toward the bathroom. Rylee, Zayden, and I all look at each other. Rylee's brows are pinched down.

"I'm worried about her," she says quietly, as if nervous that Savannah may overhear her.

"Why?" I ask. I have my suspicions, but I want to get Rylee's take on it before I say anything.

"Have you noticed how much weight she's lost the last couple of months?"

I sigh and rub the back of my neck. No longer hungry, I push back the plates I started making for me and Savannah and lean against the counter. The worry I've felt over the last couple of weeks that I've been trying to ignore comes to the forefront of my mind.

"I have. I was wondering if it was only me who noticed."

Rylee's eyes move to me. "It's definitely not only you."

"Maybe it's just stress from school," Z suggests, wrapping a comforting arm around Rylee's waist. "We all know how tense it's been."

Rylee shakes her head. "I don't think that's it. School has always been a breeze for Savannah. She's naturally smart, and I know for a fact she hasn't been struggling." She looks down as she begins picking at her nails. "Savannah has… always battled with anxiety regarding her weight. I don't know why, her parents are great, and Lord knows she's never even come close to having to worry about being overweight."

She looks up and meets my eyes. I flinch as guilt fills my stomach. All the taunts I threw at Savannah about her weight feel like fucking acid eating away at me.

"You had no way of knowing, Oliver," Rylee says, guessing my thoughts.

Her soothing voice does nothing to calm the rage coursing through me. No goddamn wonder Rylee got pissed anytime I mentioned Savannah's appearance. Or the look of hurt on Savannah's face she always tried to hide. That pain is what fueled my taunts, knowing that it bothered her.

I should be sucker punched about five hundred times for that.

I clear my throat of the lump nearly choking me. "What exactly do you think's going on?"

"I don't know. I asked her a few days ago what was going on and she said she's been having stomach issues. She was supposed to make herself a doctor's appointment, but I'm not sure she ever did. I've tried bringing it up, but she always gets pissed at me when I do."

"Well, she's just going to have to suck it up," I growl.

"Oliver, we have to approach this delicately." She walks over and places her hand on my arm, looking up at me imploringly. "I'm afraid if we come on too strong, we'll push her away."

I grind my molars. I get what she's saying, but I don't like it. The last thing Savannah needs is to feel like we're attacking her, but fuck if I'll let her neglect her health.

"Fine," I grunt. "What do you suggest we do?"

"Let me talk to her."

Rylee's right. They've been friends for years, while I've put her down again and again about her weight. And together now or not, if I approach her with this, I have no doubt the outcome won't be good.

"You know she's right, Oliver." Zayden gives his opinion with a frown. "You and her don't have a good history, these last few weeks excluded. She'll go on the defensive and it'll backfire."

"I fucking know, okay." I take a deep breath. "Tonight. I want you to talk to her tonight."

Rylee nods. "I will."

I turn away from both of them and grab my beer. My nerves are shot and the knot in my stomach grows tighter. I don't know how bad this thing with Savannah is—it could be nothing for all we know, but there's no way I'll take a chance.

I think back to what she looked like when we met in my kitchen last year, when her sharp tongue laid into me for the first time. Her weight was perfectly proportionate. I remember being blown away by her looks and the shape of her body. She's definitely lost weight since then. And I noticed over the last few weeks she's losing more and more. While I've had some concerns, I also know how girls go crazy over their body image. Constantly trying new diets and weight loss programs. But for the most part, it doesn't get out of hand. I don't know what Savannah's doing to lose weight, but it's definitely getting out of hand.

Just this morning, when I woke up in her bed and pulled a creeper by watching her sleep, I noticed her hip bones sticking out too much above the hem of her shorts. I passed it off as how she was laying.

What if it's something more?

What the fuck are you doing, Savannah?

eighteen

SAVANNAH

"Hey." Rylee knocks lightly on my bedroom door right as I'm slipping the towel from my damp hair. She peeks her head in to make sure I'm decent before coming the rest of the way inside.

"Hey." I rub the towel along the ends of my hair to sop up the remaining water before tossing it in a nearby laundry basket.

"You got a second?" She gently closes the door behind her.

"Um, yeah. What's up?" I arch a brow, confused by the cautious way she's approaching me.

She crosses the room and takes a seat on the edge of the bed, patting the mattress next to her. "Sit," she requests.

"Okay," I draw out, gingerly taking a seat next to her.

"I have something I need to talk to you about. And I need you not to get upset, okay?"

"Why do I get the feeling I'm not going to like what you're about to say?" I swallow past the nervous knot that forms at the base of my throat.

"It's about your weight." She pauses, gauging my reaction—when she gets none, she continues. "I know we talked about this a while ago and you said you were having some stomach issues. Did you ever make that doctor's appointment you we're talking about?"

"Is this because I didn't want Chinese food?" I gape at her. "For fuck's sake, Rylee. Really?"

"It's not just about the Chinese food, it's about *all* food. You think I haven't noticed, but I have."

"Noticed what exactly?"

"How you rarely ever eat and when you do, half the time you end up getting sick."

"What exactly are you implying?" I try to keep my temper at bay. Flying off the handle will surely give me away, and the last thing I want to do is play into her hand. I know her. I know what she's fishing for—the telltales that she's looking for. And I'll be damned if I give them to her. Clearly, my best friend is a lot more observant than I was giving her credit for.

"I'm not implying anything. I'm asking. Are you really okay, or is there something else going on?"

"There is something going on. I've already told you. I'm having issues with my stomach. I think maybe it's an ulcer or something."

"You're sure that's all there is? Because if something else is going on, you know you can tell me."

"What is this?"

"What do you mean?"

"This." I gesture between the two of us. "I feel like you have something you want to say and for some reason you're skirting around it like you're afraid to say it."

"I'm worried you have an eating disorder." She pushes the words out in a rush. "And I'm not the only one that thinks so. Oliver and Zayden have noticed too."

Anger pulses through my veins, and while she may have hit the nail right on the head—though I would never admit it out loud—the fact that they've been discussing my eating habits behind my back is both embarrassing and hurtful.

"You guys have been talking about me?" I draw back slightly.

"It's not like that. We're just worried about you."

"I already told you. I think it's a stomach ulcer." I try to reel in my emotion.

"Then why haven't you gone to the doctor?"

"Who said I haven't?"

"V." She gives me a knowing look.

"Fine. I haven't. But it's only because I've been so busy. It's not like my doctor is around the corner. I have to drive all the way home."

"All the way." Rylee nearly rolls her eyes. "Savannah, it's like a thirty-minute drive. Try again."

"Yeah, it's only a thirty-minute drive. But then I'll have to stop and see my parents. They'll insist I stay for dinner. And then the next thing you know, one doctor's appointment has cost me an entire day."

"But when something isn't okay, you need to prioritize these things."

"I'm not a child, Rylee," I bite, growing tired of this conversation.

I don't see what the big deal is. Okay, I've lost some weight. And while yes, I know I have a problem, I also know that I can handle it. I wish she'd stay out of my business this one time and leave me be.

"And I'm not trying to treat you like one. But, V, I love you. And if there's something wrong with you, I'm going to worry about you until it's taken care of."

"Fine. I'll make a doctor's appointment first thing tomorrow. Will that satisfy you, *Mother*?"

"Stop it." She nudges me gently with her elbow. "Now what do you say you come out and try to eat something. I got you your favorite." She smiles in an effort to lighten the mood.

Unfortunately, it doesn't have the effect she's going for, because after everything she's just said, I'm feeling beyond agitated and a little panicked.

One thing is for sure, I'm going to need to be a lot more careful when it comes to eating around her, and apparently, Oliver and Zayden too. I don't relish the thought of forcing myself to eat when I don't want to, but I can't have them all whispering behind my back either. Until I can get this thing under control, I need to pretend like everything is perfect.

"I told you I already ate," I remind her, not wanting to backtrack now. "Besides, I have some school work I need to catch up on. Maybe I'll heat up some leftovers later."

"School work?" She gives me a weird look. "I thought you were hanging out with Oliver tonight."

"I was. I mean, I am. I just have a few last-minute things I need to get done before the break. You go eat. I'll just be a few more minutes."

"V...." She hesitates.

"Please, Rylee. For the love of God, I'm fine. But if I tank this assignment because you won't leave me alone for five minutes, I most definitely will not be okay."

"Okay. Okay." She holds her hands up in front of herself, pushing to a stand moments later. "What should I tell Oliver?" She pauses next to the door.

"Exactly what I just told you; that I'll be out in a few minutes."

"Okay, but you know he's a shitty listener. I can't promise he won't come back here anyway."

"Well, I'll deal with him if he does." I push to my feet, trying to act as normal as possible even though I feel anything but.

"Okay." She hesitates a moment before leaving my room, pulling the door shut behind her.

I take a deep breath in and let it out slowly.

I don't know why I'm so mad. I should be happy that I have people in my life that care so much about me. But to be the topic of conversation—especially when I'm not included in said conversation—it bothers me... a lot. Probably more than it should.

I grab my bag from the floor and drop it on my bed, emptying the contents onto the mattress. I lied to Rylee. I have no school work. I just didn't want to walk out there and have everyone's eyes on me —especially knowing what they're all thinking. But to make the lie believable, I toss open a few books and take a seat on the bed.

As Rylee predicted, less than ten minutes pass before Oliver pushes his way into my room without so much as a knock. His gaze goes from me, to the mess of books on my bed, and then back to me.

"What are you doing?" he asks, quietly closing the door behind him. He seems hesitant and given the way I'm feeling at the present moment, he should be.

"I had a few things I needed to finish up really quick."

"And it couldn't wait?"

"No, Oliver. It couldn't," I snap.

"Calm down there, killer. It was just a question." He makes his way toward me, shoving a couple books out of the way before taking a seat directly in front of me. He tucks his left leg in and leaves his right hanging over the side of the mattress.

"Sorry," I mumble. "I just really wanted to get this done."

"Don't apologize. I get it. The last couple of weeks I've been up to my fucking eyeballs in ridiculous assignments. I swear, how they think any of this shit is going to help us in the real world is beyond me."

"Yeah," I agree, fidgeting with the pencil in my hand.

"Are you done now?"

"Huh?" I question, not sure I follow.

"With your school work…. Are you done?"

"Oh." I look around the bed. "Yeah." I nod once.

"Well, then let's get this shit cleaned up." He picks up a notebook and two textbooks before turning to drop them on the floor.

"What are you doing?"

"Moving this shit."

"Why?"

"Because I can think of a lot better use of this space." He gives me a knowing look and instantly my skin prickles.

"Is that so?" My earlier tension from my conversation with Rylee starts to fade into the background.

This is what I need. A distraction. Something to make me feel semi-normal when I feel anything but. And while I'm irritated with Oliver for taking some part in why Rylee came in here to talk to me in the first place, I don't want to think about any of that right now.

"It is." He grins, shoving the remaining books to the floor as he pushes to his knees and crawls toward me.

"So." Oliver's hand traces up and down the back of my arm as I lay tucked into his side. "What's this I hear about us going to your parents' for Christmas dinner?"

My back goes rigid as I lift my head off his chest and peer up at him.

"What do you mean *us*?" I croak.

I invited Rylee, as my mom requested. And I knew that she had invited Zayden, because let's be real, she doesn't go anywhere without him these days. But I wasn't aware anyone had told Oliver about it. I had zero intentions of inviting him.

"You know…. Me, you, Rylee, and Z."

"You are *not* coming to my parents' house," I tell him, not missing the slight twinge of hurt that crosses his face.

"Why the hell not?"

"Because."

"Because is not a reason. You don't want me to come?"

"It's not so much that." I knead my bottom lip between my teeth. "It's just… well, my parents are really sweet people. They uh, they're not really accustomed to being around someone like you."

"What the fuck is that supposed to mean? Is there something wrong with who I am?" He sits up, bringing me up with him.

"No, that's not what I'm saying." I shift in the bed so that I'm facing him.

"Then what exactly are you saying?"

"No offense, but you're kind of crass. And you have a really dirty mouth."

A smile tugs at his lips.

"So, you don't want me to meet your parents because I have a dirty mouth?" He seems amused, which is better than being mad.

"I heard how you spoke in front of your father," I remind him.

"That's different. He's my fucking father. I'm honestly kind of offended that you don't think I know how to conform to an audience. Fuck, I've spent my whole life doing just that."

"Well, it's not like I've known you for very long. Not really anyway."

"I don't know." He reaches out and cups my bare breast. "I think we've gotten to know each other pretty well over the last few days." He smirks.

"Stop it." I swat his hand away. "You know what I mean."

"What if I promise to be on my very best behavior? Then can I come?"

"Why do you even want to? I thought family gatherings weren't your thing."

"When it comes to my family, yes. But I think I'd rather like to meet the people who brought you into this world."

Something about the way he says it makes my heart pick up speed.

It's so strange. How quickly I went from hating him to being completely taken with him. He's not perfect by any means, but honestly, that's one of the things I love about him the most. He is who he is, and he doesn't apologize for it.

Did I mention love in reference to Oliver Conley?

I shake off the thought. I can't love someone that I barely even like. But then again, even I know that's not true. He's gotten under my skin in a big way. I'd be lying if I said I wasn't absolutely smitten by him…. And his dirty mouth.

"No cursing, especially at the dinner table. And you can't get mad when my father asks you twenty questions, or my mother force feeds you a million calories worth of pie—because she will." I pause. "And if anyone asks, we are not serious."

"But we are," he disagrees.

"Oliver." I give him a knowing look.

"What? We are serious."

"Are we really, though?"

"What would you call it?"

"Casually dating." I shrug. "Hooking up," I tack on.

"There's nothing casual about this for me." He tugs me toward him, pulling me into his lap. His hand sweeps across my shoulder as he pushes my hair away from my face. "I'm all in."

"All in?" I swallow around the question.

"All in," he repeats. "As in, I want to be your boyfriend. Your very, very serious boyfriend. I don't take what we're doing here lightly, and I don't want you too either. We started out unconventional, I'll give us that." He chuckles. "But I want this, V. I want you. It's fucking scary as hell to admit that, but it's the truth. You're mine now."

"You say that like I don't have a choice in the matter."

"Because you don't." He turns abruptly, my back coming to rest on the mattress moments later as he pins me beneath him. "Now say it."

"Say what?" I stare up at him, stunned by how gorgeous he looks hovering over me.

"That you're mine." He wedges my legs open, settling his hips in between my thighs. His thick erection presses into my core, and I swear it feels like tiny fireworks begin going off just under my skin.

"I'm yours." I have to bite back the moan that threatens to spill from my throat when he rocks forward.

"And I'm yours." He smiles, knowing full well what he's doing. He's using his sexual abilities to force me into submission. Not that I'm complaining. "No games. I want all of you. I want to know every part of your life."

God, I love this side of him. I love that he seems so desperate for me. It's a high I've never experienced before.

"Fine, you can come." I let out a dramatically playful sigh.

"As your boyfriend?"

"Ugh." I roll my eyes. "If you promise to control that wicked tongue of yours."

"I thought you liked my wicked tongue." He leans down and kisses me, slowly and deeply, my fingers finding the back of his hair as I tug gently on the strands.

"You know what I mean," I say when he breaks the kiss.

"I do." I feel his smile against my cheek as he kisses his way down to my jaw and across the side of my neck. "I promise to be good." He nips at the skin along my collarbone.

"I'm curious to know what that looks like." I giggle when he squeezes my side.

"Well, you're going to have to wait." His face comes back up to mine. "Because right now, I'm going to be bad." He licks his lips. "Very, very bad."

nineteen

OLIVER

We pull up to a medium-sized, white farmhouse. It's nothing like I pictured Savannah's childhood home to be like. In my mind, I saw her growing up in a sleek, modern home with big pillars, the perfect landscape, and a huge wrought iron fence. This most certainly isn't that.

The house is old, but still very well taken care of. Big trees litter the large property—a tire swing hanging from one of the low branches—and a porch that wraps around to the back of the house. There are a few Christmas lights hanging from the roof and a big blow up Santa in the yard. It looks homey and comfortable. Like a happy family lives inside.

Savannah fidgets beside me, and I reach over and grab her hand. "Hey. You okay?"

Her eyes slide to me. "Yeah."

I lift a brow when she starts nibbling her bottom lip. "You're nervous."

"Kinda." She lifts and drops her shoulder. "I'll be honest. I've never brought a guy home before."

This makes me grin. "So that makes me special or something, right?"

She snorts and rolls her eyes. "Or something," she mutters.

Chuckling, I lean over and plant a kiss against her lips. When I pull back, she still looks uncomfortable. Her anxiety doesn't sit well with me.

Grabbing her chin, I turn her face my way.

"If you really don't want me to be here, I can leave. I don't like the thought of you being uncomfortable in your own home."

Even though I don't want to leave, I still make the offer. I've never wanted to meet the parents of girls I'm involved with, but for some reason, I do want to meet Savannah's. They have to be good people if they brought someone such as their daughter into the world.

Some of her worry melts away. "No. I'm being ridiculous. I want you here."

"You sure?"

She smiles. "Yep."

There's a tap against the window and Rylee's face appears through the glass.

"You guys coming, or are you going to hang out in the car the rest of the day?"

One more peck against the lips later and we're climbing out of the car. The four of us opted to take two cars since Savannah is planning to spend the night with her parents and Z and Rylee are going to his dad's house for a bit after dinner. With reluctance, I chose to go to my father's house for the night. Z's dropping Rylee back at home later tonight and will pick Savannah up tomorrow afternoon on his way back there.

It's difficult as hell having three families to worry about during the holidays.

It's cold outside, so when I see Savannah shiver as we walk up the drive to the front door, I wrap my arm around her shoulders to try to warm her up.

"I can't believe it's been three months since I saw Nora and Silas last," Rylee comments. "I'm used to seeing them almost as much as I saw my own parents."

"They've missed you. Especially Mom."

"I've missed them too."

When Savannah opens the door, a wave of delicious scents assail us. I drop her overnight bag by the door right as a loud squeal pierces the air.

"There's my girl!"

An older woman who looks like Savannah hurries across the floor in a blur. My arm drops from her shoulders as the woman yanks Savannah forward into a tight embrace. After a moment, she lets her go with a loud kiss to her cheek before she stands back. Keeping hold of Savannah's arms, she runs her eyes from the top of her head to her feet.

"What in the world are you doing to yourself, Savannah? You're practically skin and bones. It's a good thing I've got a table full of food."

Savannah giggles nervously, her eyes darting to Rylee before coming back to her mom. "It's nothing. I've just been having some stomach issues lately. And before you ask, I have a doctor's appointment next week. I think it's ulcers." She wrinkles her pert nose.

Rylee and I share a look. An unspoken agreement to watch Savannah during dinner to make sure she eats. Ever since Rylee talked to her about our concerns, we've kept a close eye on Savannah. Thankfully, we both noticed her eating more. Rylee's concerns, on top of my own, really scared the shit out of me. Eating disorders can be very dangerous.

A huge wave of relief came over me when she started eating more and began taking better care of herself.

Letting go of her daughter, Savannah's mom turns to Rylee and gives her the same tight hug and loud kiss.

"You, young lady," she gives Rylee a pointed look, "have waited too long to come see Silas and me. How have you been?"

Rylee smiles softly at the older woman. "I've been good, Nora. Sorry I haven't been by. It's been a little hectic with school."

Nora's lips tip up. "Don't fret. So long as you're doing good, I'll forgive you." Her eyes leave Rylee and slide to Zayden. "You must be Rylee's boyfriend, Zayden. Savannah told me she'd be bringing you."

"It's nice to meet you, ma'am." He holds out his hand for Nora to shake.

"Please, call me Nora."

Her eyes move to me next. She doesn't say anything at first, instead quietly assessing me. It makes me want to shuffle my feet.

"And who might you be?" Her questioning gaze flickers to Savannah. "You didn't tell me you were bringing a gentleman along."

"Sorry, Mom. This is Oliver, Zayden's best friend. He's uh…."

She stumbles over her words. I have no idea what she plans to tell her mom about my role in her life, but I decide to take matters into my own hands. Stepping forward, I hold out my hand.

"I'm her boyfriend. It's nice to meet you, Mrs. Reynolds."

Her brows jump up and she looks momentarily surprised. After a moment, she fits her hand into mine.

"Well, this sure is a surprise," she says, a smile forming on her face. "It's great to meet you too, Oliver. Please drop the missus. Nora will do just fine."

With a nod, I step back. Glancing at Savannah, I tense, unsure if she's going to reprimand me for telling her mother I'm her boyfriend or be okay with it. Seeing the small smile on her face says she's fine with it.

Thank fuck.

"Where's Dad?"

Nora tosses her thumb over her shoulder. "Out back getting some firewood."

I'm about to ask Z if he wants to come with me to help Savannah's father, but a door slams in the back of the house. A moment later, a tall older gentlemen appears in the hallway carrying a shit load of wood. Because I want to make a good impression and also because I worry that the ridiculous amount of wood the man is carrying will break his back, I step forward and grab a few pieces from the top.

"Thanks," he grunts.

I follow him into a room off to the side. There's a huge decorated Christmas tree over by a window with a couch, love seat, and a couple of end tables close by. Lights, figurines, and garland are everywhere. It looks like Santa threw up all over the place. Even with the crazy amount of decorations, it's still tastefully done.

It's nothing like what our house looked like during the holidays when I was a kid. My mother always had a professional decorator come in. The Christmas tree was artfully done, and we only had a few strategically placed decorations. Certainly nothing of this magnitude.

It's a nice change.

Stopping at the fireplace, I drop a couple logs onto the dwindling fire and set the rest on top of the pile Savannah's father made. After poking the coals a few times, he replaces the poker in the holder and stands up, brushing off the front of his shirt.

As if he just realized a complete stranger is standing right in front of him, he gives me a strange look.

"Who are you?"

"Sorry, sir." I wipe my hands down my pants before offering him one. "The name's Oliver. I'm Savannah's boyfriend."

He glances down at my hand. "My daughter doesn't have a boyfriend."

It's not often I get nervous around people, but Savannah's dad's accusing eyes damn sure has me fighting the urge to step back from him.

Before I get the chance to retract my hand, he reaches out and grips it tightly. I keep my expression neutral and strengthen my grip. Not in a domineering way, but to show him I'm not some weak punk that can be easily intimidated.

"Savannah and I recently started seeing each other," I explain.

"Daddy!" Savannah yells, hurrying over to us. "What are you doing? Trying to scare off Oliver?"

He lets my hand go and faces his daughter. "I'm doing no such thing." A grin breaks out across his face. "I'm just sizing up your new boyfriend here. He's got a firm grip." He shoots me a wink. "That's a point in his favor."

"You're such a brat sometimes," Savannah says with a laugh.

"Get your butt over here and give your daddy a hug." He yanks her forward and she wraps her arms around his neck.

I step back to give them privacy but stop when her dad shoots me a look over her shoulder. He releases his daughter.

"Oliver, right? I'm Silas. So long as you treat my daughter good, we'll get along right as rain."

There's no mistaking the threat behind his words. If he gets wind I've been treating his daughter wrong, he'll break my kneecaps. *Got it.*

Jerking my chin up, I tell him, "Looks like we'll be good friends then."

"Food's ready!" Nora calls, popping her head around the doorway. "Silas, honey. Will you bring up a bottle of merlot from the cellar?"

"Sure thing, sweetie." After a gentle pat to Savannah's shoulder, he walks out of the room.

"Your dad's something else," I tell Savannah with a grin. "I like him."

She smiles, looking more relaxed than when we first got here. "What can I say? He loves me and wants to make sure my man treats me right."

"Just the way it should be."

"Come on." She grabs my hand. "They're all waiting on us."

"So, Oliver," Nora starts, sipping from her wine glass. "Tell us about your dad. Obviously, we know Rylee's mom married him. That is, if I'm not getting you mixed up with someone else."

I set my napkin down beside my plate and pick up my water glass. "Yes. It's been what?" I look at Rylee. "About a year now?"

"Yeah. They married right before Christmas."

"What kind of work does he do?"

"He's a lawyer. Real Estate."

"And your mom?"

"She's in Tennessee. I'm not sure what she's doing right now." I pause. "We don't stay in contact much these days."

Understatement. I'm currently pissed at the woman and have no desire to know what she's doing.

"I'm sorry. It must have been hard when they divorced."

I shrug. "It is what it is. No sense in dwelling on it."

Rylee looks at me with a lifted brow. Yeah, too bad I didn't feel that way sooner. It would have saved a lot of heartache and pain for several people—mainly Rylee.

"What are you in college for? What are your plans after you graduate?" Silas asks.

"Honestly? I don't have a clue. It's still up in the air. My father wants me to follow in his footsteps, but I'm not too keen on becoming a lawyer."

Reaching over the table, Nora pats my hand. "I'm sure it'll come to you soon. It's difficult deciding what you want to do with the rest of your life."

It is. Especially when you can't think of one damn thing you're good at.

"How about you, Rylee? How's college been treating you?"

While the rest of the table discusses Rylee and Savannah's college life, I glance over at Savannah. More specifically her plate. I'm happy to see over half of her food gone.

A few minutes later, Nora pushes back her chair and stands. "Savannah, Rylee, why don't you help me clear the plates and bring out the desserts?"

"Sure thing, Nora."

Dropping her napkin on the table, Rylee stands and grabs both hers and Z's plate. When Savannah reaches for mine, her elbow hits her glass of water and knocks it over. Straight into her lap.

"Crap," she mutters, staring down at the water soaking her clothes.

"Scratch that," Nora says. "You go change, Savannah. Your dad can help me and Rylee."

"That's really cold."

Laughing, I grab my napkin and drop it in her lap. I lean over and whisper in her ear, "Need help changing?"

Her eyes turn hooded when she looks at me, her lips quirking up. "As much as I love that idea, Mom and Dad aren't stupid. Unless you want a bullet hole in your backside, I would highly suggest you *not* help me change."

I grin. "It would be worth it."

With a laugh, she presses a quick kiss against my lips and gets up from her chair. "Stay here," she says sternly. "I'll be back in a minute."

Unable to help myself, I watch her ass sashay out of the room, barely refraining from laughing at the big wet spot on the back of her pants.

twenty

SAVANNAH

"Well, look at what the cat drug in?" I say, opening the door to find none other than Charles Pierce lounging on the couch like he owns the place.

I don't know Pierce that well—not as well as Rylee does anyway—but I absolutely adore him just the same. He's one of those people you just can't help but love. He just has this quality about him. It's hard to explain unless you meet him for yourself.

"I was wondering when I was going to get to see your fine ass." He grins, pushing to a stand. I shove the door closed and drop my purse on the chair before wrapping my arms around his middle and giving him a tight squeeze.

"Damn girl, you're tiny." He leans back, easily taking me off my feet.

I ignore the comment. Everyone keeps saying how much weight I've lost, but I don't see it. I think they've all lost their minds.

"You're squeezing me to death." I laugh. He chuckles in my ear, setting me to my feet seconds later. "When did you get in?" I ask, taking a step back.

"A couple of hours ago."

"Where's Rylee?"

"Changing. We're going to meet that hotter than sin man of hers over at some Mexican restaurant. You should totally come with us."

"Oh, she's coming with us." Rylee appears at the mouth of the hall.

"I am?" I hitch a brow.

"Yep. And Oliver is too."

"Oliver?" Pierce's gaze swings to Rylee. "Oh, that's right." Something seems to dawn on him. "You're dating sexy devil spawn." He gives me a playfully pointed look.

"Devil spawn?" Laughter bubbles over my words.

"Son of Satan. Demon. Lucifer himself. You take your pick. He may be F.I.N.E. Fine, fine, fine, but he's also quite the piece of work."

"You don't have to tell me that." We exchange a look.

Pierce wasn't the only one who had a front row seat to the hell Oliver put Rylee through. Sure, he was there, witnessing it all happening, but then I was the person she came home and called.

"And yet, you're the one dating him." He clucks his tongue on the roof of his mouth, running a hand through his blonde hair. "I gotta admit, when Rylee told me you two were doing the nasty, I was shocked. The last time I saw you, you were fit to be tied. I thought I'd come back to visit, and Oliver would be buried in a shallow grave somewhere because you killed his ass."

"Don't think I wasn't tempted."

"A couple of times I thought it might actually happen," Rylee interjects, sliding up next to Pierce. "You about ready?"

"Yep." He rocks back on his heels.

"V?" Her gaze slides to mine.

I look down at my outfit and assess myself. Black leggings and a dark gray sweater. Not really what I would have chosen for a normal dinner outing, but it's also not bad enough that I really feel the need to change either.

"Well, considering you didn't give me much of a choice," I grumble in mock annoyance.

"Awesome. And then after dinner—we're all going out!"

"Going out? Going out where?"

"Girl, we got fake I.D.s for a reason. I don't know about you, but I'm ready to put mine to use. I might even go wild and have a margarita at the restaurant."

"That's my girl." Pierce turns, high-fiving Rylee.

"We're walking, so it's not like any of us have to worry about driving," she explains. "Oliver recommended this bar a couple blocks from the restaurant. I guess it's a hot spot for college kids. They have a live band on Friday nights too." She grins at Pierce, the two sharing a look.

"Can I drag you away from Z-man long enough to tear up the dance floor?" he asks.

"I think that can be arranged." She loops her arm through his. "You ready?" Her gaze swings back to mine.

"Actually." I hesitate, my eyes doing a quick sweep of her body. She's not dressed up by any means, but she looks a hell of a lot better than I do. Leggings and a sweater might be okay for dinner, but definitely not for drinks and dancing afterward—especially if Oliver's going to be there. I'm not really sure why I care that much, as he's seen me in a lot worse, but for some reason I do. "Can you give me a minute to put something else on?"

"Why? You look great?"

"I look like I've been lounging on the couch all day," I tell her knowingly.

"Fine," she grumbles through a smile. "But make it quick. Z and Oliver are probably already at the restaurant."

"You can't spring this on me last minute and still expect to get there on time. That's your own fault." I point my finger at her as I slide past her, heading to my room.

I quickly change into dark skinny jeans, black heels, and a form fitting long sleeve black shirt with tears down the sleeves. It's cute and stylish but also comfortable. At least this way I don't feel like a total bum.

Less than five minutes later, I re-enter the room to find Pierce and Rylee laughing in the kitchen.

"What are you two doing in here?" I ask, peeking my head around the corner.

"Pierce decided he was going to starve and decided to have a snack," Rylee explains.

"And that's funny why?" I ask, covering my mouth when Pierce turns to face me. He gives me a wide smile, revealing two hot dogs instead of teeth.

"There's something not right with you," I tell him, shaking my head.

He pulls the hot dogs out of his mouth, shoves one back in, and starts to chew.

"Says the girl who's dating Oliver Conley." He purposely pokes fun, just trying to get under my skin. "Some might argue there's something not right with you."

"And they'd probably be right." I shrug. Hell, sometimes I think I've lost my ever-loving mind. I still don't know how it happened. Not really anyway.

One minute we were on opposite ends of the battlefield preparing for war, and the next we were fighting on the same side. It all happened so fast I honestly don't think I've completely wrapped my head around it.

There are times when I think I must be going through some sort of mental breakdown. But then there are times, especially when he looks at me a certain way or smiles, that I feel like I've never seen things more clearly.

And then there are my parents, who absolutely loved him. I didn't really know what to expect when I brought him home last week, but I was pleasantly surprised by the whole ordeal. He was polite, well-spoken, helpful. By the time he left, I think even my mom had a little crush on him. Not that I can blame her. He really was the perfect gentleman.... If only they knew.

"We should get going," Rylee speaks up, elbowing Pierce, as he shoves the second hot dog into his mouth with a big, cheeky grin.

"You feeling okay?" Oliver slides up next to me at the table where I'm currently nursing my second drink of the night.

"Yeah, I'm good." I smile.

Truth be told, I've been feeling quite sick since dinner, but not wanting to draw any attention to myself, I made it a point not to go to the bathroom.

"You sure?" He quirks a brow, not seeming so sure.

"Yeah." I point to where Rylee and Pierce are dancing. "Those two are quite the pair. I'm surprised Zayden lets her dance like that with another dude."

"If it was anyone else, he'd likely have his head in a vice, choking the life from him." He chuckles. "Come on." He pushes away from the table and extends a hand to me.

I look down at it like he's crazy.

"Dance with me," he requests, the look on his face so freaking cute I have no idea how I could possibly refuse, even though dancing is the last thing I feel like doing right now.

The bar is packed. There are people crammed from one wall to the other. There's barely room to move, let alone dance, yet, they're still making it work.

"I don't know." I take a sip of my drink.

"Oh, come on, Savannah." He takes my arm and tugs me to my feet—not really giving me much choice in the matter.

I reluctantly go with him, nodding to Rylee when we slide up next to them on the dance floor. The band has spent the entire evening playing all the hits. The ones that you can't help but sing along to.

"Oh, we're halfway there," Oliver sings the words to Bon Jovi's *'Livin on a Prayer'* as he pulls me into his arms. His hips sway effortlessly against mine, and before long, I forget about the sour feeling in my stomach and concentrate on the man in front of me.

He's got moves—I'll give him that. Then again, I'm learning there's very little that Oliver isn't good at.

He steps back, spinning me under his arm before pulling me back into his chest. I drop my head back on a laugh. Oliver has this innate ability to pull me out of my head and force me to enjoy myself. I both love and hate that about him.

Eventually, the song ends and another one begins. If I had hoped that I could satisfy him with one dance, I was wrong. Especially when a slow song replaces the heavy beat and several people exit the dance floor, leaving only couples out on the shiny tiled floor. Out of the corner of my eye, I see Zayden cut in on Rylee and Pierce's dance. Pierce steps back, bows his head like he's straight out of the eighteen hundreds, and saunters off toward our table.

"This is nice." Oliver nuzzles his face in my neck and breathes in deeply. "Fuck, you smell good. As much as I'm enjoying this, I think I might want to get out of here soon."

"And why's that?" I smile around the words, already knowing the answer.

He pulls back, meeting my gaze. "I think you know why." A mischievous grin tugs at his lips.

Before I can say anything, Pierce reappears, tapping on Oliver's shoulder. "Can I cut in?" he asks.

I have to bite back a laugh, because the look Oliver gives him says he's seconds away from tearing his face off. But to my surprise, he releases his hold on me. Pressing a kiss to my lips, he steps back, giving Pierce room to slide in and take my hand.

"One wrong move and I'll stomp your ass into the ground," he warns Pierce, who seems completely unaffected by the threat.

With another quick glance in my direction, he turns and walks away, leaving me and Pierce alone.

"He's intense," Pierce says as soon as he's out of earshot.

"Ya think?" I snort.

"You know," he pulls me in closer, "when Rylee first told me about you two, I couldn't see it. But now, I don't know, I get it."

"What do you mean you get it?" I question, our faces lingering a few inches apart.

"Oliver's a prick. He always has been. If I didn't have such a crush on him in school, I probably would have hated the ground he walked on."

"Wait." My eyes go wide. "You had a crush on Oliver?"

I'm aware Pierce is bi, and so Rylee says Pierce doesn't care what anatomy they have—he's attracted to the person. But for some reason, it never occurred to me that Oliver might have been one of those people.

"Um, hello. Am I blind?" He laughs. "I mean sure, I thought he was a self-serving, conceited asshat, but that doesn't mean I couldn't appreciate the pretty package he came in. Still do." His smile widens.

"Did you ever tell him?" I ask for the hell of it. I already know he probably didn't.

"Do I look like I have a death wish." We laugh in unison. "Anyway, he's always been hot. But his personality kind of left a little to be desired. But tonight, I don't know, he seems different."

"Different how?"

"Well, he hasn't taken his eyes off of you all night for starters. The Oliver I knew before treated and discarded women like chewing gum. He'd pop a piece in, give it a taste, and spit it out as soon as it lost its flavor. But with you…. Let's just say that doesn't appear to be the case." He pauses. "So, I'll refer to my previous statement. I get it. I didn't before. But seeing you two together has changed my mind."

"Thanks, I think." I crinkle my forehead, not really sure what to say.

"You really like him, don't you?" he guesses.

"God help me, I don't even know why." I give a defeated sigh.

"Sometimes it's hard to pinpoint why we feel a certain way. But when the chemistry is there, you simply can't deny it. My advice? Enjoy the ride. If you waste too much time questioning why or how, you end up missing out."

"I guess." I think over his words. "What about you? You seeing anyone?"

"Me?" He shakes his head. "Nah. College is all about experimenting, playing the field. I don't want anything serious. I'm having too much damn fun. But, I will say, that if the right person came along, I wouldn't turn them away. For now I'm living in the moment."

"Okay, times up." Oliver's deep voice washes over me from

behind, causing goosebumps to scatter across my skin. Seconds later, he appears next to me.

"Well, he let us go longer than I thought he would." Pierce winks before releasing his hold on me. "She's all yours," he tells Oliver, who steps in to take his place. "I've got my eye on a pretty redhead by the stage. I'll catch you two later." With that, he takes off, disappearing into the crowd of people.

"I hope you enjoyed that." Oliver tugs me in closer, his hands sliding over the top of my ass cheeks. "Because it's never happening again." He runs his nose along the side of my throat.

"Why's that?" I smile, wrapping my arms around his neck.

"Because you're mine, Savannah Reynolds. And in case I didn't mention it before, I do *not* share what's mine." He straightens his posture, his intense gaze burning into mine.

"Noted." I grin. "But for the record, I hardly think me dancing with Pierce is sharing."

"He's got a dick, doesn't he?"

"Um, I would assume so. Though I've never asked him to verify."

"Ha. Ha," he mocks me. "You think you're so funny." He leans in so close that our noses are touching. Despite the upbeat song now blaring from the stage, we're still swaying slowly side to side.

"No, I know I am." I stick my tongue out playfully.

"Keep that up, and I'll have your ass over my shoulder in two seconds flat."

"Oh, yeah? Why's that?"

"Because if you're going to have that tongue out of your mouth, then it might as well be on my cock."

"Do you always have to be so dirty?" I ask, trying to act unaffected by his words. Truth be told, the instant they left his lips, my entire body flushed with heat.

I don't know how he does it. Normally, I'm repulsed when someone talks like that. But with Oliver, it's the sexiest thing ever.

"Don't pretend like you don't like it." He presses his mouth to mine, tracing his tongue along the seam of my lips. I immediately open for him, moaning when he kisses me slow and deep without a single care of who might be watching. "That's what I thought," he murmurs as he pulls away, clearly seeing the effect he has on me.

"Shush." I grin, going in for another kiss, sucking his bottom lip into my mouth before dragging my teeth gently over it.

"Fuuccckkk," he groans. "You keep doing that, and I'm going to fuck you right here."

"I think they might have us arrested," I point out on a giggle.

"Maybe...." He gets that mischievous look in his eyes again. "But I have another idea." With that, he steps back and snags my hand, tugging me through the crowd toward the back of the room.

"Oliver... what the—?" I holler over the loud music as he squeezes by several people lining the hallway waiting for the bathroom before he shoves his way out the back door.

The instant the door closes behind us, it's like entering a whole other world. It's so dark I can barely see anything, and eerily quiet too. In fact, other than the muffled noise of the music from the bar, I don't hear anything.

I glance around, realizing we're in a back alley of sorts. The bar resides in a strip mall sitting smack dab in the middle of four other establishments. There's another strip of stores behind it, so essentially we're sandwiched into the roughly ten feet of space that separates the backs of the buildings.

"What are we doing out here?" I ask.

"What do you think we're doing?" Oliver backs me into the door, his fingers sliding inside the waistband of my pants.

"Oliver." I gasp when he tugs my pants and panties down to the middle of my thighs.

"Shhh." His hand slides between my legs where I'm already so wet you'd think he'd been touching me for a few minutes rather than a few short seconds.

"Oliver," I groan when he slips one finger inside, quickly followed by a second.

"Fuck, you feel so fucking good." He pants, his hand working faster.

"Oliver," I object again, my hands going to his shoulders in an effort to stabilize myself. I feel like my legs are going to give out beneath me at any moment. "We cannot have sex out here," I tell him.

"Why the fuck not?" He removes his fingers, and with quick work, slides open the front of his pants.

I look both ways down the dark alley. "Because anyone could walk out and see us," I tell him.

"No one is going to come out here. And if they do, they won't be able to see us," he reassures me. "Now turn around."

"What?" I gape at him.

"Turn around." He grabs my biceps and forces me in the opposite direction. Pressing on my shoulders, he leans me over, and I feel the warmth of him settle behind me. "Are you on birth control?" he asks.

"What?"

"Birth control. Are you on it?"

"Yes, but…." Before I can get another word out, Oliver slides inside of me so hard and fast that the action nearly knocks the wind right out of me.

twenty-one

OLIVER

Fisting my hands in her thick blonde hair, I rock my hips so my cock slides deeper into her warm mouth. Groaning, I drop my chin to my chest and open my eyes.

"Fuck, woman. You look sexy as hell down on your knees with my dick in your mouth."

She hums and the vibration sends shock waves up my spine. I hiss and tighten my grip on her hair. With a steady glide and a twinkle in her eye, she slips more of my length into her mouth until the head hits the back of her throat. My knees damn near buckle when she keeps going, deep throating my shaft. The tightness of her throat and the warmth of her mouth is too fucking much.

"Shit," I groan gutturally. "I'm gonna come, baby."

Tingles lick up my spine and my balls draw up. She doesn't move away, but instead works me over faster, deeper.

"Sava—"

A loud banging has me jerking awake.

Opening my eyes, my vision is filled with pretty blonde hair. I bury my face in the thick mass and take in a long lungful of air. Flexing my hips, my hard cock is met with the plump softness of Savannah's amazing ass.

"Mmm...." she moans, pressing back against me. "Feels like someone is happy to see me this morning."

I slip my hand under her shirt and palm her tit. "He's always happy to see you." I tweak her nipple. "Especially when I have dreams like the one I was just having."

"You were dreaming about me?" I hear the smile in her voice.

"Yeah. A really hot dream."

We're in my dorm room and the beds are tiny as fuck. Savannah carefully maneuvers around so she's laying on her back. Her eyes are lit with interest.

"What was I doing?"

Before I get a chance to answer by suggesting we reenact the dream, there's another loud bang on the door, reminding me of what woke me up in the first place.

I shoot the door a glare, wishing the person on the other side to hell. With a grumble, I get up from the bed. Behind me, clothes ruffle as Savannah slips on her panties and jeans.

I glance at her over my shoulder. "Those come back off once I get rid of whoever this asshole is."

With a smirk, she snatches up the t-shirt I was wearing last night from the floor and slips it over her head. It falls to her knees and looks really fucking good on her. I'm sliding my jeans up my legs when the knocking comes again.

"Hold your fucking horses," I holler, and yank open the door at the same time.

At first, I'm shocked at the woman in the hallway who is staring back at me. Then anger takes hold. My teeth clench together, but I manage to grit out, "Why the hell are you here?"

What's up with my parents showing up for unannounced visits lately?

My mother's brows jump up in surprise at my outburst, but the look quickly fades into irritation.

"Can you not curse in front of me, Oliver?"

"No, I fucking can't. Now answer my question. Why are you here?"

My mother looks down at her hands clasped in front of her. When she lifts her head, her expression is filled with remorse. A few months ago, I would have fallen for her crap. I would have pulled her into my arms and comforted her. I would have done anything to make her feel better.

But the wool has been lifted from my eyes, and I see past the phony expression. She was damn good at using my love for her to her advantage.

That shit stops now.

"Your games no longer work with me, *Mother*. So you can wipe that fake-assed look off your face."

Her lips tighten, causing little lines to form around her mouth. "Why are you being so mean to me?"

"Probably because I see you for what you are now, and I really don't like it. Using your son, cheating on your husband, lying to your family to make you look like the victim. Should I go on?" When she doesn't answer, I again ask, "Why are you here? And who the hell is the guy standing behind you?"

Lifting my eyes, I acknowledge the man who's been silently standing behind my mother this entire time. I can tell by the hard clench of his jaw that he wants to say something about my attitude toward my mother. He's either playing it smart by keeping his mouth shut because he's afraid, or he's keeping quiet out of respect for my mother.

I take a closer look at him and realize he looks familiar. It only takes me a moment longer to recognize who he is. It's uncanny how much he and my father look alike.

My eyes shoot down to my mother. "You actually brought him here?" I growl.

She lifts her chin and straightens her shoulders. She gives me the look I've seen her give my father. The one where she curls her lip up in disgust.

"I wanted to see you," she says angrily. "Believe it or not, I do love you, Oliver. Benjamin," she reaches back for his hand, "wanted to come and meet you since he's never met his nephew before."

I have a death grip on the doorknob. "Great," I say dryly. "He's met me. Now both of you can leave."

"Can you stop being a brat and show a shred of respect?"

My eyes fall to her. "You lost my respect when you up and moved over halfway across the United States without telling me. You lost it when you cheated on my father—not just once, but twice

—and lied and told me it was him who cheated so I would hate him and not you. And you damn sure lost it when I realized all the times you manipulated me into thinking all of your and my father's problems were him."

I'm just about to slam the door in their faces when there's a tap on my shoulder. In my heated anger at seeing my mother and her new lover, I forgot Savannah was right behind me.

I turn so I'm facing the door jam, still keeping my mother and Benjamin in my sights.

"I'm gonna go," she says quietly, briefly flicking her eyes to my mother. "To give you guys some privacy."

Gripping her hand, I tug her to my side. "There's no need. They were just leaving."

"Hi," my mother says, shoving her hand in front of me for Savannah to shake. I barely restrain the urge to slap it away. "I'm Maria, Oliver's mother. And who might you be?"

Savannah hesitates, glancing up at me. She knows my issues with the woman who gave birth to me. If not for me telling her before, she damn sure heard me a moment ago. But Savannah, being the good person she is, won't snub her like I'd prefer she would. After a moment, she clasps her hand with my mother's.

"I'm Savannah."

"Savannah. Such a pretty name."

I roll my eyes.

"Thank you," Savannah responds.

"And this is Benjamin." She gestures to the still silent man. "He's Oliver's uncle."

"And my mother's fuck toy," I mutter darkly.

"That's it, young man," Benjamin growls, releasing my mother's hand and stepping forward. "I've heard enough of you disrespecting your mother."

Pushing Savannah behind me, I turn to face him fully. White hot anger has my hands clenching into fists. "Back the hell up, old man. I don't give two fucks that you're my father's brother. I won't hesitate to lay your ass out."

Savannah grabs the back of my shirt and my mother puts her hand on Benjamin's chest, pushing him backward.

"There's no need for violence?" She steps in front of my uncle and turns back to me. "Oliver, please. I came all this way to see you. Can you at least give me a few minutes of your time?"

As much as I want to tell her to fuck off, I know she won't give in until she gets what she wants. I get my stubbornness from both of my parents.

"Fine," I grit out. "Give me a minute."

I slam the door, not waiting on her reply, and turn to Savannah.

I press a kiss against her lips. "Aren't you glad we decided to stay here last night?"

She wrinkles her nose and smiles, the look scrunching up her face adorably.

"We definitely could have done without that kind of wake-up call." She cups my cheek. "I know you're angry with her and you have every right to be, but I think it's good you're letting her in to talk."

"Yeah," I mutter.

Turning away from her, I grab a clean shirt and slip it over my head, feeling Savannah's eyes on me. I'm sure I look like I'm on the verge of strangling someone. I damn sure feel like it. I've always had a hot temper, and I hold grudges longer than most people. My reaction to my mother's actions may appear extreme to a lot of people. But I'm fed up with everything. Her actions have not only affected me and my father, but it's because of her cheating and lying that I did what I did to Rylee and Zayden last year. Had she not lied and told me my father was having an affair, I wouldn't have blamed him and Evelyn for everything, and by extension, Rylee.

"Do you want me to leave?"

I turn at Savannah's question and walk to her. Looping my arms around her back, I pull her toward me until she's against my chest.

"Do you want to leave?" I ask. "I really wouldn't blame you. It's about to be a shit show in here."

She shakes her head. "That's not what I asked. Do *you* want me to leave?"

I drop my forehead to hers. "Not really. You'll be the only good thing in the room once they come in."

"Okay." She smiles. "I'll stay."

I press a kiss to her lips, lingering longer than I should, and my mood lightens. Savannah does that for me. Even back when we were spewing hate at each other, she always managed to make me forget all the bad things in my life.

All too soon, I pull back. "Once I get rid of them, I'm taking you back to your place and your bigger bed. I plan to spend the next few hours getting lost in your delectable body."

Grinning, she gets to her tippy toes and gives me a peck on the lips. "I can't wait."

My good mood plummets when I let her go and walk back to the door. Pulling it open, I scowl when I find my uncle with his arm wrapped around my mother's waist, her hand laying on his chest. Without a word, I turn on my heel, leaving it up to them to follow.

Savannah's sitting on the bed, so I go sit beside her. I don't fully understand why, but when she grabs my hand in hers, some of my anger melts away. I give her hand a squeeze.

My mother walks into my room and Benjamin follows. She takes a moment to look around. I bet it's eating her alive to see my room in such disarray. She was always such a neat freak, insisting on everything having a place and every surface being dusted daily. Of course, she never lifted a hand herself in keeping the house clean. It was the household staff who did that.

Spotting my desk chair, Benjamin grabs it and gestures for my mother to sit. She does so primly before settling her eyes on me. Benjamin stands behind her, his arms crossed over his chest like some protective asshole or something.

"How have you been?" she asks quietly, breaking the silence in the room.

I keep my answer short. "Fine."

"Are you enjoying college?"

"It's college. Who really enjoys it?"

She blows out a breath, and her eyes roll to the ceiling before coming back to me. "I'm really trying here, Oliver. Can you make it a little easier on me?"

I bite my tongue, holding back a nasty retort. If it was just the three of us, I wouldn't, but Savannah's already seen and heard enough of my family's drama, so I'm trying to keep it as civil as possible.

I unclench my teeth. "It's been fine. Grades are good."

She nods. "That's good." She takes her purse from her shoulder and props it upright on her lap. "You're still planning to apply to Harvard, right?"

"I'm not going to law school."

"What? Why on earth not?"

"Because I've got no desire to be a lawyer like my father."

"That's been your plan for years. You'll make a good lawyer someday."

"No. That's never been my plan. It was yours and my father's. I just went along with it to keep the peace."

"This is stupid, Oliver," she objects. "Being a lawyer will ensure you have a fruitful life. Why in heavens would you give it up?"

"Fruitful life?" I laugh derisively. "You mean money. Not everything is about money. Maybe I want to do something that'll bring *me* happiness."

"Money brings happiness," she retorts.

"No. It brings greed. It causes hatred."

My anger mounts. Feeling the tension radiating off me, Savannah presses her shoulder against my side and tightens her grip on my hand. I blow out a breath and let it out slowly.

"Not everything is about money, Mother." My eyes lift to Benjamin before dropping back to her. "My father had a shit ton of it, but it obviously wasn't enough for you."

She's quiet for a moment, but I see the wheels turning in her head. The subject is a dead one for me, and she must know it, because she doesn't say anything else on the matter.

Benjamin changes the subject. "Your mother and I were wondering if you'd come for a visit in Tennessee this summer."

My eyes bounce in disbelief between his and my mother's. "You're serious?"

"We'd both love to have you," he replies.

"How fucking stupid do you think I am to want to spend even a second longer than I have to in your presence?"

His eyes turn hard. "There's no need to be a shit about it. While I don't like it, I get your aversion to me, but Maria is your mother."

"And a shit one at that."

"Oliver Conley!" my mother shouts, getting to her feet. "I've heard about enough."

"I haven't even gotten started." I get up and walk toward the door. "I'm done here. I suggest you both leave if you don't want to hear more."

I glare at both of them and they glare right back. Benjamin grabs my mother's hand and pulls her behind him.

"Let's go, Maria. This was a waste of time."

She trudges behind him but stops in the doorway where I'm standing. "I would really love it if you could come for a visit this summer. There's something important I need to speak with you about."

I ignore her suggestion. She's ludicrous if she thinks I'd visit her while she's with my uncle.

"You may be my mother, and I still love you. But I can't stand to look at you any longer. When the time comes that I can, I'll call you."

This woman has no idea how much she's hurt me with her lies and deceit, but from the look on her face right now, she might have an inkling.

After another long look at me, she turns and walks away.

Instead of slamming the door behind them, I close it quietly.

twenty-two

SAVANNAH

"Well that was... interesting." I swallow hard, watching Oliver stalk back across the room toward me.

Last night when I agreed to stay the night at his dorm, I might have reconsidered had I known what we would be waking up to. Not exactly the way I had envisioned meeting his mom for the first time.

"Yeah, interesting," he grunts, dropping back down beside me on the bed. "I'm sorry you had to witness that. I don't know what the hell she was thinking showing up here—and to bring him of all people."

"You don't have to apologize to me. I'm just sorry that you have to deal with any of this at all. I can't imagine how I would feel if my mom cheated on my dad. Especially if she did it with a relative or close family friend. That just adds a whole other level to the betrayal."

"Yeah." He blows out a heavy breath. "You know, the fucked-up thing is, if she had just been honest with me, it would be different. I would have been mad, sure. But I would have gotten over it. But for her to play the victim, to make me believe for years that my father was the villain. She deepened the wedge between the two of us and for that, I don't know if I'll ever be able to forgive her. My father is no saint, and while somedays I'd like to throat punch the condescending asshole, he's still my father. And then there's Evelyn and Rylee. Fuck." He runs a hand through his already messy hair. "I was so fucking awful to both of them because I believed my mother when she said it was my father who ruined their marriage. Not that it excuses my behavior toward them, because it doesn't, but knowing I could have saved myself and everyone else around me a lot of fucking hurt had she just been fucking honest…."

"Hey." I reach over and snag his hand, giving it a comforting squeeze. "What's done is done. You can't change the past. But you can learn and grow from it. You're not doing yourself or anyone else any good by beating yourself up over the way you acted. I'll be the first to say that your actions were despicable."

"Why don't you tell me how you really feel?" His eyes slide to mine.

"You know it's not in my nature to sugar coat things. But your past actions don't make you irredeemable either. But Oliver." I knead my bottom lip between my teeth nervously. "The way you treated your mom just now…. I get that you're angry, but the damage is already done. And she's your mom. You can't stay mad at her forever. She made mistakes, just like you did. Are you really going to make her continue to pay for them?"

"Fuck yes, I am. She deserves to sweat it out for a while. After all the lies and deceit, she deserves a hell of a lot more than me giving her some attitude."

"That wasn't just attitude," I argue, hoping I'm not overstepping. "I don't think I could ever speak to my mom the way you spoke to yours. No matter what she had done."

"Well, that's the difference between you and me." He tugs his hand away and pushes to a stand. "Besides, you have no fucking clue how you would handle this situation because you have good parents."

"You're right. I can't say for sure how I would react because I've never dealt with anything even close to this before."

"No, you haven't. And I really don't need you judging me right now or making me feel guilty for how I behaved."

"That's not what I'm trying to do." I stand, stepping up directly in front of him. "I'm just trying to give you an outsider's perspective."

I can tell he's trying really hard not to let his irritation get the better of him, and for a moment I wonder if maybe I'm out of line by even commenting on what transpired between him and his mom.

"Look at me." I grab his chin, forcing his gaze down to mine. "I am on your side. Do you hear me? But Oliver, where would you be if everyone chose not to forgive you for the mistakes you've made?" I let him ponder that for a moment. "I get that you're angry. Trust me, I do. And I understand why. But what good is holding onto all this anger really doing? I'm not saying forgive and forget. But treating your mom like she's dirt on the bottom of your shoe? I don't get how that's going to accomplish anything. You don't want to see her, fine. You don't want to talk to her, that's okay too. But she's still your mom. Don't you think she maybe deserves just a little respect?"

"Respect?" He draws back like my words have physically assaulted him. "She deserves shit because she is shit."

"Oliver."

"No. Fuck that. I shouldn't have to treat her like she's fragile china because she's my mother. She fucked up, and I'm allowed to be pissed about it. And I'm allowed to let her know that I'm pissed about it."

"You are," I agree. "But there are better ways of going about it."

"You know what? Fuck this." He takes a full step back. "Maybe you should leave too." His nostrils flare.

"Oliver. I didn't mean to make you feel bad about anything. But I'd be remiss if I didn't speak up and say something when I feel like your behavior resembles that of a spoiled child."

"A spoiled child?" He laughs, the sound riddled with anger. "A spoiled child." His heated gaze meets mine.

I know immediately that I've gone too far, and as much as I wish I could take it back, I can't. I didn't mean for this to take the turn that it has. My intentions were good, but now I can see that I should have kept my mouth shut.

"I'm sorry. Look," I blow out a slow, controlled breath, "I get that you're angry. And you know what, you have a right to deal with that anger anyway you see fit. It's not my place to tell you how you should feel or how you should act. I guess I'm just not used to seeing someone talk to their mom that way. I'd be lying if I said it didn't bother me a little."

"You have to understand that not all relationships are like the one you have with your parents. Not all moms are like your mom. Being a mom doesn't automatically make someone a good person."

"I know that."

"Do you? Because from where I'm standing it sounds to me like you feel like I should put on a happy face and pretend like everything is okay. That's not me, Savannah. That will never be me. And if you can't accept that I am who I am and that I'm going to lash the fuck out when I'm pissed—no matter who you are—then you might as well walk away now, because this is me."

"You're so convinced that everyone is against you that you can't even see when someone is trying to help you."

"Help me? How is you siding with my lying, whore of a mother helping me?"

"I'm not siding with her. I'm trying to make you see that the way you treat her is directly affecting you. This isn't about her, Oliver. It's about you. It's about this anger that you're carrying around. It's about how the mere mention of your mom sends you into an absolute rage. It's about the guilt I see in your eyes, because even after everything she's done, you still feel guilty for being angry with her. That isn't good for you. It's not good for anyone."

"So what? You're telling me I should go easy on her for my sake?" He snorts.

"Yes. That's what I've been trying to say this whole time. I'm sorry if it didn't come out that way, but God, you're infuriating to talk to sometimes."

"I'm infuriating? You should try being on the other end of this conversation right now." He gestures between the two of us.

"I never said I was an easy person to deal with," I counter.

"I never said I was either." A trace of a smile tugs at his lips.

"I'm sorry." My shoulders sag forward. "I really was just trying to help."

"I know." He shakes his head, the anger melting from his face. "I'm sorry too. I have a bad habit of letting my anger get the better of me."

"You?" I quirk a brow. "Never," I say sarcastically.

"Alright, smartass." He steps into me, snaking an arm around my waist before pulling me flush against his chest. "Maybe you're right. Maybe I should find a different way to deal with my anger." Something flashes in his eyes, and I'm not sure if I should be more nervous or excited.

"I stopped listening after you said I was right." I yelp when he lays a hard smack to my ass.

"You're asking for it, woman," he warns, backing me toward the bed.

"And what exactly is it that I'm asking for?" I play innocent, batting my eyelashes dramatically.

"For a fucking ass whooping is what." He grins against my lips as he presses his mouth to mine.

"How about no." I wrap my hands around the back of his neck, deepening the kiss. "But I do have something in mind that might make you feel better," I whisper against his mouth.

"Oh, yeah?" He draws back, sucking in a sharp breath when, without a word, I drop to my knees in front of him. "Savannah." He groans when I release his already hard erection from the confines of his pants, holding his weight in my hands. "It's like you knew exactly what I was dreaming about."

"You were dreaming about this?" I gaze up at him, the look of lust on his face undeniable.

"I always dream about you."

His words propel my action. I stroke my fingers slowly up and down his shaft before leaning forward to swirl my tongue around the head. His fingers tangle in my hair and an unintelligible slew of words fall from his mouth.

I grip him harder, suck him in deeper, feeling his legs shake beneath his weight as I do.

As much as I love sex with Oliver, and believe me, I do, there's something just as pleasurable about this. Something so satisfying about the power I feel in this moment. The control I know I have over him.

I continue to work him up and down, my hand and mouth working in unison to satisfy his entire length. It's not long before I feel him tense. Before I hear the guttural moan rip from his throat and hot liquid spills into my mouth. I drink it all up, swallowing every ounce of his release. I slow my movements, trailing my tongue slowly from root to tip. Oliver twitches, his breathing still labored as he leans down and pulls me to my feet.

"That was...." He shakes his head like he can't even find the words for what that was.

I smile, feeling quite pleased with myself at the moment.

"Does that mean you forgive me?" I give him a hopeful look.

"Forgive you? Fuck, I don't even remember being mad anymore." He chuckles, adjusting himself back into his pants before tugging me into his arms. His lips brush the top of my forehead.

"I really am sorry." I wrap my hands around his back and nuzzle my face into his chest.

"Don't. I know you were just trying to help."

"Do you?" I pull back and look up at him.

"I do." He slides his nose against mine. "And I love you for it."

I don't think he means he actually loves me, but damn if my heart doesn't flip against my ribcage just the same.

Is that what I want? For Oliver to love me? For this to be something more than it already is? Honestly, I hadn't given it that much thought. To me, it's always been a matter of when this ends, not if. But the more time I spend with Oliver, the more I realize that I don't want it to end.

It's hard to explain.

I don't know if it's the realization that I might actually have real feelings for Oliver that makes me suddenly feel lightheaded, but when I move to straighten my posture, it feels like the whole floor moves with me. Everything goes topsy-turvy, and my knees give seconds before Oliver's grip on me tightens, keeping me from going to the floor.

It happens so quickly. One second I feel like I'm spinning, and then the next everything snaps back into focus.

"V." There's panic in Oliver's voice as I regain my footing. "Are you okay?" He pushes my hair over my shoulder, looking down at me with concern.

"Yeah, sorry. I got a little dizzy there for a second." I force a smile. "I think maybe I stood up too fast." I give him a knowing look—just trying to lighten the mood.

"Maybe you need to eat something," he suggests. "We haven't had anything since early last night."

I'm hungry. Starving actually. And yet, even still, the thought of food makes me feel instantly nauseous. Regardless, I have no doubt that lack of food is what caused my dizzy spell. It's not the first time either. As of recent, it's been happening more and more frequently, and while I have managed to keep down some food, I know it's not enough.

"Yeah, my blood sugar might be low." I shrug like it's nothing.

"Come on. Let's get ready and we can go get muffins and coffee from the little café on the corner." He hesitates, like he's afraid to release me.

"I'm good," I reassure him.

"Well, maybe not coffee for you. Isn't caffeine supposedly bad when you have an ulcer?" He reluctantly lets me go, watching me carefully, like he's afraid I'm going to topple over at any second.

"Yeah, that's right." I nod, swallowing past the guilt that seizes at my throat.

I didn't want to lie, but when Rylee asked me about it in front of Oliver, it just sort of fell from my lips. Truth be told, I never even made a doctor's appointment. I just told them all that I did. And when that appointment time had come and gone, I knew I was going to have to say something. I just didn't intend on it being a bold-faced lie.

I know eventually I am going to have to seek some kind of real help. I've been trying so hard to manage this situation on its own. This illness. But even I'm realizing that it's beyond my control at this point.

Even still, what I do and how I do it will be my business and my business alone. It's embarrassing enough knowing I let things get this far out of hand. The last thing I want is to have to admit what I intentionally put my body through to my family or my friends. And especially to Oliver.

I try so hard to pretend like I have it all together. Like I'm so strong. When in reality, I'm probably weaker than all of them. I don't want this condition to define how people look at me. How *he* looks at me. Because suddenly, that matters so much more than I ever thought it would.

twenty-three

OLIVER

Slipping my phone into my pocket, I open my dorm door. It's eerie as hell with the halls so quiet. Most students are still away at home for the holiday. Come Monday morning, the place will be bustling again, irritating the hell out of me.

I close and lock my door, then head toward the elevator.

"Yo, Oliver!" someone calls from behind. I turn as Belamy approaches. "Glad I caught you before you left."

"What's up?"

I don't care for Belamy too much. He's a jackass who thinks he's God's gift to women, but I'm in a good mood, so I'll give him my time.

The elevator doors open, and I step inside, hoping he'll get the clue that I'm in a hurry. I hold my hand out to stop the door before it closes. I guess he's going down too, because he steps inside with me and I press the first-floor button.

"I thought you were going home for the holidays?" I ask and watch as the flashing numbers appear on the wall.

"I did, but my parents left for Florida a couple of days ago. They're staying on the beach for New Year's."

"And you chose to come back to this shit hole instead of going with them?"

He gives me a pointed look. "It's also their anniversary."

"Got it," I grunt. Old people fucking. I'd stay far the fuck away too.

"Me and a couple guys are heading over to Carter's. He's

throwing a big New Year's party at his place. You and, what's your girl's name? Savannah, right?" I nod. "You should bring her over."

"Thanks for the invite, but we already have plans."

"That's too bad. Maybe the next one."

The elevator stops and we both walk off.

"Yeah, sure," I say non committedly.

Had Belamy asked me months ago, I would have been all for it, but a quiet night with Savannah, Z, and Rylee seems much more appealing. I've always been a partier—the bigger and wilder, the better. Not so much lately though.

I'd say I was getting old and parties have lost their allure, but I'm only fucking nineteen. I just hate being surrounded by people I don't know. Back home it was different because I knew everyone.

Belamy and I part ways, and I head toward my car. I'm picking up Savannah from work on my way to her and Rylee's place. Z's picking up the alcohol and food. Our party of four won't be wild, but it'll damn sure be relaxing and satisfying.

Pulling up to the curb in front of Grinders, I reach to shut off my car to go inside and wait, but Savannah's already walking through the front door. A moment later, she's inside my car, and I lean over for a kiss.

"Hey," I murmur against her lips.

"Hey back at you."

I slide my tongue against her lips, and she opens for me. She tastes like the strawberry smoothies I know she loves.

Moments later, I pull back and look at her. She's seemed off a bit the last couple of days. Ever since we had our heated discussion after my mother and uncle's visit. Despite her saying otherwise, I was pissed at the time because it really felt like she was taking my mother's side. After thinking about it for a while though, I know she had my best interest at heart. I know I was hard on my mother, but it's equally hard for me to look past everything she's done. I need to learn how not to let it affect me so much. My mother's actions are her own, not mine. I shouldn't let what she does ruin my relationships.

After Savannah's buckled in, I get us back on the road. I reach over and grab her hand in mine, bringing it to my lap.

"How was work?"

"Eh." She shrugs. "It was work. Surprisingly not busy. I actually got off a few minutes early."

A Taylor Swift song comes on the radio and Savannah reaches over and turns up the volume. I side-eye her and groan.

"Not you too," I complain. "I already had to put up with Rylee's obsession last year."

She laughs. "I'm not a huge fan like her, but I do enjoy this song."

I can't help but crack a smile as Savannah starts to sing along. She looks happy and carefree, which is different than how she's been over the last couple of days. With that thought in mind, I let her sing her heart out. She can't carry a tune worth shit, but I'm happy she feels comfortable enough around me to make a fool of herself.

A few minutes later, I pull into the parking lot of her apartment building. Reaching to the backseat, I grab my overnight bag and climb from the car. Savannah still has a smile on her face when I open her door.

"What has you in such a good mood today?" I ask, grabbing her hand as we walk toward her building.

She grins so big her cheeks puff out. "I don't know. Today just feels like a good day."

We stop at the elevator and I press the button before turning to face her. Snagging an arm around her waist, I pull her flush against me.

"I like you happy like this."

I press my lips against hers, and the kiss turns heated. Too heated for the hallway. When I pull back, Savannah stares up at me with hooded eyes and a small smile touching her lips.

"I know what would make me happier."

"Yeah?" I arch a brow. "What's that?"

"A nice long massage with you rubbing lotion over every inch of my body."

I groan and swoop down to take her lips again. Unfortunately, we're interrupted when the elevator doors open, and an elderly couple walks out. They stop and look at us. The old man smirks while the older woman looks like she just ate something sour.

"Sorry about that," I say. "Just can't deny her when her hands turn grabby." To emphasize, I squeeze her ass.

The woman gasps and the man chuckles before grabbing his wife's hand to walk around us.

"Did you really have to do that?" Savannah asks, looking up at me wryly. Her lips twitch, giving away the laugh she's holding back.

"Yep." I pause. "And I have to do this too."

Before the doors close, I bend down low, put my shoulder to her midsection and easily hoist her up. Damn, but she weighs next to nothing.

Squealing, she pinches my butt, making my ass cheeks clench. "Put me down, you brute!"

I press the button for her floor and smack her ass. "Stay still, heathen, or I'll drop you."

She stops moving and keeps quiet as we go up several floors. When I step off the elevator, I nearly lose my footing when she lifts the bottom of my shirt, shoves her hand inside my pants, and caresses my bare ass. My ass has never been an erogenous zone for me, but I have to admit, my dick perks up as she rubs her smooth hand against it.

"I suggest you remove your hand from my pants before I fuck you right here in the hallway," I warn, my voice dipping low.

With a giggle, she pulls out her hand and goes limp over my shoulder. "Party pooper."

Since Savannah is with me and it's her place, I don't knock when I get to her door. After I close it behind us, I put Savannah down on her feet. Her face is red from the blood flow to her head, but she looks no worse for wear.

"Jerk," she snarks good-naturedly.

I grab the front of her work shirt and pull her to me. I lean down, stopping only an inch away from her lips. "You know you love me anyway."

This is the second time I've used the term *love* when talking to her. I don't know if what I feel for her is love. Only that whatever it is, it's intense. The last time I used the word, she became dizzy afterward and almost fell on her ass. This time, I don't give her the chance to think about it too much. I close the last inch of space between us and take her lips.

By the time I pull back, we're both out of breath. If it was up to me, I'd skip dinner and socializing and take her ass to bed for the evening. But I know she's looking forward to a relaxing evening to bring in the New Year.

"Come on. Let's go see what Z got us to eat."

When we walk into the kitchen, Rylee avoids our eyes, but her cheeks are blazing red. Zayden's across the room with a hand towel clutched in his hand. It hangs down in front of his crotch. He shoots daggers at me, and I return his look with a smirk.

"Y'all ready to get this party started?" Savannah yells, walking up to Rylee and bumping her hip against hers.

"Been ready. Just waiting on you two."

Going to the freezer, Savannah grabs a bottle of tequila and a couple different jugs of juice from the fridge. She grabs glasses next, and Rylee sidles up next to her.

"Wait. I didn't think about this. Isn't alcohol bad for ulcers?"

Savannah turns around, throwing one hand on her hip and using the other to poke Rylee in the chest.

"You are *not* taking this away from me." She looks at me next, and I raise my hands in the air, taking a step back. She brings her eyes back to Rylee. "I'll eat, which will help a little. I haven't had a lick of liquor in weeks. It's New Years, and I'm bringing the holiday in right."

Rylee doesn't look convinced, and I can't say I blame her. I don't know much about ulcers and didn't know alcohol would affect them. I'm not okay with Savannah doing something that could negatively affect her, but I also know she's been under stress lately. Maybe letting loose with a little bit of alcohol will help her relax better.

"Fine," Rylee grumbles. "But we eat first, then let the booze flow."

"Deal."

Savannah stops by my side after brushing her teeth after eating. She said something about chicken between her molars before heading off to floss and brush. But now she's back, sliding a kiss across my lips before she retakes her seat. I want to snatch her into my lap so I can kiss away more of her minty fresh breath.

Patience and I have never been friends, but I force myself to be until after the ball drops at midnight.

"How about we make this game a little more interesting?"

The four of us are sitting at the kitchen table playing blackjack. Cartons of food and bowls of snacks are scattered about. The tequila bottle is over half empty, and I know we're all feeling the effects.

"What do you have in mind?" Savannah asks.

Rylee looks to each of us before her brows jump up and down playfully. "Strip poker. You lose, you have to take off an item of clothing and take a shot."

I wait for Savannah's protest. There's not a chance in hell she'll agree to something like this. She almost had a conniption fit the day I seduced her into having sex while we listened to Zayden and Rylee going at it.

To say I'm surprised when I glance at her and see her contemplative expression is a huge understatement. I'm even more surprised when she grins big and says, "Let's do it."

I look at Zayden to find him looking at me. We both shrug at the same time. "We're in."

"With some rules," Z adds. "To the underwear only. Unless you want me to sock Oliver in the eyes until they're swollen shut so he can't see you."

Rylee pouts as she grabs the cards to shuffle. "Spoil sport."

"Are you saying you don't mind seeing your stepbrother's dick?" Z asks, raising a brow.

"Not particularly." She wrinkles her nose. "But all he has to do is stay in his seat."

"So, it's okay if I see Savannah's tits then? She can't hide those under the table."

If he were closer, I'd sock *him* for that comment. I hate that the words are even coming out of his mouth.

Her lips tighten and she shoots a glare at Z. "Point made. Underwear stays on."

She starts flipping cards in front of each of us. I end up with fifteen, while Savannah has an eighteen with a queen and an eight. Zayden has a total of nine with a six and a three. Rylee's face card is an ace.

Savannah stays with her eighteen points.

I tap the table. "Hit me." Rylee drops a five next to my eight and seven, and I stand with my twenty points.

I chuckle when Savannah grumbles beside me. "It's okay, baby. I won't make you take off too much."

She shoots me the bird.

"Hit me," Zayden calls and adds ten more points, bringing his total to nineteen. He's got no choice but to take another card and hope it's not more than two.

"Better luck next time, Z," I gloat when he gets a seven.

"Fuck you," he grumbles. "Beat his ass, Rylee."

She flips her face down card over, revealing a two, which brings her total to three or thirteen, depending on how she wants to play her ace. Either way, she has to deal herself another card. A three gets dropped next to her cards.

When she drops a ten next, I throw my arms up and shout, "Strip!"

"You're an ass."

Ignoring Zayden's comment, I glance over to Savannah to see what she's taking off. Thank fuck it's just her socks. I'm not sure how I'd react if she took off her shirt or pants. Sure, I agreed to play the game, but it doesn't mean I want Zayden to see her in her bra.

"You do realize if I lose again, I'm going to have to get rid of my shirt, right?" she taunts, guessing my thoughts.

I pull the hoodie I'm wearing over my head and toss it to her. "Put this on."

"That's cheating. You can't put more clothes on during the game."

I slide my eyes to Rylee. "Says who?"

"Says me," Savannah answers instead, tossing my hoodie across the room. "But good news for me, you're one article of clothing down." I narrow my eyes. "Hey, you agreed to play the game." She sticks out her tongue at me, and I'm tempted to take a bite.

"Whatever." I direct my gaze to Rylee. "Just deal."

The next hand does not go in my favor. Rylee beats us all with a perfect twenty-one. Zayden whips off his shirt and drops it on the floor to join his socks from the last round he lost.

I lose my shirt and enjoy the way Savannah looks at my chest. Flexing, I make my pecs jump just for her viewing pleasure. Her eyes jerk up to mine, and I toss her a wink. With a smug look, she grabs the hem of her shirt and slowly peels it over her head. Her lacey black bra comes into view, and my cock instantly turns hard in my jeans.

It takes me a moment to pull my eyes away from her to glance at the other occupants at the table. Rylee is busy shuffling, a small smile playing on her lips. And Zayden's smart by keeping his eyes averted from Savannah. I'm not sure I'd be able to keep myself in check if he were looking at my girl.

Shots of tequila are taken, and the next hand is dealt. I breathe a little easier when Savannah wins this round.

While Rylee sheds her shirt, Zayden glares at me as he drops his jeans. I get to my feet, keeping my gaze locked on the woman next to me. Her eyes turn to saucers and her tongue darts out to lick her bottom lip when she sees the outline of my semi-hard shaft. It's probably not good to be sporting wood with your best friend and stepsister in the room, but fuck if I can help it when Savannah is a foot away from me with the top of her tits spilling out of her bra.

With my lips tipped up, I sit back down, blocking her view.

"Deal," I tell Rylee, and pour us another round of shots.

Zayden and I probably look ridiculous sitting here avoiding looking at the other's girl. I really don't want to see Rylee in her bra, and I know Zayden won't look at Savannah out of respect for Rylee.

I win the next round, but I'm not happy about it. I'd much rather lose every article of clothing I'm wearing than have Savannah take off her pants. My hands fist on the table and a growl vibrates in my chest as she gets to her feet.

"You look at her, Z, and I'll pop your eyes out of their sockets and shove them down your throat."

"No worries, man. I've got my eyes on something else."

Savannah smiles smugly as she unbuttons and gently pulls down the zipper of her pants. Her jeans are tight, so she has to do a little wiggle to get them over her trim hips. The top edge of her panties come into view and my mouth goes dry. Seeing Savannah in sexy underwear isn't new, but I swear the woman damn near knocks me on my ass every time she gets undressed.

"Damn, girl. Where did you get that bra and panty set?" Rylee asks, knocking me out of my fantasy of dragging Savannah to her room and peeling her bra and panties off with my teeth.

"Victoria's Secret. They got in a brand-new line a few days ago. The material feels heavenly against my skin."

My chair gets knocked back as I move to my feet. "Game's over," I grunt and stalk toward Savannah.

"Agreed," Z says behind me, his own chair scraping across the floor.

I stand in front of Savannah, keeping her hidden from view. Leaning down, I grab the back of her thighs. "Legs around me," I order at the same time I pick her up. I groan when the heat of her pussy meets my hard shaft.

Rylee's giggles and the deep rumble of Z's voice comes from behind me as I stalk down the hallway toward Savannah's room. After kicking the door closed, I walk to the bed and drop her on the mattress. She bounces a couple of times before she gets to her knees.

"Guess what time it is?" she asks, walking her fingers up my bare chest.

"What time is it?" I settle my hands around her waist.

She looks up at me and grabs the back of my head, pulling me closer. "Twelve-oh-four. Happy New Year, Oliver."

I smile against her lips, having no idea that we even missed the ball dropping until this very moment. Not that I care. I would much rather be doing this anyway. "Happy New Year, baby."

Leaning forward, we both tumble to the mattress, where we spend the next couple of hours ringing in the new year in the best way possible.

twenty-four

SAVANNAH

"Hey, how was your break?" Thomas, a guy in my English Lit class slides up next to me seconds after the professor dismisses us.

I don't know the guy well. We had a couple classes together last semester and talked a few times, but that's really the extent of it.

"It was good." I shove my laptop into my bag before shrugging it onto my shoulder. "How was yours?"

"Great. Though I have to say, I'm really happy to be back here. I love my family, but after nearly two weeks with them I was going bat shit crazy."

"Yeah, I get that. That's why I only went home twice over break."

"You stayed here? All by yourself?"

"I wasn't by myself." The thought of Oliver has a smile pulling at my lips.

Thomas turns and follows me out of the classroom into the hallway.

"Well, I guess I'll see you later." He reaches out and gently grazes my forearm. It's completely innocent, but when I look up and see Oliver leaning against the wall waiting for me, I realize by his expression that he doesn't agree.

"Yeah, see you later." I swallow hard, my eyes locked on Oliver.

He looks so damn sexy in his V-neck tee and dark jeans that I'm tempted to wipe my mouth to make sure I'm not drooling. God, those shoulders. Those cheekbones. He really is so good looking it almost hurts.

His eyes follow Thomas as he turns and heads down the hallway, not coming back to me until he disappears from view.

"Who the hell was that?" he snaps when his focus returns to me.

"No one." I shrug, closing the rest of the distance between us.

"Sure as fuck didn't look like no one." He towers over me, his gaze hot on my face.

"Awe, is someone jealous?" I purposely bait him.

"I don't like other men touching what's mine."

"What's yours?" I drag my bottom lip between my teeth to keep my smile at bay.

"You. Are. Mine." He pronounces every word clearly. "Or did you miss that the last hundred times I've said it?"

"No. I didn't miss it. I just wanted to hear you say it again." I finally let my smile break free.

"You're a pain in the ass, you know that?" he grumbles, snagging my arm before pulling me to his chest.

"Pot meet kettle."

"Seriously though, who the fuck was that?" he asks, instead of kissing me like I had hoped he would.

"Relax, killer. His name is Thomas. We have a couple of classes together. Spoken a few times. It's really not a big deal. I wouldn't even call him a friend—that's how little I know about him."

"The way he was looking at you says he has no interest in being your friend, but rather getting into your pants."

"Oh my God, Oliver." I shove at his chest as I take a full step back. "Not everyone thinks that way."

"Guys do," he disagrees. "You think guys talk to girls just to make pleasant conversation?" He gives me a doubtful look. "No, guys talk to girls because they want to fuck them."

"So, you're telling me that every girl you talk to you want to fuck?" I plant a hand on my hip.

"Yep." He nods. "Or at least I did. Until a certain someone stormed into my life. Now I find myself only wanting her."

"Is that so?" I reach out and take his hand, entwining my fingers with his as we turn and head toward the exit.

"It is." He knocks his shoulder gently into mine.

"Well, if it makes you feel better, I have no interest in anybody but you, so it really doesn't matter what Thomas' intentions were for talking to me. It wouldn't get him anywhere, anyway."

"That does make me feel marginally better." He smiles down at me as we push our way through the double doors and step out into the brisk January air.

"What are you doing here? You don't have any classes this afternoon," I say, having looked over his schedule pretty thoroughly to see how our classes lined up. Unfortunately, we once again do not have any classes together. Then again, that might be a good thing, because I doubt I'd learn a single thing with Oliver there to distract me.

"I thought I'd see if you wanted to grab lunch."

"I actually had a sandwich right before class." It's not a *complete* lie. I did eat a sandwich. Well, like two bites of one. But hey, that's progress, right?

"Yeah, I already ate too." He laughs when I throw him a confused look. "I just needed an excuse to come see you."

"You know you don't have to have an excuse. If you want to see me, just say so."

"Fine. I just wanted to see you." He releases my hand and drops an arm over my shoulder when a small shiver runs through me. "Can I give you a ride back to your apartment?" he asks.

"I don't know. I think maybe I'd rather go back to your dorm."

"Oh, yeah. And why is that?"

"Because it's closer." I give him a knowing look, to which he responds with the sexiest damn smirk I've ever seen.

"My dorm room it is."

"Can I ask you a question?" I pop my head up from Oliver's chest and look up at him.

We've been lying in his bed for the better part of two hours, and even though I have to be at work at five, I have zero motivation to get up.

"Sure." He glances down at me.

"You and your dad—have things always been tense between the two of you?"

"We're lying in bed naked and you want to talk about my father?" He cocks a brow.

"I just.... I don't know. I want to know more about you. About your family. About your past."

"It would take me days to try to explain to you the complicated relationship I have with my father."

"Condense it for me. Tell me about when you were a kid? What was it like growing up in your house?"

"Honestly?" He blows out a breath. "Lonely. My father was always working. My mother was MIA most of the time. I mean, we spent time together when I was little. But as I got older, we sort of grew apart." He shifts, rolling onto his side so we're facing each other. His hand slides around my waist and he scoots in so close that our noses almost touch.

"But you have to have some good memories, right? I'm sure you did things together as a family. Game night. Vacations. Stuff like that."

"Not really. We went on vacations, but that usually equated to my mother at the spa or drinking by the pool and my father working in the office of whatever house we rented for the week. It wasn't your typical family vacation."

"I'm sorry. That must have been really hard."

"It was. But as a kid, it was my norm. I never thought a whole lot of it. As I got older, I liked the freedom. Though it got me in a lot more trouble than I'd like to admit."

"I can't even imagine what that must have been like. My parents were always so involved. We spent so much time together that all I wanted was to be alone."

"Take it from someone who practically raised themselves, you're lucky to have the mom and dad that you do."

"I know," I agree. I've never questioned that.

"Z made things easier. Fuck, for years he felt like the only family I had. He was my brother. He *is* my brother."

"Yeah, I feel the same way about Rylee. Growing up as an only child, she was the sibling my parents never gave me. She was a part of my family, and I was a part of hers. I've always referred to Evelyn as my second mom, because when I wasn't at home, I was there. We were pretty much inseparable as kids. So, I guess I didn't just have one great mom, I had two."

"Hence why you hated me so much for the shit I pulled last year."

"You made it pretty easy to dislike you," I agree, running my fingers gently up and down his bicep.

"I guess I did."

"But don't worry, you're starting to redeem yourself," I tease.

"Starting to?" He draws back.

"Okay, you have," I admit on a laugh. "But in all seriousness, you really have surprised me."

"What do you mean?"

"I don't know. You're not the person I thought you were at all. I had you pegged as this egotistical, malicious, spoiled rich kid who thought the world owed him something, and that we should all bend to his will. But the more I've gotten to know you, the more I realize that's not who you are at all. Well, except maybe for the egotistical part." I grin, letting him know I'm only kidding. "You, Oliver Conley, are a closet good guy."

He grunts. "I don't know if I'd go that far."

"I would," I disagree. "You make me feel a way no one has ever made me feel before."

"And what way is that?" His fingers start moving, trailing circles along the small of my back.

"Wanted," I admit. "When you look at me, I don't know how to explain it. It's like you don't see any of my flaws. When you look at me, it's like I'm the most beautiful girl in the world. I've never had anyone look at me like that before."

"Because you are the most beautiful."

"I'm not," I quickly disagree. "And that's okay. There will always be someone prettier, more talented, or smarter than I am. That's just the way of the world. I've never tried to compete with anyone else. I didn't need to, because nearly my entire life I've been in competition with myself. But with you? You make me feel okay with who I am. If that makes any sense."

"It does." He pulls in a deep breath. "Because that's how you make me feel too. You see who I am, fucked up parts and all. And yet here you are. Other than Z, I don't think anyone has accepted me quite so fully." He leans in and presses a soft kiss to my lips. "And for the record, you are the most beautiful woman I have ever seen."

"Careful. You might start giving me a big head, and yours is already big enough for the both of us," I tease, giggling when his hand slides up to my side and he gives it a hard squeeze.

"You know." He falls serious again. "I wish you could see yourself through my eyes—just once. I don't think you'd ever look at yourself the same way again."

"I could say the same about you."

"V, I...." He swallows hard, the words dying on his lips when the sound of his ringtone fills the space.

I have no idea what he was about to say, but for some reason it feels like it was going to be big. Or maybe that's wishful thinking on my part. Whatever it was, he doesn't make any attempt to finish his sentence, which makes me even more curious.

"You going to get that?" I ask after a few seconds have passed and he still hasn't moved to answer the phone.

"Nope." He pulls me closer so that not even a single inch of space separates us, pressing a kiss to the tip of my nose. He places another to each cheek before making his way to my lips.

The phone quits ringing and instantly starts again.

"Fuck," he mutters against my mouth.

"Just answer it." I press my hand to his chest and scoot back as much as I can due to the small size of the bed.

"This better be fucking important." He rolls, grabbing the phone before holding it up in front of his face. "And that's a big fuck no." He silences the ringer.

"Who is it?" I ask, propping up on my elbow.

"My father." He drops his head onto the pillow and lets out a frustrated sigh.

The call no more than ends before the ringing begins again.

"Are you fucking kidding me?" He shoots up in bed.

"Hey." I touch his back, pulling his gaze to me. "Just answer it."

"I don't want to answer it."

"You know he's going to keep calling if you don't," I point out. "Answer it. I have to get ready to go, anyway. I have to be at work in less than an hour." He gives me a disappointed look as I move to leave the bed. "Answer it," I tell him again as I slide off the edge of the mattress and stand. My entire body protests the movement.

This has been one of the best days of my life, and for no other reason than because of who I spent it with. I never knew an afternoon in bed could be so enjoyable. And not just because of the physical aspect, but because of the emotional as well.

Little by little, I feel like I'm breaking down the walls of Oliver Conley, and the more he lets me in, the harder I fall.

Because as much as I want to deny it, as badly as I want to bury it and pretend like it isn't real, the truth of the matter is, I'm falling in love with him.

No, I *am* in love with him. I think I've known it for a while, but I'm just getting around to admitting it to myself. The man I swore I'd hate until my dying breath has seemingly overnight, become someone I don't ever want to live without. And this terrifies me as much as it excites me.

"Oliver." I point to the device still ringing in his hand.

"Fuck," he grumbles again, swiping his finger across the screen. "What?" he barks into the phone.

I shake my head at him, swooping down to pick my clothes up off the floor.

"This couldn't wait until later?" he grinds out, throwing his legs over the side of the bed. He pauses, presumably listening to whatever his father is saying.

I feel his eyes on me as I dress, and for this reason, I do it slow and purposeful. I don't miss the smile that toys on his lips as he watches my slow and seductive movements.

"What?" he questions, his attention so focused on me that he seems to have completely blanked on whatever his father is talking about. "I'm busy." He runs a hand through his messy hair. "I've got class." Another pause. "Why is it when I need you to make time for me, it never fucking happens, but when the roles are reversed you expect me to come running?"

"I gotta go." I step up next to Oliver and drop a kiss to his temple.

He covers the bottom of the phone so his dad can't hear him. "Stay."

"I can't," I mouth. "Call me later?" I back toward the door, sliding on my shoes before picking my bag up off the floor.

I'm seconds away from tugging the door open when Oliver pushes to his feet and struts toward me in all his naked gloriousness.

"I'm going to have to call you back," he says into the phone before he tosses it onto the bed behind him. "Did you really think I was going to let you slip out like that?" He grins, backing me into the door.

"I have to go to work," I tell him again, my skin heating with the way he stares down at me.

"And I have every intention of letting you go, but first." He presses against me before tipping my chin up.

In one swift move, his mouth closes down over mine. He kisses me so intensely that I swear I feel it radiate through my entire body.

I've never had someone make me feel so much so deeply with nothing more than a kiss. But that's what Oliver does. He devours me. He consumes me. Hell, at this point, he owns me.

And when he pulls back and hits me with a satisfied grin, I think it's pretty safe to say that he knows it too.

twenty-five

OLIVER

Tossing back a handful of Red Hots into my mouth, I turn down the tree-lined street leading to my father's house. I have the radio cranked up so loud, an old man walking his dog eyes my car like it's the most God-awful thing he's ever seen. I casually flip him the bird as I pass by.

I park on the curb in front of the house and get out, flipping up the collar of my jacket when a gust of cold wind blows in my face. I am so fucking ready for summer. I hate being cold.

When I walk inside, I'm greeted by blessed heat, and the sound of classical music. Slipping my jacket off, I drop it on a bench by the staircase and go search for my father. I wouldn't be here if I didn't have to, especially since Savannah's off work today, but dear old Dad said it was urgent I come see him this weekend. Savannah offered to come with me, but I want her nowhere near my father if I can help it.

I head toward his office, knowing ninety percent of the time when he's at home, that's where he is. I'm surprised when I push open the door and find not my father sitting at his desk, but Evelyn.

"Oh! Hi, Oliver," Evelyn chirps, looking up from the computer. "I assume you're looking for your father?"

I jerk my chin up. "Apparently, it was dire I come see him at the first opportunity."

"Yes." She smiles, but when it doesn't reach her eyes, I become suspicious. "What he has to speak with you about is very important." She gets up from the chair and walks around to the front of the desk, leaning against the mahogany wood. "He just stepped into the kitchen for a moment. We were going over the finances for the month."

I drop down into a chair and prop my feet up on the edge of the desk, getting comfortable with my arms crossed over my chest.

"You talk to Rylee lately?" I ask, making small talk. I *hate* small talk, but it's better than sitting here with Evelyn in a weird silence.

"Earlier today." She pauses. "Why? Is there something I should be worried about?"

"Nope. Not that I'm aware of."

"Oh." She laces her fingers together in front of her. "How has school been?"

"Boring mostly." I shrug. "But fine."

"How have *you* been?"

"Good," I grunt. Tilting my head, I regard the woman in front of me. "Why are you so nice to me?" I ask, having always wondered.

From the way her eyes widen and the jerk of her head, I'd say I surprised her with my question.

"You're my husband's son. Why wouldn't I be nice to you?"

"Because, up until recently, I wasn't very cordial toward you. And I damn sure wasn't with Rylee."

Her lips pinch together in a frown. "Oliver, I never thought for one moment your father marrying me would be easy on you. You're a grown man, but even men have feelings. I refuse to talk negatively about Maria, but we all know she hated me, even before your father and I got together. Paul told me you know why he and your mother divorced, and it had nothing to do with me. He also told me that Maria made you believe otherwise. I didn't blame you for hating me. You thought I broke up your family, and you lashed out. And while I don't know the extent of your treatment of Rylee, I know you weren't nice to her. I may have wanted to strangle you at times." She smiles wryly. "I also knew you were hurt and dealing with that pain the only way you knew how. You needed time, and I wanted to give that to you. It all worked out in the end."

I understand now why Rylee and Savannah always defended

Evelyn. She really is an incredible woman and mother. A damn sight better than my own. Rylee is lucky to have her.

We're interrupted when my father appears in the doorway. His eyes flick back and forth between me and Evelyn, assessing the situation. When Evelyn smiles, his shoulders relax.

"Oliver, it's good to see you, son."

With a grunt, I drop my feet to the floor and sit up straight without returning the sentiment. He walks over and hands Evelyn a plate holding a sandwich at the same time he leans down and drops a quick kiss on her lips.

"Give us a bit of time to talk?"

She nods, offering a smile. "Let me know if you need me."

"Thank you, darling."

Evelyn stops by my chair and grips my shoulder, giving it a squeeze. "No matter what you may think, Oliver, don't ever doubt that your father loves you."

With her cryptic words bouncing around in my head, she leaves the room, quietly closing the door behind her. I look back at my father, lifting a brow. "What the hell was that about?"

Instead of answering me, he walks around his desk and takes his seat. After rolling up the sleeves of his dress shirt, he props his elbow on the smooth surface. I notice something in his eyes I've never seen before. Something I *never* thought I'd see.

Fear and uncertainty.

My father has always been impenetrable. Sure about everything and fearing nothing.

It's that look that has me shifting uncomfortably in my seat. I'm not going to like what he's about to tell me.

"Whatever it is, just spit it out."

He sighs, steepling his fingers together and resting his hands against his chin.

I'm just about to get up and walk the fuck out of the room when he speaks.

"I know you've had reservations on how much I love you. For me, that has never been in question. From the first moment the doctor placed you in my arms, Oliver, I had this huge weight in my chest. Not from gaining a burden, but from my heart being truly full for the first time in my life. It scared the shit out of me how much I loved you, and I had no idea what to do with it. You were this tiny, little baby. So small, but capable of making me feel something so strong."

His eyes are intense as he stares at me. He breaks the look long enough to scrub his hands over his face. He looks tired and worn out.

"You don't need to say it for me to know I've been a shitty father to you. I've been hard on you. Not because I don't care, but because *I do*. I push you because I know you can do so much with your life. You're capable of becoming a much better man than I am. I want the best for you, and I've strived to give you that. I wanted your life to be easier than mine ever was. But I fear I've made it harder on you." He looks down at his desk for a moment before lifting his eyes again. "Instead of forcing you to do things my way, maybe I should have supported you. Let you do things your way and helped when I could. I'm sorry I haven't been there for you like I should have been."

I don't know if I should enjoy his confession of his crappy behavior toward me over the years or be weirded out by his strange behavior. Either way, it'll take more than a simple apology to make up for all the shit he's put me through.

This whole thing is a little concerning, because I never thought I'd see the day where my father would be mushy.

I sit forward in my seat and rest my elbows on my knees. "Okay, what's going on? Are you dying or some shit?"

He cracks a smile. "No, I'm not dying."

"Well, why the heart to heart all of a sudden?"

When he opens his eyes, they're filled with torment. "Because of what I'm about to tell you. I need you to know that I love you, Oliver. I will always love you, and there's not a damn thing that will change that."

He pulls in a deep breath, closes his eyes, and breathes out slowly. My sweaty hands grip the arms of the chair as I wait for him to continue.

"The first time I found out your mother was having an affair with Benjamin was twenty years ago," he begins, his voice low. "It had been going on for about a year. During that time, it had been months since your mother and I had been intimate. I'd noticed a change in her—she seemed distant and never wanted to do the things we used to do. I blamed it on me being busy at work. It never crossed my mind that she was having an affair, let alone with my brother. That was, until I came home early one evening to surprise her with a weekend getaway. I was the one surprised when I caught her in bed with Benjamin."

Hearing of my mother's affair isn't news to me, but even so, having my father describe the first time he found out makes me sick, and my anger against my mother renews.

His eyes leave mine to move across the room, staring off into space. "As I told you weeks ago, I'd confronted her, and she'd promised it would never happen again. Because I was a fool, I believed her. Weeks passed when she finally came to me. I'll spare you the details, but she wanted sex. I still wasn't ready to see past her affair and my desire for her was gone, so I denied her. She tried several more times, but I could never give her what she wanted. A couple of months later, I found out she was pregnant." His eyes move back to me. "I knew right away that the baby couldn't be mine. We hadn't had sex in over six months. That was why she came to me wanting sex. To pass the baby off as mine."

His words, and the implication behind them, has me freezing in my seat, and all the blood drains from my face. I hear and understand what he's saying, but I'm having a hard time wrapping my brain around it.

"I could have very easily divorced her. Any love I felt for her was squashed the moment I realized she was pregnant with another man's child and had tried passing him off as mine."

"Why didn't you?" I grit out, my blood pressure rising, heating me from the inside out.

"Because of you," he says simply. "You were an innocent baby. Maria loved money and what it could give her. My brother had none, and I knew he would never be able to give you the life you deserved." He gets up and walks around to the front of the desk, leaning back and crossing his arms over his chest. "Maria was all for staying married because she knew she'd be left with nothing if we divorced."

"Because you'd make damn sure she would get nothing if you dissolved the marriage. Meaning she'd have nothing to give her child."

I'm angry. No, anger doesn't cover it. I'm *livid*. My whole fucking life is a lie, and the people I'm supposed to trust the most are the ones who've deceived me.

"Yes, but not for the reasons you're thinking. You may not have been my child, but you were still my blood and deserved more than Benjamin could ever give you. After discussing it with your mother, we decided to stay married, and I would raise you as my own. We were going to tell you who your real father was once you were old enough to understand. All of that changed when I held you in my arms for the first time."

I laugh sardonically. "How fucking touching."

My father ignores my snide remark.

"You were mine in every way that mattered. I didn't give a shit that it wasn't my seed that created you. I claimed you and never once regretted that decision. I've loved you as if you were my own. I don't know if Maria ever told Benjamin that you were his, but he never showed up to dispute my claim."

I get up from my chair and begin pacing the room. Feeling my father's—or rather, my *uncle's*—eyes on me, I turn to face him.

"Why tell me now?" I demand.

"Because you deserve to know," he answers quietly, pain etched in his tone. "As much as it pains me to say this, knowing you could leave and never want to see me again, I was wrong to keep this from you. I hate Benjamin and don't think he would make a good father, but it's your right to make that decision."

I begin pacing again. I have no fucking clue what to do with this information. The only thing I do know, is that I have a fuck load of anger coursing through my system. My father claims to have loved me, despite being sired by another man, but does he really? Would he have treated me differently had I truly been his? Would my childhood have been filled with love and laughter, instead of ridicule and judgement? Would he have held and comforted me when I fell and scraped my knee, instead of telling me to man up and get over it? Would there have been picnics and family game nights, instead of being pawned off on nannies?

I'll never know the answers to those questions. I'll never know if things would have been different. Which angers me even more.

"I'll support whatever decision you make, Oliver."

I spin around and face him, and not for the first time, but for entirely different reasons, I look at him with disgust.

"You will because you've got no choice. You no longer get a say in what happens in my life. You've had that ability way too long, and it stops now."

"I know you hate me—"

"Hate you? Right now, I fucking despise you. My whole life has been a lie. Who I thought was my father, the man who never made me feel loved, isn't my father. And the man who actually is, is an asshole who steals a married woman from her husband. And my mother," I laugh humorlessly, "is a manipulative bitch, who would rather stay with her husband because of the money he has. The three of you can go fuck yourselves and stay out of my life. I'm done."

He calls my name, but I stalk across the room toward the door. Yanking it open, I leave without a backward glance. Evelyn is following me, calling my name, but I ignore her too. I need to get the hell out of this house filled with lies and deception.

I DON'T KNOW how many hours pass before I'm stumbling up the steps to Savannah's apartment. Time seemed to cease to exist a while ago. Probably about the time I had my sixth shot of whiskey. The elevator in the lobby was taking too damn long to reach the bottom floor, so I said fuck it and made my way toward the stairs. Not sure if that was a good idea or not, because it seems like I've been climbing stairs for hours.

Squinting my eyes, I throw my hands in the air and yell, "Hallelujah," when I spot the number four through my blurred vision.

I guess I lean against the door too hard because it slings open and slams against the wall. "Oops." I laugh.

I stagger from left to right as I approach Savannah's door. Or at least I think it's Savannah's door. I tip forward, staring at the number. When it becomes one number like it's supposed to, instead of two, and I realize that it's for sure Savannah's door, I grin.

Gripping the knob, I try to twist it, but it doesn't budge. Why the hell isn't it opening?

Frowning, I bang on the door.

When she takes too long to answer, I bang on the door even harder. "Saaavannaaah!" I call, hoping she can hear me.

I stumble forward and almost smash my face onto the floor when the door suddenly opens. Barely catching myself on the frame, I look up at her and give her a silly grin. "Hey, you."

"What in the world are you doing?" My smile drops at her hissed words. "You're going to wake the neighbors."

"Nah." I hiccup. "It's like seven in the evening. They're all awake, anyway."

"Oliver, it's two-thirty in the morning."

"Oh." My eyes ping pong around and my vision becomes dizzy. "Where the hell did the time go?"

"Get in here before someone calls the cops." She grabs my arm and tugs me inside.

"What? That's dumb. Why would anyone call the cops?"

"Because you're drunk and being obnoxiously loud."

I pout and reach for her, then scowl when she steps away.

"Did you drive here?"

"No. Uber." I take a step and reach for her again. "Now come 'ere. I need some lovin'."

She shakes her head and turns away from me. "What you need is some water and to sleep off all the alcohol you've consumed."

Scowling, I follow her into the kitchen. Finding her at the sink filling a glass of water, I walk up behind her, pin her hips against the counter, and wrap my arms around her waist.

"No water," I mumble and bury my face in the crook of her neck. She stiffens, and I really don't like it, but I ignore it and lick her sweet skin. "I need to fuck you. That'll make it all go away."

She relaxes fractionally. "Make what go away?"

I run my nose up her neck and nibble her ear. "I don't want to talk about it."

Grabbing my wrists, she unlocks my arms enough for her to spin around to face me. She gazes up at me with concerned eyes, and it reminds me of the look my father gave me right before I walked out of his office. I hate that look. Especially on Savannah.

"What happened? You said you were going to see your father this afternoon. Obviously, something happened between you two."

"I told you I don't want to talk about it."

When I try to lean down and steal a kiss, she denies me by pressing her hands against my chest. The move pisses me off.

"What the hell, Savannah?"

"You're drunk, Oliver, and it's obvious something happened with your father. You don't need sex, you need to talk. And if you don't want to talk, then you need to sleep."

"Nooo." I draw out the word. "What I need is for you to get undressed and get with the program. I came here hoping you'd help me blow off some steam. What I'm getting is you nagging at me to talk about my *feelings*."

"Is that all you came here for?" She looks hurt. Ordinarily that would bother me, but in the state I'm in, it annoys me. "Sex? Is that all you want from me?"

I push away from her and stagger back a few steps. "Right now. Yes. Are you denying me?"

"Yes."

"Why?"

Her eyes turn glassy and she hugs her arms around her middle. "Because you're being an asshole right now, when all I want to do is help you."

"I already told you how you can help me!" I yell.

She flinches, but a second later, her expression turns hard. "Sex doesn't fix everything, Oliver. You may want it, but you don't *need* it. And I refuse to have it with you while you're in this state."

I laugh, the sound strangled, and I flip my arms in the air. I teeter to the side but catch myself on the counter.

"I should have known you'd be like them. My father, who isn't really my father, treats me lower than shit and has lied to me my whole life. My mother is a whore who leaves her husband and son for her brother-in-law," I hold up a finger and wiggle it around, "who also happens to be my *real* father. Why the hell would you be any different? The moment I need you, you're not there."

"Oh, Oliver, I'm so sorry." She shakes her head and gives me a crestfallen look that only amps up my anger. "Is that why your father wanted to talk to you? Is that what this is about? Talk to me."

"I told you, I don't want to talk about it."

"You just found out your dad isn't really your dad. I can't imagine what you must be feeling right now."

"Good. You feel sorry for me. Does that mean you're going to put out now?" I try to capitalize on the look of pity written all over her face.

The stubborn set of her jaw is my answer.

"Doesn't matter. You were good while it lasted, but I think I'm done with you. I believe I'll go find something better." I rake my eyes up and down her body. "Someone with less… meat on their bones."

I grin and shoot her a wink. I know I'm being an asshole, and I'll likely regret my actions tomorrow, but right now, I don't give two shits if I hurt her feelings. I started drinking tonight to dull the pain in my chest after I left my father's place. It worked. Until I got here and Savannah's watchful and worried eyes reminded me of what I lost today. I'm a bastard, literally and figuratively. Lashing out is what I do best. When I hurt, I want the people around me to hurt too.

Savannah's bottom lip wobbles, and my first reaction is to go to her. But for some reason, I don't. A tear trickles past her thick lashes, and I swear I feel the heat of it on my own cheek. Angrily, she bats the tear away and straightens her spine.

"So, that's it? You're breaking up with me because I won't give you what you want?"

"Pretty much."

"Wow." She's surprised, hurt even, but her anger far outweighs every other emotion on her face.

"I don't know why you seem so surprised. You knew I was only in this for one thing."

Having heard enough, she pulls her phone from the front pocket of her hoodie and swipes across the screen. "I'm calling Zayden to come get you."

"No need. I'm out of here."

I turn on my heel and stalk toward the front door. I was drunk when I first got here, but some of my buzz has dissipated. That needs to be rectified.

Being sober means the pain will come back, and I'm fucking done with pain.

twenty-six

SAVANNAH

"What the hell is going on?" Rylee stalks through the front door, Zayden fast on her heels.

"Where's Oliver?" Zayden asks, looking around the room.

"He's gone," I say solemnly.

"V, what's going on? I could barely make out two words that you said over the phone." Rylee crosses the room, crouching down in front of me where I'm sitting on the couch.

"I don't really know," I answer honestly. In truth, I'm so confused right now I'm not sure what to think. I feel like I've entered some weird alternate universe. Everything seems slower and harder to process. Almost like it's a dream.

"Start from the beginning."

"Oliver showed up here so drunk he could barely stand up straight. He was trying to get me to...." My eyes dart to Zayden before going back to Rylee. "To have sex with him." I lower my voice. "But I knew something was wrong, and I said no. I was trying to get him to talk to me. You should have seen him." I shake my head, tears once again springing to the surface.

"Did he say what happened?" Z interjects, stepping up directly behind Rylee.

"Well." I swallow hard. "He said that his dad isn't his dad." I blink up at Zayden.

"Wait. What?"

"He was hard to understand, and he wouldn't really tell me

anything, but he said he found out that his dad isn't really his dad. His uncle is."

Zayden steps back like he's been physically forced backward, concern the most prominent feature on his face. "Where is he now?"

"I don't know. He was drunk. I told him I was going to call you and he bolted."

"Fuck." He runs his hair through his hands. "I have to go find him," he tells Rylee directly. She nods once and he's out the front door before I know it.

"V." Her gentle voice pulls my gaze back to hers.

Without warning, I burst into tears, all the emotion I've been holding in for the last few minutes boiling over.

Her arms come around me, and even though I know she's curious about what exactly happened, she doesn't press for any information. Instead she just holds me.

I don't know how much time passes. Five minutes. Thirty. All I know is that when I finally pull away and look at Rylee, my eyes ache and there's this heavy weight sitting directly on my chest.

"Stay here. I'll be right back." Rylee stands, disappearing into the kitchen moments later.

I don't know what happened. I don't know what I did to deserve for Oliver to treat me the way he did. I know he's hurting—that much was abundantly clear. But the things he said to me? They were inexcusable. Unforgivable even.

My mind drifts back to the way he looked at me. The way he spoke to me. Like I was some worthless piece of shit that held no value to him or anyone else. And then for him to throw out the comment about my weight. That was low, even for him.

I startle when Rylee drops on the couch next to me, so lost in my thoughts I hadn't heard her re-enter the room.

"Here." She hands me a glass of water.

I take it, offering her a small nod of thanks before lifting the glass to my lips and taking a long drink.

"V." She waits until I lean forward and set the water on the coffee table before continuing. "Tell me what happened."

"Honestly, I don't know," I croak, my voice hoarse. "He showed up here, beating on the door so loudly it's a wonder no one called to complain. I knew he was drunk as soon as I opened the door, and he almost face planted into the apartment. He treated me… he treated me like I was just some object, something he could take his anger out on. I've never had anyone make me feel the way he did. Like I meant nothing. Like I am nothing."

"Hey." She reaches over and slides her fingers around mine, giving my hand a squeeze. "You know that's not true."

"Well, according to him, that's exactly how he views me." I swipe angrily at the tears still falling from my eyes.

"You said he found out Paul isn't his father… How is that possible?"

"I don't really know. He wouldn't talk to me. He was rambling incoherently about his parents. About his mom being a whore. And about how his dad isn't really his dad. I couldn't really follow him, but from what I understood, his uncle is his real father."

"Oh my God." She holds her hand up to her mouth. "Poor Oliver. I wonder if my mom knows."

"I can't imagine Paul would tell Oliver and not clue Evelyn in."

"Yeah," she agrees, blowing out a breath. "This is crazy."

"It is. And I get that he's probably so confused and hurt right now, but the way he came at me, Ry, the way he spoke to me…"

"He shouldn't have done that."

"He ended things."

"What?" She seems even more surprised by this news.

"He said I was only good for one thing, and since I wasn't going to give him what he wanted, he was going to go find someone who would."

"Oh, V. I'm sure he didn't mean that."

"You didn't hear him. You didn't see him. The way he looked at me. It was like he was a complete stranger, yet the exact person I always thought he was. I think maybe I was just kidding myself. That he was actually this good guy deep down. Turns out I should have listened to my gut."

"Savannah."

"I'm serious, Rylee. What kind of man treats someone he cares about the way he treated me? What kind of man purposely tries to hurt people simply because he's hurting? He pushes away the people who care about him. He makes them pay when something in his life doesn't go right. Well, I'm done. I refuse to be anyone's fucking punching bag." I push to a stand and start to pace the living room. "And you know the most fucked up part? I actually thought I meant something to him."

"You *do* mean something to him." Rylee watches me from the couch.

"You know he called me fat." I stop mid-stride and turn to face her.

"He what?"

"Oh, yeah. Said he was going to go find someone with a little less meat on her bones." My voice shakes.

Even though I know my weight is so low it's bordering unhealthy, I still can't stop that little voice in my head from reaffirming how right he is.

"Jesus." She blows out another breath, pushing to her feet. "Listen, I won't make excuses for him. I've been on the other end of Oliver's wrath, and I know firsthand how vengeful and hurtful he can be. But Savannah, he cares about you. So much. You have to know that."

"No, what I know is that he's a self-serving, manipulative asshole that uses people before he discards them the first chance he gets. You think I haven't been listening when Zayden makes comments about how Oliver was in high school? Or that I missed all the times you'd tell me how he had a different girl in his room every other night, and you couldn't understand what they saw in him, because he treated them like absolute dirt? This is a pattern, Rylee. This is who he is."

"You don't really think that. People change. Oliver has changed."

"Oliver is still the same vindictive son of a bitch he's always been. You only think he's changed because he wants you to think he has. Don't you see? That's who he is. He plays nice for Zayden, but do you think he'd keep up that charade if Zayden wasn't in the picture? Hell no. He'd turn on you so fast your head would spin, and deep down, I think you know I'm right."

"You're hurting."

"Hell yes, I'm hurting! Because I let myself fall in love with a man I knew wasn't capable of loving me back."

"You love him?" Her words are a whisper on her lips, and I realize that this is the first time I've ever admitted to how I truly feel about Oliver out loud.

"*Loved*," I correct.

"You can't just unlove someone because they hurt you, V. That's not how love works."

"I knew he'd hurt me," I continue on like she didn't even speak. "I knew it, yet I still let him spin me into his web. How could I have been so stupid?" I toss my hands up in the air.

"We don't always have control over who we fall for. No matter how crazy it may seem at the time, it's true what they say. The heart really does want what it wants, and it doesn't matter what our heads say. All reason and logic go out the window and we follow our hearts blindly, because in truth, I don't think we really have a choice in the matter. Do you think I wanted to fall for Zayden? Do you think I wanted anything to do with him after how he treated me? I was so sure I knew exactly who he was, but you know what, V? It turned out I didn't know him at all. I only knew what he wanted me to see. But then things changed, and I started to see the real Zayden, and I gotta tell you, it's not easy loving a difficult man, but it's damn worth it."

"Oliver is not Zayden."

"You're right, he's not. But believe it or not, they aren't that different, either. Oliver loves you, Savannah. I know he does. Even if he doesn't realize it yet. I can see it when he looks at you. But that also means you're going to be the first person he pushes away. Because he's hurting. And he's afraid you're going to hurt him too.

And while I won't defend the way he spoke to you or the things he said, I will say that I would bet my life he didn't mean a single word of it."

"You act like you know him so well. Honestly, how well can you really know him?"

"You're right. Maybe I don't know him as well as I'd like to think I do. But if Zayden has taught me anything, it's how to look past the tough exterior Oliver exudes. At the end of the day, he's just as scared and uncertain as the rest of us. And he's been going through a lot lately. Things that neither you nor I could even pretend to comprehend. I'm not asking you to excuse his behavior, but I am asking that you not let it lead you to make a rash decision that you'll regret down the road."

"What decision? He broke up with me. Pretty sure the decision has already been made." I hate the ache that swirls in my chest at the thought.

I can't stomach it. The thought of never feeling Oliver's lips on mine again. Of never staring up into those incredible eyes of his and losing myself in their depths. Never getting to hear his laugh vibrate against my ear as I lay on his chest. Never seeing his smile as he hovers over me, the weight of him so sweet inside of me.

I try to pull in a breath, but my lungs feel restricted, like something is sitting on my chest making it almost impossible to breathe. Tears once again fill my vision as the reality of it sinks in.

Because right now, the things he said, the way he acted, it's still not enough to dull the loss of him. The loss that I feel everywhere.

"V."

"Don't." I hold up my hand to stop her. "Don't you dare say he didn't mean it. You don't know that. You have no way of knowing that. Because let me just tell you, he was pretty fucking convincing."

"He was upset and drunk."

"Alcohol is a truth serum. Isn't that what they say? You know what I think? I think he meant every word. I think he was using me, and I think I've known it all along. I was a challenge. I was probably the only girl to ever hate him. He had to work for me and that's what made it so fun. But the chase is over now and suddenly I've lost my luster." My gaze goes to Rylee. "And before you tell me I'm wrong, think about it for a minute. He went from hating my guts to not being able to get enough of me overnight."

"But didn't you kind of do the same thing with him?" she asks gingerly.

"That's different."

"How is it different?"

"Because he pursued me. It's not like I woke up one day and was like—huh, I think I'll start liking Oliver now. No. He pursued me. He wore me down. Not the other way around."

"So, then what? That's just it? You're done."

"Yes. I'm done. Or well, he's done. Either way, we're done. And that's that."

"The Savannah I know would never give up that easily on something she wants."

"Well, maybe I'm not that Savannah anymore." My chin quivers as I feel another wave of emotion wash through me. "I'm not going to fight for someone who can dismiss me so easily, as if I never mattered."

"Just…." She starts, but her words die on her lips when her phone starts ringing. She reaches into her pocket and pulls it out, immediately answering it. "Did you find him?" I watch relief fill her face. "Okay, yeah. That's good. I'm going to stay with V." She pauses, presumably listening to Zayden speak on the other end of the line. "Okay, I will. I love you, too." She ends the call, her gaze slowly coming back to mine. "Zayden found him lying on the front steps of his dorm, barely conscious. He took him upstairs and he's sleeping now."

As angry as I am with him, as hurt as I am, I won't deny that I feel a small sense of relief knowing he's home safe.

"He's going to stay the night there just to be safe. He said Oliver is in pretty rough shape."

"He was," I confirm.

"Well, at least now he's sleeping it off. Speaking of which." She glances at the time. "It probably wouldn't hurt for you to get some sleep."

"I don't think I could sleep if I wanted to."

"Come on." She steps forward, sliding her arm through mine. "I'll lay with you."

"What am I, five?" I grumble, allowing her to lead me down the hall.

"You might be too stubborn to admit it, but I think we both know the last thing you want right now is to be alone. I may not be as sexually appealing to you as Oliver, but you should know by now that my snuggles are beyond compare."

I smile in spite of the fact that my insides feel like they're being torn apart. I've never felt like this before. So torn up over the thought of losing a guy. But here I am, feeling like I'm seconds away from crumbling to pieces on the floor. And over a guy I've only been dating a few short weeks. Over a guy who's shown me time and time again that he doesn't deserve my tears. He doesn't deserve my heart. And he sure as hell doesn't deserve my love.

I wish I knew how to turn it off. How to unlove someone I never should have let my heart love to begin with. And I would if I could. Because I'd rather feel nothing at all, than feel the way I do right now.

Rylee turns down the blankets and waits for me to climb into bed before sliding in next to me. She doesn't say anything, offering a silent comfort that she somehow knows I needed.

It's not long before my mental and emotional exhaustion starts to take hold. Rolling to the side, I pull my legs into myself and snuggle deeper into the covers, tears still sliding down my face as sleep takes me under.

twenty-seven

OLIVER

Hearing the click of my door opening, then the loud slam of it closing, I crack open my eyes and glare at the intruder. I'm not the least bit surprised when I find Zayden staring back at me.

"Get out," I grunt and close my eyes again.

"Not happening."

"How the hell did you get in my room, anyway? The door was locked."

"Have you forgotten how many times we broke into your father's office when we were kids to steal from his liquor stash?" My blanket is ripped off me. "Shit, Oliver. When was the last time you showered? You fucking stink."

"Then leave, so you don't have to smell me." I push up to a sitting position and lean against the headboard of my bed. "And he's not my fucking father."

Zayden knocks a pile of clothes off my desk chair and takes a seat. Which means he's not leaving like I told him to. I don't have the energy for the conversation he's going to try to have with me. And even if I did, I damn sure don't want to talk about it. It's why I've been avoiding him the last couple of days.

"Talk," he demands.

"Fuck off." I flip him the bird and grab the box of Red Hots from my desk. My mouth tastes like something died in it, so I use the cinnamon flavor to mask the awful taste until I can brush my teeth.

"Again. Not happening." He kicks back in the chair and throws his sneakered feet on my bed. "I'll sit here all damn day if that's what it takes. I've given you time to wallow in pity, but that shit ends now."

I grumble under my breath and fold my arms over my bare chest, staring across the room and pouting like a child. It only lasts for a few seconds before I realize how ridiculous I must look. I lean my head against the wall and close my eyes when my head begins to pound.

"Paul isn't my father," I say, breaking the silence. "Apparently, my mother had been having an affair longer than I was originally told."

"You mentioned something of the sort the other night, but I couldn't make out much of what you were saying because you were so hammered." He pauses. "Shit, man. That's rough."

I snort. "That's putting it mildly. I feel like my whole life was a sham. My father, or rather, *Uncle Paul*, claims he never thought of me as anything less than his son, but it explains so much. His treatment of me. The lack of compassion. The careless way he regarded me. I used to always try so hard to impress him, to make him love me, but it was all pointless. How could he love me when every time he looked at me, I reminded him of his wife's infidelity? And the kicker is, I don't really blame him for feeling that way. I'm not sure I would have felt differently if I were in his shoes."

I spend the next few minutes outlining my meeting with Paul. While Z tried to get it out of me the other day, I was too hungover to really explain anything to him. I just needed sleep and thankfully, he let me be. I should have known it was only a matter of time before he showed up demanding to know what the fuck was really going on.

"Have you spoken to him since he told you?" he asks after I'm finished.

"Fuck no. I've got nothing to say to him. He ceased to exist to me the moment I learned he lied to me my entire life."

Several moments of silence pass between us.

"Have you tried to look at it from his point of view? To get a better understanding on why he lied?"

I roll my head to the side and give him an icy look. "Who's fucking side are you on?"

"Yours. But I'm also trying to rationalize why he would keep this from you. I mean, what would be the point? Especially if he's as heartless as you claim he is."

"Like I claim he is?" I growl. "You know the piece of shit father he's been."

He nods. "I do. And I'm not excusing his behavior, but I don't think it's because he doesn't care. If he didn't, then he would have used the knowledge that someone else fathered you to hurt you." He sighs, dropping his feet to the floor and bending so his elbows rest on his knees. "Some people don't know how to be good parents. Especially those who were raised by shitty parents themselves. It doesn't mean they don't care. They just don't know how to show that they *do* care."

I don't give a shit what Paul's excuse is. Maybe it's the little boy in me who felt neglect by the man he idolized. Would I have been better off with my real father? The few times I heard my grandparents talk about Benjamin, they didn't have many good things to say about him. He was the black sheep of the family who expected everything to be handed to him, but never wanted to work for it. I always thought of him as a spoiled brat.

"What about your mother? Have you confronted her? She's not blameless in this. She could have just as easily told you as Paul could have."

"I'm not ready to talk to her. I need time to come to grips with the fact that Paul isn't my father before I deal with my issues with my mother."

"Understandable."

I grab my phone off my desk and check my notifications. Disappointment hits that there are none from Savannah. Why the hell would there be? I treated her like shit. Remorse has a knot forming in my chest when I remember some of the things I said to her. My memories of that night are fuzzy from the amount of alcohol I consumed, but I can very clearly remember the hurt look on her face right before I left her in the kitchen. Every time a flash of her broken expression comes to mind, I want to jam pencils in my ears to scramble my brain and make them go away. Instead, I forced the memory to appear over and over again as a reminder of what an asshole I am. I never deserved Savannah, and my actions from that night prove it.

I draw my legs up and rest my arms on my knees. Picking at a scab on my knuckle from when I punched the wall outside Savannah's apartment building, I ask Z a question I desperately want the answer to, even though I don't deserve to know.

"How's Savannah?"

He takes so long to answer that I glance over at him. His jaw is hard and the pulse at his temple throbs.

"Not sure if I should be telling you anything about Savannah. Not with the way you treated her that night."

I drop my chin and avoid his eyes, shame making my face heat. "You're right," I respond. "I was an asshole and there's no excuse for my behavior. I was hurting and needed someone else to hurt too. I lashed out at the wrong person. I have no right to ask about her, but I am anyway. I know it doesn't seem like it, but I do care about her."

"If you do, then why haven't you tried calling her and asking *her* how she's doing?"

My head thumps against the wall, jarring my teeth. "I'm sure she's already deleted and blocked my number. And if she hasn't, she damn sure won't answer. I'm the very last person she'd want to talk to."

"You won't know if you don't try."

"I don't deserve her. I've known that from the beginning, but I was selfish and went after her anyway."

"Do you really think if Savannah felt that way, she would have gotten involved with you?"

I grit my teeth so hard my jaw aches. "She wouldn't have known better because I didn't show her the real me. She got a taste of that when we first met. She hated me because of the shit I did to Rylee. I'm no better than the man she originally thought I was."

All of a sudden, the pillow I'm leaning against is jerked out from behind me, and I thump against the wall.

"What the fuck?" I growl, sitting up to glare at my best friend.

"You are so fucking stupid," Zayden says calmly. "I'll give it to you that you have a shitty way of dealing with stress, but that doesn't make you a shitty person, Oliver."

I rub the back of my head where it banged against the wall, then sling my legs over the side of the bed. The movement has the air stirring. Shit, I really do stink.

"The only reason you say that is because you're my best friend and you have to say it."

"Stop being a fucking girl fishing for compliments."

Getting up from the bed, I glower at him as I cross the room to the tiny closet. "Fuck you, too."

"Look." He sighs and jams his fingers through his hair. "I'm not perfect either. I did shit to Rylee too last year. Do you think of me as a piece of shit?"

"Right at this moment?"

His lips twitch.

"Yes, but in general, no," I answer and turn away from him. I yank down a hoodie and a pair of jeans from their hangers.

"Do you really think you'd be my best friend for as long as you have been if I thought you weren't a good person?"

My answer is a grunt. Pulling out a pair of boxers and socks, I send them sailing across the room to the bed.

"And to answer your earlier question, Savannah's in rough shape."

I jerk around to face him, fear lodging itself in my throat. "What does that mean?" I croak.

Tossing the pillow on the bed, he crosses an ankle over his other knee.

"Relax. I just mean the shit you pulled the other night really hurt her. She's strong and tries to hide it, but she's got dark rings under her eyes, man. I don't know what all you said to her, but knowing your sharp tongue, it wasn't nice."

My gut clenches and a sharp pain stabs me in the chest. I wasn't just 'not nice', I called her fucking fat. I used the worst weapon I had because that's what I do. I hurt the ones who mean the most to me.

"Is she taking care of herself?" I voice my question through a dry throat.

When Zayden doesn't answer right away, I glance over at him. Concern draws his brows down and the look sends panic through me.

"I don't know. I haven't been around much so they can have girl time, but Rylee's concerned. Savannah's been pushing her away, opting to stay in her room most of the time when she's not in class or at work. Anytime she comes out, she acts like nothing's wrong, but Rylee says it's fake."

"I'm sure Rylee wants to maim me right about now."

Z smirks. "You're definitely on her shit list. But she knows you were hurt and lashed out because of it. It doesn't excuse your behavior, but she understands it."

I grab my clothes, along with a bottle of shampoo, and stuff everything into a gym bag. Turning, I hunt down a towel and put that in my bag as well.

"What are you going to do?"

Without looking at him, I mutter, "Nothing."

"Oliver—"

I cut him off and turn to face him. "Even if I did deserve Savannah before all this went down, I damn sure don't now. Not after what I said to her that night. Besides," I blow out a breath, "she'll never forgive me."

"You don't know that if you don't try," he says stubbornly.

"And what happens the next time something shitty happens in my life? I keep hurting her and she keeps forgiving me? That's not a healthy relationship. I won't keep doing that to her."

Before he has a chance to respond, I snatch up my bag and stalk to the door.

"I'm hitting the shower."

I leave before he can say anything else.

As much as I want to go to Savannah and beg for her forgiveness, I know I don't deserve it. I've already caused enough damage and I refuse to do anymore.

Even if that means the pesky organ in my chest feels like it's slowly being shredded by a meat grinder.

twenty-eight

SAVANNAH

"Hey, V, will you do me a favor and take this order?" Rylee pulls my attention away from where I'm restocking cups to the register. "I have to pee so bad," she says in way of explanation.

"Yeah." I nod, setting the sleeve of cups onto the countertop before heading toward her.

"Thank you." She gives my arm a squeeze, her eyebrows knitting together when she does. "Your arms are nothing but bone," she tells me, but I ignore her comment and turn my attention to the group of college kids on the other side of the register from me—proceeding to take their order.

I feel her eyes on me for a few long seconds before she turns and walks away. I know she's concerned. If I didn't feel like I was dying inside, maybe I'd be concerned too.

Things have gotten bad. Like really bad. I can't eat. I can barely sleep. And each day seems to drag on forever, like there will never be an end to the pain that's consuming me from the inside out.

I feel like a walking zombie. I have no energy. No motivation. No drive to do anything. Hell, this is the first time I've even been to work in nearly a week. I've missed just as much school too. And while I feel like it shouldn't hurt this bad—losing Oliver after a few weeks together—it does. It hurts so bad that sometimes it's all I can do to force myself out of bed.

I finish making the coffee order and I'm setting the finished drinks on the pick-up counter when Rylee comes back out of the bathroom, a damp paper towel still clenched in her hand.

"Thanks for that." She tosses the towel into the trashcan and sidles up next to me.

"Sure." I turn to go back to what I was doing, but her hand on my forearm stops me.

"V." She waits until my gaze swings to hers. "I'm worried about you."

"Me?" I ask like I don't understand why she would be. "I'm fine," I lie the same way I've done for days now.

The truth is, I'm not fine. I know it and based on how she's looking at me, she knows it too. But the last thing I want to do is talk about Oliver. In fact, I haven't so much as spoken his name out loud since the night we broke up.

I had a good cry and that's all he's getting from me. Or at least, that's what I keep telling myself, even if it's so far from the truth it's laughable.

"You look awful," she tells me point blank. "You've barely come out of your room in a week. I haven't seen you eat once during that time. Your cheekbones are sunken in and it looks like you put your eyeshadow on under your eyes—that's how dark they are."

"Wow. Thanks." I snort, not trying to hide how offended I am by her comment.

"I'm serious, V. You look like death."

"I already told you…."

"Yeah, you're fine. I got that," she cuts me off.

"What do you want from me exactly?" I snip, growing tired of this conversation.

I know she's only trying to help, and I love her for it, but right now I want to be left alone. Maybe I'm treating this situation like it's a bigger deal than it should be. Maybe I really should be fine. But I can't force myself to feel any way other than the way I feel. And right now, I feel like something in me is broken, and for the life of me I can't figure out how to piece it back together.

"I want you to talk to me. Tell me what I can do."

"Erase the last two months of my life. Think you can handle that?" I bite out in frustration.

"Why are you treating me like I'm the enemy all of a sudden?" She draws back, a little taken aback by my tone.

"I'm sorry." I blow out a slow breath, trying to calm myself. I don't know what's wrong with me all of a sudden. The last couple of days I feel like I've been hanging on by a thread. My emotions are all over the place, and I find myself having these intense bouts of anger where I want to break everything in sight.

I'm upset by what happened. Hell, I'm devastated. But something tells me this isn't only about Oliver anymore. Something is going on with me. Something I can't control. I feel like I'm losing my damn mind.

"I know you're trying to help," I continue after a long moment. "But really, Ry, I'm okay. I just need some time."

"And I totally get that. But I can't sit back and watch my best friend self-destruct and not say anything about it. You're my sister, V. If you're hurting, I'm hurting. And I want to help. But I can't if you won't talk to me."

"There's nothing to say. I let myself get carried away with a man I knew would hurt me, and that's exactly what he did. Case closed. I'll get over it."

"Will you?" She arches a brow.

"Seriously." My nostrils flare, and heat creeps up the back of my neck. "Are you implying that he's someone I can't get over?"

"I'm not implying anything. And this isn't just about Oliver. Not anymore. This is about *you*. There's something going on, and I'm not going to stand by and let it happen. Not without doing everything I can to help you."

"I don't need your help." I clench my back teeth. "And I don't want it either."

"This isn't you. Listen to yourself. Why are you so angry?"

"Maybe because you don't know when to shut up and mind your own business." I rip off my apron and shove it into her arms.

"Tell Vince I'm not feeling well." I spin on my heel and quickly exit the coffee shop.

I have no idea where I'm going, given that my shift wasn't supposed to end for another two hours, but I couldn't stay in that place another minute. I feel like I'm suffocating, and no matter where I am, the weight on my chest continues to get heavier and heavier.

I rub my hands up and down my arms, wishing I had thought to grab my coat before storming out. Then again, I haven't thought many things through as of late.

I have just rounded the corner when my cell phone springs to life in the back pocket of my jeans. I ignore it, figuring it's probably Rylee.

I know she's only trying to help, but right now I need to handle this on my own. I wish she could understand that.

Eventually, my phone stops ringing, only to start ringing again seconds later. Letting out an audible groan, I reach into my back pocket and pull the device out, seeing my mom's name flashing across the screen.

I consider answering it. Maybe talking to my mom will help. Then again, I doubt it would. It would take her two seconds to pick up that something was wrong and then she'd worry, and right now, I don't need that on my plate too.

Even though it's been days since I've spoken to her, I send the call to voicemail and take the next right, heading toward my apartment building. I'm less than a block away when I start to feel a little woozy and have to stop and lean on a lamp post for support.

Shaking my head, I try to right myself, but the ground still ends up going sideways. Hanging onto the post, I'm somehow able to keep myself in a standing position. Panic grips at my chest at the realization that something is really wrong.

Grabbing my phone, I fumble with the screen as I punch in Rylee's number. It rings four times before her voicemail picks up.

Hitting end, I scroll through my contacts to find the number to the coffee shop, which is easier said than done because of the little white lines that have suddenly started dancing in front of my vision. My stomach twists and my knees shake beneath my weight.

Finally able to locate the number, I click on the contact and press the device to my ear. It rings only once before Rylee's voice comes on the line.

"Ry," I croak before she can get through her normal greeting.

"V?"

"Something's wrong," I tell her, tears welling in my eyes.

"What? Where are you?"

"On the corner of Shaker and Vine. Everything is off balance and there's something wrong with my vision." My voice shakes. "I'm scared."

"Stay there. I'm on my way." The phone line goes dead.

Fearing I might actually pass out, I carefully make my way to the far side of the sidewalk where I can press my back against the wall of a small boutique shop that Rylee and I have shopped in a few times. My back scrapes the brick as I slowly lower myself to the ground.

I pull my knees into my chest and take a few deep breaths, feeling slightly better now that I'm not standing.

I blink, and the spots in my vision also start to clear.

Relief floods through me.

Here I thought I was about to die and turns out I was probably just having a panic attack or something.

I've barely had time to process the thought when Rylee rounds the corner in a full-on sprint. She slows when she reaches me, crouching down to assess me as she tries to catch her breath.

"Are you okay? What's going on?" She pants, concern clear on her face.

"I'm okay," I tell her calmly. "I think I was on the verge of having a panic attack," I admit, honestly a little embarrassed.

"A panic attack?" She dips down lower, her eyes darting across every inch of my face. "You're really pale," she observes. "Come on, let's get you home." She straightens, leaning down to take my hands.

"Vince is going to end up firing us both." I silently curse myself for calling her when I should have let the moment ride out.

"Vince will get over it."

"I'm sorry about earlier too," I tell her. "I didn't mean…."

"You don't have to apologize. I know you're having a rough time right now. And I'm sorry I pushed." She tightens her grip on my hands and angles her body a step back to give her the leverage to hoist me up.

As soon as I'm upright again, the dizziness returns with a vengeance. I reach out and grab Rylee's shoulder to steady myself.

"Whoa." She grips my biceps. "V, what's going on?" She sounds distant, like she's talking through a tunnel.

"I don't…." My words die on my lips.

One minute, I'm standing upright with Rylee right in front of me. The next, everything blurs. It's the strangest sensation. Almost like being in a dream, but not in a dream at all. I feel my weight give. Feel the air swirl around me as I fall. Feel the impact of the ground as my body crumbles to the pavement. And then everything goes black.

twenty-nine

OLIVER

My tires squeal when I turn into the emergency room parking lot and search for an empty spot. Gritting my teeth when I can't find one, I decide to park under the overhang in the drop off section—uncaring about the ticket I'll no doubt end up with—when I see a car backing up out of a spot. I snag it before anyone else can. I barely turn the ignition off before I throw open my door. As I sprint across the parking lot, my heart pounding so hard I feel it in my ears, I recall the phone call I got fifteen minutes ago.

"You need to get to the hospital. Savannah's been admitted," Zayden says, his voice grave.

"What?" I shouted, jerking up from my desk chair. "What the hell happened? Is she okay?"

"She collapsed. Rylee was with her when it happened and called an ambulance. That's all I know."

"Fuck!" I spun around and snatched my keys and wallet from my desk before I bolted toward the door. "I'm on my way."

Zayden's grave tone as he told me Savannah had been admitted into the hospital will forever haunt me. It's only been fifteen minutes since we hung up, but it feels like many long and torturous hours.

The sliding glass doors are barely open wide enough for me to shoulder through them before I'm rushing inside. My eyes immediately locate the reception desk.

"Oliver!" someone shouts my name when I'm only a few feet away.

Spinning around, I find Zayden jogging over. Rylee's right behind him. My stomach drops when I notice her puffy eyes and red splotchy cheeks. She's been crying.

"What happened?" I manage to get out through the huge lump in my throat.

Zayden wraps an arm around Rylee and tugs her close.

"We were at work," Rylee starts, then pauses to clear her throat. "She was acting strange, very temperamental. We had a slight disagreement and she stormed out of the coffee shop." Her bottom lip begins to wobble. "A few minutes later, she called the shop and said she thought something was wrong. I rushed out to check on her and found her a block away. She looked so pale. When I tried to help her to stand to take her home, she collapsed. She just went down like a ton of bricks, and I couldn't get her to wake up."

Zayden pulls Rylee to his chest and kisses the top of her head when tears begin to slide down her cheeks.

My chest constricts, robbing me of breath.

"What have the doctors said? How long has she been back there?"

"She hasn't been back there long, and they haven't told us anything."

I fist my hands and shove them into my pockets before I do something that may get me kicked out of the hospital. Like throw my fist through a wall. She hasn't been here long, so I'm sure they don't know anything yet, but damned if I don't want to demand answers right this minute.

"How has she been the last few days?" I ask Rylee, assuming she's been around her more than anyone else.

"Distant. Closed off." She wipes her nose with the sleeve of her jacket. "She hasn't been eating," she adds quietly.

"Fuck," I mutter, spinning away from them.

Guilt burns like a blazing ball of fire going down my throat knowing my words from that night might be the reason Savannah's in the hospital. According to Rylee, Savannah's had eating issues for a while, but I thought she was getting better. Rylee even said she thought the same thing. I have no doubt in my mind that my hateful words that night didn't help the situation. I don't think either of us truly bought the ulcer story, and yet when I had the chance to push, I didn't.

I tip my head back and close my eyes, taking in a deep breath and letting it out on a silent prayer to the man above.

Please let her be okay.

When I drop my head and open my eyes, I look across the room. I spot Savannah's mom and dad standing in a quiet corner with Evelyn and none other than my father/uncle—*Paul.*

The need to hurt something—or someone—is almost overwhelming. I hate that he's here when he's the reason why I went off the rails that night.

"You need to let your anger go, Oliver."

Clenching my jaw, I look down at Rylee, who's come to stand beside me. "I'm not sure if I know how to."

Her hand is warm when she reaches down to grab mine.

"You need to figure it out. I understand you're angry with him—you have every right to be. I don't know Paul like you do, but I like to think I've gotten to know him some over the time I lived in your house. I don't see him as being purposely malicious." She squeezes my hand before letting it go. "People make mistakes all the time. Sometimes those mistakes are made with the best of intentions. But you can't let what he did affect your life. You need to let it go." She moves so she's standing in front of me, her eyes filled with sadness. "Savannah told me some of the stuff you said to her, but I know it wasn't true. You care for her deeply. I'm afraid if you don't let go of what Paul and your mom did, you'll be in a never-ending cycle of hurt and pain. Which isn't what Savannah needs."

After she walks away, I follow her and Z to the waiting area. I take a seat as far away from the others as I can. With my head in my hands, I repeat Rylee's words over and over in my head.

I know she's right. Paul may have been a shitty father and his decision to keep my parentage a secret was wrong, but in the grand scheme of things, my childhood could have been worse. I may not have gotten the love and affection a child should get from their father, but at least he was there. He provided for me and gave me anything I asked of him. The few times he did act like a loving father, he did so wholeheartedly. He did that when he didn't have to. He could have divorced my mother and threw us both out on our asses. Instead, he stayed with a woman he hated. And he said he did it out of love for me. I don't know if that's true, but I know he wouldn't have done it if he didn't at least care. Paul doesn't do anything he doesn't want to do.

I don't know how long I sit there contemplating on my problems regarding my father when someone takes the seat beside me.

"How are you holding up?"

I glance up and meet Silas Reynolds' tired eyes.

"Could be better."

He nods. "I bet that can be said for all of us."

I grunt and look down at my clasped hands dangling between my knees.

"Our Savannah's a strong girl. Whatever's ailing her won't keep her down."

I nod my agreement, unable to look into his eyes anymore. If he knew my role in her being here, I'm sure he'd be dragging me out by the scruff of my jacket before beating my ass into the concrete.

We both jump up when the double doors leading to the back open and a doctor walks out. Everyone in the waiting room follows suit.

"The Reynolds family?" the older doctor calls.

Nora and Silas approach him with the rest of us trailing behind.

"I'm Dr. Novak. I was the one who assessed Miss Reynolds when she was brought in."

"How is she?" Nora asks, her voice trembling.

"She's stable, but she was very malnourished. My main concerns are her low electrolytes and kidney function, which aren't working at full compacity. With those two issues, if the problem isn't taken care of, we could be looking at kidney failure. We've done an electrocardiogram and an echocardiogram. Her heart is fine at the moment, but that can change with this type of illness."

"I don't understand. What illness? What's wrong with her kidneys? And how can this affect her heart?"

The doctor's eyes soften when they meet Nora's. "Mrs. Reynolds, your daughter is suffering from an eating disorder called bulimia nervosa. This type of illness weakens the body because it's being starved of the nutrients it needs to survive."

She clutches her chest and Silas wraps a comforting arm around her. Beside me, Rylee hiccoughs on a sob. My own chest feels like someone punched through my sternum and is squeezing the life out of my heart.

Bulimia nervosa.

I don't know much about the disorder, but I know it has to do with eating and then forcing yourself to vomit the food back up.

"Bulimia?" Nora croaks. "How in the world could we have not known about this? I noticed she was losing a lot of weight, but I thought it was the stress from school and being out on her own. I never…." She shakes her head, tears sliding down her cheeks. "My poor baby."

"Many people who suffer from eating disorders tend to hide it from those around them," Dr. Novak explains. "If they don't want you to know, you won't. At least not until it gets so bad they can no longer hide it. She's resting now," he continues. "The next several months are going to be a struggle for her. For now, we've got her on an IV to bring up her electrolytes, which should increase her kidney function. We'll keep a close eye on it. I'd like to keep her here for a few days to monitor her. We have a psychiatrist and a nutritionist I'd like for Savannah to speak with as well."

"Thank you, doctor," Silas states gruffly. "When can we see her?"

"Give the nurses a few minutes, and one will come get you. I'd like to limit visitors to only two for the first day. She's not only been through something physically taxing, but it's also been highly emotional. We don't want to overwhelm her. If you have any questions for me, let one of the nurses know and they'll hunt me down."

After the doctor leaves, I turn away from the group. My whole fucking body sags. Relief that the situation wasn't worse than it could have been, worry that Savannah won't accept the help she needs, and guilt that we didn't notice how serious her condition was until now eats away at me.

Finding a dark corner, I slide down the wall and bury my face against my knees.

SEVERAL HOURS LATER, I quietly crack open the door to Savannah's room. My heart is in my throat and it's damn near choking me.

I was surprised when Nora came to me a few minutes ago and asked if I wanted to go see Savannah. I wasn't going to ask, because as much as I want to see her, I don't really deserve it. Not after saying the things I did to her and being one of the reasons she's in the hospital. Nora and Silas don't know that, though. They don't even know we broke up. Apparently, neither Savannah nor Rylee told them. I'm sure if they knew what transpired between us, they would have never let me near their daughter again.

Rylee told me Savannah was awake when she left her a few minutes ago, so I'm nervous. I have no idea how Savannah will react to me being here.

She's facing away from the door as she lays on her side and stares out the window. Her blonde hair is spread out on her pillow behind her. She looks so fucking tiny in the bed. It's not until this moment, looking at her slender arm lying limply over her waist, that I realize just how small she is. I knew she lost a lot of weight over the last few months, but she's practically skin and bones.

Another wave of guilt slams into me. I hate myself for the part I played in her being this way, and for not realizing what was going on with her.

My shoes squeak on the floor, drawing her attention. She turns her head slowly toward me. The sharp plains of her cheekbones and the sunken appearance of her eyes gut me.

"Hey," I say gently, taking a few steps closer to her.

She watches me, showing no emotion at all. "What are you doing here?" she asks, her voice dead.

"I was worried about you."

Her eyes roll and she lets out a soft snort. "You have to care about someone in order to worry about them. All you care about is yourself."

"I do care about you, Savannah."

"The only thing about me you cared about was what I could give you and how good it made you feel."

Stuffing my hands into my pockets, I venture a step closer, but the look Savannah shoots me has me stopping.

"What I said that night, that was a lie. I was in a shitty place and lashed out. I'm sorry."

"And so you wanted to drag me into your shitty place? To make me suffer right along with you?" She turns to face the window again. "How very nice of you," she says snidely.

I deserve every bit of anger and resentment she sends my way. It's no worse than the hatred I feel for myself.

"Savannah—"

"Just leave, please. I don't want you here."

I don't want to leave. I want to plant my ass in the chair by the bed and stay there for as long as she's here. I made her suffer when I was going through bad shit. I need to be beside her as she navigates her own issues, enduring every bit of pain she's going through.

But I won't because I get the sense my being here is making it worse. And that's the last thing I want. I've hurt her enough already.

I look at her for several more seconds, taking in her frail form. She may look sick and unhealthy, but she's still the most beautiful woman I've ever seen.

"I'll leave for now because that's what you need," I tell her quietly. "But I won't be gone long. I know you hate me and think I don't care about you—both with good reason. But I'll prove to you that you're wrong on both counts, especially the last one."

She doesn't say anything, doesn't even acknowledge my words, so I turn around and leave her room, softly closing the door behind me.

It's been forty-eight hours since Savannah was admitted into the hospital. Forty-eight hours of torture for everyone who cares for her. I haven't left the hospital since I walked in two days ago, frantic for answers. Neither have Nora and Silas, until about an hour ago, when they decided to go home to shower and change. Rylee and Zayden have gone home each night to get a few hours of sleep, but they've been back each morning. Paul and Evelyn left a couple of hours after hearing the news of her condition, but Evelyn's called Rylee several times for updates. To say we're all stressed is putting it mildly.

Thankfully, the doctor just left with some good news. Her electrolytes have come up and her kidney function has improved. She's still not all the way out of the woods, but he's hopeful she'll be ready to leave in a few days. The question is, where will she go once she's discharged. Nora and Silas, at the request from the doctor, want her to check into a rehab facility, but Savannah's reluctant. She realizes she needs the help and wants it but hates the idea of being "locked away"—as Savannah puts it—in a medical facility.

Luckily, according to Rylee, she's been in a fairly good mood, considering everything going on.

It's been difficult, but I haven't been back to see her since she told me to leave two days ago. It's a good thing Rylee's kept me updated, or I might have forced my way back inside her room. As it is, I'm getting ready to head back up there now. I've given her time. Now it's time to remind her that I'm still here and not going anywhere.

"Oliver."

I stop and turn around, gritting my teeth as Paul and Evelyn walk toward me.

"I thought you guys were at home," I say, attempting to keep my voice calm, but knowing I'm doing a shit job of it.

Evelyn smiles. "We wanted to stop by and check up on Savannah." She holds up a bag. "I wanted to bring her a few things."

Kissing Evelyn's cheek, my father asks, "Why don't you go on up while I speak with Oliver?"

After he watches her walk away, Paul turns to face me. I really don't want to do this right now. I've got more important things on my mind—like wondering if Savannah is going to kick me out of her room again. But I also don't want to make a scene in the hospital and take the chance of being booted out.

"How are you?" His voice is low.

"How do you think?" I ask bluntly, then silently curse myself.

Calm your shit, Oliver.

He nods. "You're right. Stupid question. I know you care for Savannah, so I'm sure this is hard on you."

It's strange seeing him like this. So uncertain, and if I'm not mistaken, nervous.

"Have you been home yet, or have you been up here the entire time?"

I lean against the wall behind me and cross my arms over my chest. "I'm not leaving here until she can."

He nods again, as if he understands. "Evelyn and I can stop by your dorm and grab you some clothes. The cafeteria food is always horrible in hospitals, so we can grab you some food too."

"Zayden's already brought me some clothes, and I ate not long ago." I look directly at him. "Just stop, okay? I've lived for nineteen years without a concerned father. There's no sense trying now. Especially since you're *not* my father."

"I'll always be your father, Oliver. Not only does your birth certificate say so, but *I* say so. I don't give a shit if you're not biologically mine. The question is, are you okay with that?"

That is the fucking question, isn't it?

Blowing out a breath, I give him the only answer I have right now. "I don't know. I need time to think and come to grips with everything. When I have an answer, I'll let you know."

"I can live with that."

Evelyn comes back out a few minutes later, and her and my father leave shortly after. I take the elevator up to the third floor. My palms sweat as I approach Savannah's room. The door is open, and I look around the frame before I step inside to make sure there are no doctors in with her. She's alone, the TV mounted on the wall in front of her turned on, the volume down low. She has a tray of food in front of her, and I watch as she spoons something and brings it to her mouth. She's on a special diet to help keep her electrolytes up. Relief hits as I watch her take another bite.

Her head jerks my way when I enter the room, and her expression falls when she notices it's me.

"How are you feeling?" I ask, approaching her slowly.

Her lip curls up into a sneer. "I was fine until you showed up. Now I feel like I might throw up."

My face pales and my stomach bottoms out.

Noticing my expression, she rolls her eyes back to her food. "Oh, relax. I'm not going to puke. But you might want to leave before I put too much *meat on my bones*."

I flinch, her words hitting me harder than any punch could.

"Why are you here?" she demands, shoving part of a banana into her mouth.

I'll take any abuse she sends my way, so long as she continues to eat.

"I told you I wasn't leaving," I remind her.

"Well, you should. You're not wanted here. Why don't you go call that something better you said you were going to find the other night?"

A vague memory of me telling Savannah I was done with her and was going to search out someone else flashes in my mind. My close friend named "guilt" makes another appearance.

"I never looked, and I had no intentions of doing so. I only said that to hurt you, and it's another thing to add to the growing list of things I'm sorry for."

"Well, you did a bang-up job of hurting me. Congratulations on that. You said your apologies, and I don't accept them, so you can leave now."

Instead of doing what she requests, I snag a chair with my foot and pull it toward me. Facing the TV, I plop down in the seat.

"What are you doing?" she asks.

I gesture toward the TV with my chin. "Watching *Gilligan's Island*."

"I don't want you in here."

Keeping my eyes on the TV, I say, "We don't always get what we want."

"Clearly," she says dryly. A moment later, she sighs. "Don't make me call a nurse in here and have you escorted out."

Her words give me pause, but only for a moment. I decide to test her statement and her willpower against me.

Ignoring her warning, I prop my feet up on the end of her bed and get comfortable.

She growls, and the sound brings a tiny smile to my face. Of course, I hide it from her. No need to poke the bear, not when I need to tame her first.

"Whatever," she mutters. "I'm going to sleep. Turn the TV off when you leave."

My smile grows when the lights above her bed flick off, and I hear her blankets ruffling behind me.

It may take time, but I'm a stubborn son-of-a-bitch when it comes to things I care about. I've known for a while that I'm in love with Savannah.

And before it's all said and done, *she'll* know and believe I love her.

I won't accept anything less.

thirty

SAVANNAH

"How's she doing?" I stir at the sound of Rylee's voice, the hospital room door snapping closed seconds later.

"She's been sleeping for a while." My stomach twists when it's Oliver's voice I hear next.

I don't know why I'm surprised that he's still here, but I am. I thought for sure he'd have left. Then again, he said he wasn't going to, and I haven't known him to be someone who doesn't do exactly what he says he's going to. He's hard headed like that. That much I know to be true about him.

"Does she know you're in here?" she asks.

"Yeah, though she threatened to have a nurse escort me out."

"A lot of good that did her, I see." I hear the smile in my best friend's voice.

"You know me. You can't get rid of me that easily."

Even though I'm tempted to roll over and demand that he leave, just to prove a point, I don't move. I keep my eyes closed and do my best to remain as still as possible while I listen to the two of them talk.

"She still isn't talking to you, I take it?"

"You mean other than telling me to leave? No. She's pretty stubborn."

"Well isn't that the pot calling the kettle black."

"I guess I can't argue with you there."

I hear footsteps shuffle against the tiled floor. "Just give her some time. I'm sure she'll come around," Rylee reassures him.

"Will she?" I hear the uncertainty in Oliver's voice, and it seems misplaced. I've never known him to be uncertain about anything.

"She's been through a lot."

"Thanks to me."

"You didn't do this to her, Oliver. This has been going on far longer than that. If anything, this is my fault." A pang of guilt slides through my chest. I hate that anyone feels responsible for what I put my own body through. "I should have seen the signs sooner. I should have pushed harder when she started making excuses. I knew something wasn't right, but I was trying to find a balance between being a good friend and completely overstepping."

"Why would she do this to herself?" Oliver asks.

"I wish I knew." Rylee blows out a breath. "She's always struggled with body image issues. She's never been able to see what we all see—how beautiful she is."

"I just can't help but feel like I made this so much worse."

"Well, you certainly didn't help matters. I'm not going to sugar coat it for you and say you played no factor. But Savannah was on this path well before you came along. I think it was only a matter of time before it peaked. Honestly, I'm just glad it's all out there, and now she can get the help she needs."

"Why do you think she didn't tell us? She had to know there was a problem."

"I think she was embarrassed. Wouldn't you be?"

"I guess." Even though I can't see him, I can imagine the rise of his broad shoulders as he shrugs. "She didn't give me the option to help her then, but I really wish she'd let me help her now."

"V is as hard headed as they come. She isn't going to forgive you that easily."

"I know. I just wish I could find a way to make her see…." His words fade off.

"Make her see what?" Rylee asks after several beats of silence filter between the two. "That you're in love with her."

I swear my heart kicks against my ribs so hard that it's nearly impossible to remain still.

"I am."

My heart kicks again, pounding so hard in my chest that the sound resonates in my ears.

"Have you told her?"

"No."

"Why not?"

"Because I don't want her to think I'm only saying it because she's here, lying in a hospital bed."

"Maybe that's exactly why you should say it. She needs us right now. She needs to know that she's loved and supported. And Oliver, she loves you. For the life of me, I can't figure out how you managed to get her there after how much she hated you, but you did. She loves you and you treating her the way you did, you walking away from her, it destroyed her. Even when she tried to act like she was okay, I could see it. She wasn't okay."

"Are you trying to make me feel fucking worse?" he grumbles.

"Of course not. I'm trying to make you see how much you mean to her. And clearly, she means a lot to you."

"She means everything."

"And there's my point. We don't get a guaranteed number of days on this Earth. You can't wait for the right time to say you love someone. You have to tell them every chance you get, because you never know what tomorrow will bring."

"But what if after I tell her, she still wants nothing to do with me?"

"Since when have you ever rolled over and accepted something so easily?" The smile in Rylee's voice is obvious.

Oliver lets out a soft grunt.

"If you two would stop self-destructing, maybe you could actually find some semblance of happiness. Lord knows after everything, you both deserve it."

"Do I?" Oliver croaks, his voice strained. "Do I deserve it?"

"Oliver, everyone deserves to be happy."

Tears begin to build behind my eyes, but I keep my lids pressed closed. As angry as I am with him for the way he treated me, at the end of the day I know why he did it. He was hurting. He was angry. And I was an easy target. And while that's not an acceptable excuse, for the first time since everything went down, I'm starting to realize how much he regrets it.

I'm not innocent either. I pushed him away at times. I kept secrets. I never truly allowed myself to be whole with him, instead choosing to give him little pieces of what I thought he wanted to see.

"After everything, I'm not sure that's true. Think about it, Rylee. I've been doing shit like this my entire life. Hurting the people I care the most about. Acting out when shit goes south. Sabotaging my own happiness for reasons I can't even begin to understand."

"Then maybe it's time to break the cycle." She pauses. "And you can start by being honest with V."

"And when she tells me to go fuck myself?"

"She won't." I hear the sound of soft footsteps padding across the room before the door opens.

"Where are you going?" Oliver asks.

"I'm going to go find Zayden. I'll be back in a little bit."

"Okay," Oliver says, the door snapping closed seconds later.

The room goes silent.

I'm not sure what to do. On one hand, I could roll over and he would know that I listened to their entire conversation. On the other, I don't want that to be the way he tells me. If he loves me like he says he does, then I need to hear him say it to me and not to another person.

It's torture. Lying so still, when all I want to do is crawl out of this bed and throw myself into his arms.

I'm not sure how much time passes. But I listen to the tick of the clock on the wall as the seconds pass and the low hum of the television as my mind swirls around everything Oliver said to Rylee.

He loves me....

He loves me?

It shouldn't even be a question, should it?

If you take away what happened last week, things between us

have been amazing. The way he touches me, like he can't get enough of me. The way he holds me, like he only wants to be near me. The way he seems to show up every time I turn around, simply because he misses me.

Deep down, I think I've known how he feels about me for a while. It just took until this moment for me to realize how true it is. And not because of his words—because of his actions.

My life is a mess right now. An utter fucking mess. But one thing remains true when everything else in my life is uncertain—I'm in love with Oliver Conley. And I don't want another moment to pass without telling him so. Like Rylee said, tomorrow is not guaranteed. We have to tell the people we care about that we love them, and we have to do it every chance we get, because we don't know how long we'll get to do it for.

I roll to my back, my eyes connecting with Oliver's the instant I look his way.

"Hey." He smiles softly.

"Hey," I push out past my dry throat.

"You sleep okay?" He still seems hesitant. Given that our last conversation revolved around me telling him to get out, I guess I can understand why.

"Yeah." I scoot up, propping some pillows behind me so that I'm sitting in an upright position. "This isn't your fault," I blurt, knotting my hands in front of myself. He shifts the chair so that he's facing me, and even though I can tell he wants to say something, he lets me continue without interruption. "I know you think it is. And while yes, you have made some comments over the last few months that did not help this situation," I watch him wince, "you didn't cause this. The truth is, I've been struggling with this disease since I was fifteen."

I have no idea why I'm telling him all this. In a way, I think I just need to say it out loud.

"I had just started dating my first boyfriend—Hunter. I was gaga over him in the way that only a young teenager can be. One day after school we went back to my house. My parents weren't home, and we started fooling around."

His fists clench and the thought brings a touch of a small smile to my lips. Even hearing me retell something that happened years ago with another guy seems to put him on edge.

"He took my shirt off, and as he looked down at me, he did something, something that shouldn't have been that big of a deal, but for some reason to me, it was. He pinched the fat on my stomach. I tried to play it off like he was trying to be funny, but it ate at me for days. Then, a few days later, I overheard him telling one of his friends that he was thinking about breaking up with me, because I was too thick for his taste. I don't know how to explain it. Something in me snapped. It was innocent enough at first. I'd go a full day without eating, or I'd let myself eat only once a day. I did that for years. Sometimes it would get better. Sometimes it would get worse. But as I got older, it became harder to not eat. People noticed. One day, after binging on way too much pizza with Rylee, I decided to try another tactic. I made myself get sick. And the weird thing is, it felt good. It felt good to eat whatever I wanted and expel it later so there was no guilt. I never intended for it to go as far as it did. I didn't want any of this. But it became a bigger problem than I could control. Eventually, I didn't need to make myself sick anymore, because every time I would eat, my body would do it for me."

"The first time we met—I made a comment about your weight." He leans forward in the chair, resting his elbows on his knees.

"You did." I nod. "But this problem was already in full swing. You didn't cause this. You have to know that."

"No, but I sure as hell didn't make it any better either."

"Sometimes you did." I give him a soft smile. "Sometimes you would look at me, and I don't know, I felt beautiful—comfortable in my own skin in a way I never had before."

"Because you *are* beautiful." In a matter of seconds, he's out of the chair and sitting on the side of the hospital bed, his warm fingers wrapping around mine. "You are the most beautiful woman

I've ever met, Savannah. Even when I hated you, I couldn't deny my body's reaction to you."

I bite down on my bottom lip to keep my smile at bay.

"I tried to stop. You made me want to stop. But I couldn't at that point." I clear my throat. "I just need you to know, to understand, that you didn't put me here. This is all on me."

"So, what now? Are you going to do the treatment?"

"I don't want to," I admit.

"I think you should." His gorgeous eyes remain focused on mine. "This isn't only about what you eat, it's also about how you view yourself. You need to start seeing yourself the way I see you. Because if you did, you'd never feel the need to change what you look like. You'd know without a doubt just how beautiful you are—and not only on the outside."

"I'm scared," I admit, my chin quivering slightly.

"You don't have to be scared. You are the strongest person I know, Savannah Reynolds. And you won't have to do this alone. You have your parents, Rylee and Zayden, and everyone else who loves you who will be right by your side."

"Does that include you?" I ask, my voice catching.

"Do you want it to include me?" His expression is hopeful.

"I do," I admit after a long moment.

"Does that mean you forgive me? Because I am sorry. I'm so fucking sorry. For all of it. I didn't mean any of it. I don't even know why I said what I said. I was hurting and I wanted you to hurt too. I know it's fucked up and unforgivable, but I'm hoping you'll give me a chance to fix this. To fix us."

"On one condition." I hold up a finger. "You promise me that the next time you feel like the world is caving in on you, you let me help shoulder some of that weight instead of making me the enemy."

"That's a promise."

"Then I forgive you."

"V." He scoots in closer. "You're going to get through this. And I'm going to be here every step of the way. Because I want you to get better. No, I *need* you to get better. Because I don't want to live this life without you. I never thought I'd meet someone who would completely upend my life in the best fucking way. But then here you came, with your spicy attitude and your sharp tongue. And I knew pretty early on that I was in trouble. I love you, Savannah Reynolds. I love you so fucking much."

I swear, it feels like my entire body levitates off the bed—like I'm about to float away on a cloud. I feel weightless. And even though I heard him tell Rylee he loved me, it wasn't the same as hearing him say it directly to me. His hand is warm on mine. His expression vulnerable and open in a way I've never seen before. It only reaffirms my own feelings.

"I love you so fucking much too," I repeat his words back to him, not missing the smile that slides across his mouth as he leans in and presses his lips to mine.

It's gentle and brief, but it still makes my entire body heat like I've stepped into a boiler room.

"Promise me you'll get the treatment," he murmurs, dropping his forehead to mine.

"I'll get the treatment," I concede, knowing he's right. I have to do this the right way if I have any hopes of beating this illness—both mentally and physically.

"I love you." He pulls back, tipping my chin up with his index finger.

"I love you."

"Say it again."

"I love you," I repeat.

"Again."

"I love you." I try not to smile but fail miserably.

"Again."

"Oh my God." I drop my head back on a laugh. "I love you, okay?"

"I'm sorry. I never thought I'd hear you say those words. I just needed you to repeat them a few times so I could make sure this is real—that I'm not dreaming."

I wrap my hands around the back of his neck and pull him in close.

"This is real. You are not dreaming. And I love you, Oliver Conley."

"And I love you." He presses another kiss to my lips.

I don't know what the future holds or where we go from here, but I do know that I don't want to do any of this without Oliver. Yes, he can be selfish and crass, and he has a temper that tends to get him into trouble. But he's also protective and sweet and funny and so many other amazing things that I can't list off the top of my head.

He's far from perfect, and so am I. But together we make sense. In some weird way, I think we always have.

epilogue

OLIVER
Six Months Later....

Tipping the beer bottle to my lips, I smile around the rim as I watch Savannah and Dani, Z's sister, gush over the engagement ring Z gave Rylee last night. The three squeal like little girls before crushing each other as they hug.

"You know this is going to go badly for you, right?" Z remarks from beside me, his voice holding a hint of mirth.

I shrug. "Not really."

"Now that I've asked Rylee to marry me, Savannah's going to want the same."

"I know." I slide my eyes to him and give him a knowing look.

He arches a brow. "You sure you're ready for something like that?"

"Not right this minute. I'd like to wait until after we graduate, but yes. I've never been more sure that I want to spend the rest of my life with her."

"Never thought I'd see the day when you and Savannah would get along, let alone hear you say you want to marry her." He chuckles. "For a while there, I thought I was going to have to bury a body somewhere."

I grunt, but he's right. Savannah and my relationship started out brutal. On more than one occasion, I wanted to wrap my hands around her pretty little neck and squeeze until she couldn't spew her hate at me anymore. And I'm sure she's mentally kicked my balls quite a few times.

Now, I still want to wrap my hands around her neck, but in a much more enjoyable way.

I look around the backyard of my childhood home. My eyes land on my father and Evelyn speaking with Nora and Silas. All four have a beer in their hand and the conversation they are having must be amusing, because Evelyn and Nora are both laughing.

My relationship with Paul never went back to normal. That's not to say our relationship will never be mended. It's also not to say I've completely forgiven him. Our relationship now is… *complicated*. He's changed over the last six months. More involved in my life; calling me regularly and asking how school and my life are going. He even calls just to chat, which kinda freaked me out the first couple of times. He's acting how a true father should act. I don't completely trust the change yet, but I'm working on it.

I've spoken with my mother a few times. Our relationship is more strained. What my father did hurt, but what my mother did hurt even more. Her and Benjamin came for another visit a couple of months ago. With Savannah's pleading, I agreed to meet with them for lunch. In which I found out that Benjamin did know about me, but felt it was best he not seek me out so Paul and Maria could work things out between them. It was a stressful hour, to say the least. I told them both, that while Paul may not have been a perfect father, he is *still* my father. I'd get to know Benjamin as my uncle, but I'll never view him as my father.

"Life's pretty good for you boys, isn't it?"

I glance over at Allen, Z's dad.

"Damn straight, it is," Z answers.

"Congrats on the engagement, son," Allen says, slapping Z on the back. "You picked a good girl to latch yourself to."

Z smiles proudly. "The best."

"You gonna wait until you graduate to get married?"

"Fuck no, I'm not waiting that long. I'll marry her as soon as she'll let me."

Chuckling, Allen turns to me. "So, when are you going to pop the question to Savannah?"

A small smile tugs at my lips. "Soon."

I already have the ring hidden away in my and Savannah's apartment. I'm just waiting on the perfect time to ask.

I moved out of the dorm a month ago and moved in with Savannah, since Rylee and Z now have a place of their own. It seemed like the logical thing to do, since I was there all the time, anyway.

"Can't believe both my boys want to get married."

"You better believe it, old man."

"You getting married so young I can handle, but you better not give me any grandbabies until you've graduated and got a steady job." He points his beer bottle to Z.

"You got it."

"That goes for you too, Oliver," he warns, shooting a glare my way.

"No worries. As much as I'd love to have kids with Savannah, I'm not ready to share her yet."

My eyes move to Savannah as she loads a couple of plates full of food from the picnic table my father set up. An image of her with a round belly full of our baby flashes through my mind. I may not be ready to share her yet, but I'm definitely looking forward to sharing that part of our life together.

As if sensing my thoughts are on her, she looks up after setting the plates down. She smiles and starts walking my way.

"Hi," she says, stopping right in front of me.

"Hey."

I wrap both arms around her and pull her flush to my chest. Dipping down, I plant a kiss on her lips.

Savannah has gained weight over the last six months. Healthy weight, and it looks damn good on her.

Once she left the hospital after her collapse, she entered rehab. The first couple of weeks were tough on her. She hated being there, but knew it was where she needed to be. She was there for six weeks, and it was a trying time. Family and friends could only visit once a week, on Saturdays. I was there, along with Rylee, Zayden, and her parents every single one of those Saturdays. It was amazing to see the transformation in her at our weekly visits. By the end of the six weeks, it was like she was a whole new person. Her face was fuller, her arms and legs weren't skin and bones, her ribs and hip bones no longer protruded. And her ass and tits.... Let's just say, they've become my new favorite parts of her.

Speaking of her ass, I grab a handful of it and give a squeeze.

"You having fun?"

"I am." She nods. "And this weather is amazing. I might have to take a dip in the pool later." Her eyes turn hooded. "Maybe you can join me."

My dick goes from soft to semi in three seconds flat. "I'll definitely join you."

Savannah left rehab not only *looking* healthier, but she also left seeing herself differently. I know she still struggles every so often—her doctor said she'll always battle poor self-image—but with the right support system and motivation, she can overcome those struggles. I've caught her looking at herself in the mirror a couple of times, a frown creasing her brow. Those times, I held my breath and sent up a silent prayer. But every time, after a couple of minutes of self-analyzing, the frown disappears from her face and she smiles, repeating something her therapist taught her to say to herself when she doubted her appearance.

"I am beautiful just the way I am."

I am so proud of her in those moments. She doesn't realize the strength she has, but the people around her do.

Lifting to her tippy toes, she pecks my lips before stepping out of my arms. She reaches for my hand. "Come on. I'm starving."

I grin as she leads me over to the table where she left our plates. She sits the proper way at the picnic table, while I straddle it facing her. I always use every opportunity presented to me to look at Savannah. This is just another one. She's called me a creeper on numerous occasions because of it.

Rolling her eyes because she knows what I'm doing, she picks up her burger and takes a big bite. Now that she's not watching what she eats and no longer has the urge to puke it back up, my girl can put away some food.

I grab my own burger and begin scarfing it down.

Z and Rylee take a seat across from us.

"Oliver and I are hitting the pool later. You and Zayden should join us."

I narrow my eyes at the side of her face. Her lips twitch around her bite of food and she gives me the side-eye.

"The pool was supposed to be ours," I grumble. But an idea pops in my head, and a slow smile slides across my face. "But they're more than welcome to join us. Could be interesting."

"No!" Savannah and Rylee shout at the same time."

Z and I laugh, enjoying the red coating both of their cheeks as we all remember the time we got off to the sounds of the other through the wall.

Dani comes running up to our table, stopping just shy of hitting the end. "Daddy said me and my friend Samantha can go swimming after we eat and our food settles. Want to come with us?"

I groan and drop my forehead to Savannah's shoulder. It shakes with her laughter.

"We were already planning on swimming," Z tells her with amusement lacing his tone. "We'd love for you and Samantha to join us."

So much for having my way with my girl in the pool. That idea flew way out the window fast.

Lifting my head, I kiss Savannah's bare shoulder before looking up at her. She's so fucking beautiful, she damn near steals away my breath.

"I love you," she says quietly.

I'll never get tired of hearing her say those words.

"I love you too."

She smiles again, like she'll never get tired of hearing me say them either.

Which is good, because I plan to tell her every day, multiple times a day, for the next sixty or seventy years.

Acknowledgments

There are so many thanks Melissa and I have to give for the creation of Malicious! First, we'd like to thank Melissa Gill with Melissa Gill Designs. The cover turned out so much more gorgeous than we could have hoped for!

To Rose with Rose David Editing. Thank you for making Malicious even better than it was before! Your amazing editing skills couldn't be more spot on!

To our proofreaders. Many many thanks to you for polishing up our book baby and making it the best it can be!

Thank you to all of the bloggers, our author friends, readers, and anyone else who helped get Malicious out into the world!

To our reader groups, Alex's Jaded Angels and Melissa's Mavens. You guys are truly amazing! Thank you for everything you do for us!

And last, but certainly not least, to our readers. It is because of you that Malicious was born. You gave Treacherous a chance and fell in love. Then demanded more. We can't thank you enough!

Other books by Alex Grayson

JADED HOLLOW SERIES

Beautifully Broken

Wickedly Betrayed

Wildly Captivated

Perfectly Tragic

Jaded Hollow: The Complete Collection

THE CONSUMED SERIES

Endless Obsession

Sex Junkie

Shamelessly Bare

Hungry Eyes

The Consumed Series: The Complete Collection

HELL NIGHT SERIES

Trouble in Hell

Bitter Sweet Hell

Judge of Hell

Key to Hell

The Hell Night Series: Complete Collection

WESTBRIDGE SERIES

Pitch Dark

Broad Daylight

BULLY ME SERIES

Treacherous

Malicious

EVER SERIES

Forevermore

Everlast

ITTY BITTY DELIGHTS

Heels Together, Knees Apart

Teach Me Something Dirty

Filthy Little Tease

For I Have Sinned

STANDALONES

Whispered Prayers of a Girl

The Sinister Silhouette

Lead Player

Just the Tip

Uncocky Hero

Until Never

Other Books by Melissa Toppen

ALL THAT WE ARE

VIOLETS ARE NOT BLUE

LOVE ME LIKE YOU WON'T LET GO

HOW WE FALL

WHERE THE NIGHT ENDS

TEQUILA HAZE

TEN HOURS

THE ROAD TO YOU

CRAZY STUPID LOVE

FORCE OF NATURE

A THOUSAND CUTS

ALMOST NEVER

About Alex Grayson

Alex Grayson is a USA Today bestselling author of heart pounding, emotionally gripping contemporary romances including the Jaded Series, the Consumed Series, The Hell Night Series, and several standalone novels. Her passion for books was reignited by a gift from her sister-in-law. After spending several years as a devoted reader and blogger, Alex decided to write and independently publish her first novel in 2014 (an endeavor that took a little longer than expected). The rest, as they say, is history.

Originally a southern girl, Alex now lives in Ohio with her husband, two children, two cats and dog. She loves the color blue, homemade lasagna, casually browsing real estate, and interacting with her readers. Visit her website, www.alexgraysonbooks.com, or find her on social media!

About Melissa Toppen

Melissa Toppen is a USA Today Bestselling Author who specializes in New Adult and Contemporary Romance. She is a lover of books and enjoys nothing more than losing herself in a good novel. She has a soft spot for Romance and focuses her writing in that direction; writing what she loves to read.

Melissa resides in Cincinnati Ohio with her husband and two children, where she writes full time.

Website
Facebook
Goodreads
Twitter
Instagram
Pinterest
BookBub
Book and Main

Made in the USA
Columbia, SC
29 July 2022